"What any of us want and what happens isn't always the same,"

Rigg said. "If I could change this…"

He was tormented in ways Shanna couldn't begin to comprehend but felt a desperate desire to change. "I'm sorry," she whispered.

She shouldn't touch him, risk her separate self, and yet she'd shared more of herself with Rigg in the few hours she'd known him than she had with any other man. How could she possibly walk away from him now?

Eyes closed, she gave herself up to the sensation. The fear died, only to be replaced by need.

De'ninaah. De'ninaah. As Rigg kissed her, an insistent voice filled the room—a voice it seemed only she could hear.

She pushed free. "Did you say something just now?"

Rigg tensed. His body began to chill. "Get your things," he said, his tone low, tortured. "You're leaving. Now."

Dear Reader,

This month Shadows is pleased to take you to the Southwest for an eerie adventure in romance with Vella Munn's *Navajo Nights*. Heroine Shanna Whitmore wants only to solve the secrets of her past—and drive away the voices chanting in a strange language inside her head—but what she finds is so much more. Because in the high, dusty desert of New Mexico she comes face-to-face with Rigg Schellion, a man whose past seems somehow connected with hers—and whose future she wants very much to share.

In months to come look for more eerie entertainment—and expect to be possessed by passion—here in Silhouette Shadows. The dark side of love has never been more alluring.

Enjoy!

Leslie Wainger
Senior Editor and Editorial Coordinator

Please address questions and book requests to:
Silhouette Reader Service
U.S.: 3010 Walden Ave., P.O. Box 1325, Buffalo, NY 14269
Canadian: P.O. Box 609, Fort Erie, Ont. L2A 5X3

VELLA MUNN

NAVAJO NIGHTS

SILHOUETTE® *Shadows*™

Published by Silhouette Books
America's Publisher of Contemporary Romance

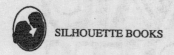 SILHOUETTE BOOKS

ISBN 0-373-27058-5

NAVAJO NIGHTS

VELLA MUNN

grew up the daughter and granddaughter of teachers, and from childhood on she was in love with the written word. She turned to writing when her first child was born and now has twenty-nine contemporary and historical romances to her credit. Vella says that she was drawn to the Silhouette Shadows line because she loves the unexplainable. She is the mother of two grown children and lives in southern Oregon with her husband.

From meadows green where ponds are scattered,

From there we come.

Bereft of limbs, one bears another,

From there we come.

Bereft of eyes, one bears another,

From there we come.

By ponds where healing herbs are growing,

From there we come.

With these your limbs you shall recover,

From there we come.

With these your eyes you shall recover,

From there we come.

—Song of the Stricken Twins,
Navajo Night Way Myth

PROLOGUE

Changing Woman. Earth Mother. How could this happen?

"I'm so sorry. We tried to protect her. But he—"

Juanica White Wind pushed past the blond policeman and into the airy two-bedroom house where her best friend had lived—until this morning. Suddenly numb, Juanica stopped and stared at the living room she knew almost as well as she did her family's hogans. "Where is she?" she whispered.

"Mrs. Parrish? In the bedroom. You don't want to go in there."

Of course she didn't; anything but that. The young Navajo ran her fingers through her long, black hair and wished with all her heart that she was at Shiprock or White Horse Trail or Redbird Pass, anywhere but here. "Cindy. Debby's daughter. Where is she?"

"In the kitchen. A neighbor's with her."

Juanica's heart broke as she thought of the beautiful two-year-old, a child with hair the color of petrified sand dunes and eyes like spring storm clouds. But she forced herself to remain in the room she'd helped Debby and Sam paint. "Was—is Cindy all right?"

"I think so. Why he didn't hurt her, considering what he did... I just wished to hell I understood more. But the girl's too young to tell us anything," the officer said.

What was there to tell? A monster had murdered Cindy's mother, he'd murdered her father just one week before. "I wanted to stay with Debby and Cindy. I should have been here. My father...I think he was trying to protect me by keeping me with him. I let him. Damn it, I deserted her!"

"Maybe he would have gotten to you, too, Miss White Wind. You're lucky—"

"I would have killed him," Juanica said, cutting him off. She clamped her arms around her waist, her fingers closing around the silver concha belt that held up her multicolored, floor-length skirt. "If I'd been here, I would have killed him."

The policeman stared at her but said nothing.

"I should have—" she began. Muffled male voices stopped her from telling the policeman that her father, a Navajo shaman, had asked her to help her grandparents shear sheep yesterday and that by the time they'd finished, she'd been so tired she'd spent the night on the reservation.

They were coming out, two grim-faced men carrying a body wrapped in a bloodstained sheet. Juanica stared at what remained of her best friend—her only Anglo friend.

Grief, shock, anger and an overwhelming fear swamped her.

Changing Woman. Earth Mother. Stop him!

"Where is she?" one of the men asked in a harsh whisper. "The little girl. I don't want her seeing her mama like this."

Juanica took a half step toward the kitchen, then turned so quickly that her moccasins slipped on the inexpensive carpet. She reached out and touched the auburn hair that protruded from under the sheet. "Forgive me, please," she whispered. "I promise I'll keep Cindy safe. Whatever it takes, she'll be safe."

"Safe?" the policeman asked, puzzled. "You must have seen what's out there. We got him. Finally."

Oh, yes, she'd seen the short, beefy Navajo sprawled facedown on Debby and Sam's front lawn. She hoped he'd felt pain for a long, long time—if he was capable of feeling pain.

Juanica wrenched herself from her thoughts. She told the men she'd make sure Cindy stayed in the kitchen until they'd left with her mother's body.

Cindy was sitting at the table, an elderly woman wearing a robe and slippers hovering over her.

"Hi, Button," Juanica whispered shakily.

Instantly, the child launched herself at her. Sobbing, Juanica clutched Cindy to her breasts.

"Where's Mommy, Aunt Wannie? My mommy. I need her, now!"

"I know you do, sweetheart," she managed to murmur while the neighbor mouthed that she hadn't been able to keep Cindy at her place. "But..."

Cindy was shaking like a leaf in a fierce wind. "He hurt me." She gingerly touched her arm, forcing Juanica's attention to a dark bruise that all but covered her delicate little upper arm. "All those police—is it like when Daddy dieded?"

Yes, precious. It's just like when your daddy 'dieded.'

White-lipped, the older woman explained that she'd heard screams first thing that morning and had looked outside. She'd seen that pickup parked out front, remembered it from when Sam had been killed. "Debby had told me *he'd* escaped," the neighbor said, with a meaningful look at Cindy. "I thought the police were protecting Debby, but... All I could think about was that poor little girl."

"Debby refused to go into hiding," Juanica whispered. "Maybe it was because of losing Sam. She couldn't think, couldn't believe it would get any worse, that he wouldn't leave her alone."

"She was wrong. He... I called the police, but I couldn't sit there and wait, not when I heard Cindy crying, along with those horrible screams. I snuck around to the back and looked in the kitchen window. That's when I saw Cindy. The poor little thing—how she got loose I don't know. Somehow I got her to unlock the door, grabbed her, ran outside with her. He was still here when the police came." The woman shuddered.

"He kept coming at me," a masculine voice said. Juanica turned to see the policeman who'd let her in. She noticed that the young man's eyes showed too much white and his hands trembled. "It was as if he didn't care," he continued. "Either that or he thought he was invincible."

"You—you're the one who killed him?"

"It took so many bullets. So many."

He isn't human; not anymore. If she said that, she'd have to explain things that neither the blond policeman nor the gray-haired neighbor could possibly understand. Things she didn't fully comprehend herself.

"What's going to happen to her?" The neighbor indicated Cindy, who still clung tightly to Juanica. "Poor baby, to lose both her parents."

"She hasn't lost me." The air felt hot, then cold. Still holding Cindy, Juanica sent a prayer to Changing Woman, offspring of Earth Mother and Sky Father, that *his* soul cease to exist. "Whatever it takes to keep her safe, I'll do it."

"Safe?" the policeman asked again. "Zarcillas is dead."

Was he? Or had he become a Chinde—evil and immortal?

Would any of them be safe ever again?

CHAPTER ONE

Twenty-five years later...

Her mind drifting like a bird's feather in the surf, Shanna Whitmore pulled into her parking spot at Sparkling Shores Apartments and turned off the engine. She reached behind her for the briefcase she'd been carting to and from work for the better part of a week. Tonight, definitely, she'd get at that reading.

Unless she had to go for a walk, she admitted as she stepped out into the east-Florida heat. Despite the beating sun and humidity, which took her breath away, she wasn't sure she'd be able to deal with her restlessness and loneliness any other way except to walk it through—walk until the world became dark, and maybe much longer than that.

Walking, to stop from thinking. Exhausting her body so the dream wouldn't sneak up on her. So she'd stop asking questions that had no answers.

She slipped her purse strap over her shoulder and took a couple of steps. Then, because she'd worn heels as long as she could force herself to, she kicked out of them.

After retrieving her shoes, she walked across the complex's manicured lawn to the stack of metal mailboxes and unlocked the one assigned to her. There was a department store bill, an urgent "telegram" informing her she had only ten days to register for a chance at a million dollars, a sales flier from a tire shop and a card from the realtor who'd sold her grandparents' house, saying that if Shanna wanted to buy some property herself, she'd be delighted to work with her.

Delighted? Hadn't the woman noticed that her client had been in a state of shock?

I've got a riddle for you. When aren't grandparents grandparents?

When they lie.

A child's laugh cut through her thoughts and allowed her to strangle the lost and angry whimper trying to break free. As a woman with a toddler in tow stepped up to the mailboxes, Shanna moved away to give them room. Her attention was riveted on the easy way mother and daughter touched and laughed.

She'd never had that with her own parents. She'd always believed Jack and Connie Whitmore had died in a sudden storm that swamped their houseboat when she was two and spending the weekend with her grandparents. But now— now she didn't know what, if anything, she could believe about her life.

Remembering her grandparents, she felt a little less sorry for herself. All right, so Grandma Gina and Grandpa Josh hadn't been who she'd spent her life believing they were. But they'd loved her, raised her, kept a roof over her head. Over a stranger's head? That was the part that didn't make sense.

She walked to her apartment in a daze, and in fumbling for her house keys, managed to drop the mail. When she picked it up, she saw that a legal-size envelope had been caught in the folds of the tire flier. She started to turn the letter over; then, for the briefest of seconds, she couldn't seem to make her fingers work. There was something about the letter that made her want to throw it away without opening it. It was, she saw, from the Adult Probation Department in Farmington, New Mexico.

Probation? Farmington? She'd written to Aztec, New Mexico, because it was the county seat and the place an old letter had come from, and she'd figured that that was where she should start looking for some answers. For a past.

For the first time since moving here three weeks ago, she didn't experience that unsettling moment of wanting to do anything except walk into the sterile apartment. She put the mail and briefcase on the coffee table, the letter from Farmington on top. Then she stepped back and stared at it, irrationally willing it to disappear. What would the letter say? Could she handle it?

Get a grip, she muttered silently, and walked into her bedroom. The moment she slipped out of her skirt and wriggled out of her panty hose, her sense of dread faded. Her cotton-posing-as-silk blouse came next. Finally she hauled her slip over her head. Relief! No more dressing for semisuccess until tomorrow.

She pulled on cutoffs and one of the T-shirts she and the other agents at Worldwide Wonder Trips had received from a California coastal resort. The shirt had once sported a picture of a grinning, bronzed surfer. However, all she could say about the shirt after three washings was that it was closer to green than any other color.

She gave a brief thought to pouring herself a glass of wine before reading the letter, but she needed a clear mind. Besides, in her current mood, it was possible that one glass would lead to another, and if that happened, she'd spend the night tangled in the same unanswerable questions that had stalked her since her grandmother's death—since she'd found that old letter and a Navajo sand painting.

The letter from Farmington was typed on official stationery and looked clean, uncluttered, professional. Cool and unemotional. Still, there was a certain weight to the words. It was almost as if she could hear the writer's deep voice, almost see his dark—dark?—eyes staring back at her. She could sense his blatant and inescapable masculinity.

Ms. Whitmore, it has come to my attention that you have been in contact with the courthouse in Aztec, asking about the proper procedure for researching your past. I realize finding one's roots is popular these days, but there are limits to what can be accomplished. You wrote that all you have are first names, two of which may or may not be your parents'. Without a surname or any other information, you are asking for the impossible. My advice is that you accept the fact that you will never know more than you do now.

Sincerely,
Rigg Schellion

Limits to what can be accomplished. Asking for the impossible. Will never know more than you do now. The words slammed into her and filled her not with defeat but with fury. *Answers, Mr. Schellion! I want, I need answers. Is that too much to ask for?*

After a long, dragging breath, she felt a small measure of control seep back into her. Rigg Schellion was speaking like a bureaucrat, that's all. He couldn't bar her from continuing her search, even if it would require a little effort from the other bureaucrats he was trying to protect.

What search? that hated voice of logic asked. *You don't even know how to start.*

She flung the letter across the room and stalked back into the bedroom, picking up the nearly flat cardboard container she'd placed in her closet. Although she'd stared at its contents until she now saw them in her sleep, she lay it on her bed and once again untied the aged string. Upending the lightweight box, she shook it gently until the faded, handwritten letter and then a dinner-plate-size sand painting slid out. As always, her attention was riveted on the beautiful reds, yellows and browns depicting a dark, slim figure holding what seemed to be lightning bolts in one hand. The other hand was lifted in a protective gesture over a childish figure kneeling at its feet. Opposite the small child was something else, something shadowy, a strange contrast to the stark simplicity of both the godlike creature and the child. Sometimes she could barely make herself look at the indistinct smear. Other times, like tonight, she could almost swear she saw nothing more ominous than a poorly defined, crouching boy.

What did it mean? The day after finding this and the letter behind a stack of boxes in her grandparents' attic, she'd gone through travel brochures of the Southwest until she'd covered her desk with every picture of sand paintings she could find. They were all striking, the product of master craftsmen. And without exception, the backgrounds were simple and serene.

Hers was different. Behind the godlike figure and whatever was at his feet, the sky had been dyed a brooding gray. She couldn't look at it without thinking of an approaching storm—of something evil.

More times than she wanted to admit, she tried to tell herself this was nothing more than some tourist trinket her grandparents had picked up, but whenever she did, an insistent voice inside her rejected that explanation. She couldn't touch the rough-surfaced object without feeling something, couldn't look at it without the image haunting her for hours afterward.

And then there was the letter.

Although part of her wanted to tear that into tiny shreds and poke it down the garbage disposal, she settled herself on the bed beside the sand painting and carefully unfolded the fragile paper.

Dear, dear Josh and Gina:
I know. I promised I'd never get in touch with you again, but my father insists that Cindy—Shanna— have the sand painting. I pray she will never have a need for it, that she never know about its meaning,

even its existence, or her past. But my father wants it
kept near her, and I would never refuse him in this.
Thank you from the bottom of my heart for what
you're doing for Shanna, accepting her the way you
have. She had to leave here; I'm convinced, for her
sake, that it had to be that way. Otherwise, I would
have kept her myself. I cry for her every day. But if she
was where he could get his hands on her—the thought
makes me sick, and I will not fail her the way I did
Debby. I wish you'd known Debby and Sam the way I
did. They were wonderful people, and they didn't deserve what happened to them.

I don't want to have to tell you this, but I believe I
must. It isn't over. *He's* still here. The young policeman who shot him is dead. When they found the officer's body, there were things... The authorities refuse
to listen to the truth, but they aren't Navajo. They'll
never understand. Other things have happened, but I
don't want to burden you with that. It's enough that
you've given my little sweetheart a home and family.
I'll always love you.

                                        Juanica

P.S. The boy seems normal. I can only pray he will be
spared.

The boy. What boy? There were so many questions, so
few answers. Fingers trembling, Shanna slid the letter back
into its envelope. There was no return address, only a barely
legible postmark from Aztec, New Mexico.

Was she the child Juanica had written about? Who were
Debby and Sam? Her parents' names had been Jack and
Connie. Grandpa Josh and Grandma Gina were her
grandparents, weren't they? But Juanica had written that
they'd "accepted" her. Would the woman have said that if
she was related to Grandma and Grandpa by blood?

He. That was what haunted her more than anything else. Who was this person Juanica kept referring to? Apparently he'd killed Debby and Sam, two people who—could it be?—were her real parents. And Juanica was saying he'd killed a policeman as well.

It was insane! A black mystery she wanted nothing to do with but couldn't walk away from, any more than she could throw the sand painting against a wall and watch it shatter—because if she did, maybe she'd shatter along with it.

The boy. Could she have a brother somewhere?

A glance at the clock radio by her bed told her it wasn't yet 5:00 p.m. in New Mexico. Should she call Mr. Schellion and demand to know why he'd gotten involved? If she didn't, her search for the truth about her identity might end with his letter.

Identity. How strange, how absorbing, how terrifying the word sounded.

Barely aware of what she was doing, she pulled a pillow against her middle and started rocking. Despite the steady whir of the air conditioner, she could hear the faint hum that came from her clock. Because she'd left her closet door open, she found herself staring at her clothes. Except for an extensive collection of cotton T-shirts—compliments of her job—that advertised exotic and less-than-exotic places, she didn't care about her wardrobe. The dresses and suits and slacks filled certain professional requirements but weren't her any more than this clean and impersonal apartment with its peach countertops and off-white carpet was.

What was she? Who?

She shouldn't have sold her grandparents' house. Wasn't that what her friends had told her—that she was reacting out of shock after losing both of them within a year of each other? But she'd rattled around in the big old place until she'd thought the hollow sounds would absorb her. The dream had haunted her there, stalked her every move, until she'd called a realtor and explained that she didn't need a place that big.

While cleaning out over twenty years of accumulated possessions, she'd come across the old box containing the letter and the strange sand painting. The box that had started all the questions. And if she didn't tell Rigg Schellion what he could do with his stupid suggestion that she drop everything, she might never have any answers.

Might never know who she was.

After pushing herself off the bed, she walked into the kitchen. Ignoring the makings for a salad, she poured herself some sun tea. She swallowed deeply, telling herself that her hand was *not* trembling, that if she'd turn on the TV, she'd stop rattling around inside her head.

But she didn't want to be numbed by TV. She wanted, needed, answers.

After another long drink, she reached for the wall phone to the right of the refrigerator and, reading from the letter, punched out the number of the Farmington probation department. When the receptionist came on the line, she asked to be put through to Mr. Schellion. "You're in luck," she was told. "He just got back."

"Back?"

"From running down a probationer so screwed up he ought to be staked to an anthill. Sorry, those are Rigg's words. I should know better than to repeat them. Suffice it to say, his black humor is increasing. Hold on. I'll put you through."

Five seconds later she heard a masculine "Rigg Schellion here."

Rigg Schellion. A voice like thunder, so deep she could feel it in her bone marrow. With her hand over her throat in an instinctive and incomprehensible gesture of protection, she introduced herself. "This is Shanna Whitmore. You might be right, Mr. Schellion." She hurried the words, hating herself for sounding defensive, hating him for putting her in that position. "Trying to find out something about my parents—if they are my parents—could be like looking for the proverbial needle in a haystack. I just can't give up yet. Can you understand that?"

"Shanna Whitmore? You're Shanna Whitmore?"

She told herself he was repeating himself so he'd have time to bring her to mind, but there was something in his tone that warned her that wasn't it. He sounded not mystified, but stunned. "I don't know if I was born Shanna Whitmore," she said. "Maybe someone once called me Cindy. Cindy without a last name. You remember what I wrote, don't you?"

"Yes. I remember."

Once again she had the unnerving sensation of listening to thunder build and roll outward. "I'm confused. I contacted the courthouse in Aztec. How come you answered?"

He didn't reply. Still, an unspoken connection remained. It was almost as if he'd reached across the miles that separated them and grabbed hold of her. She felt his strong fingers on her flesh, his dark eyes—why did she keep thinking of them that way?—boring into hers, his mind sucking hers dry. "Mr. Schellion? I don't see how any of this concerns you."

"Don't you?" He sounded old, so old. "What I was attempting to do was save you both effort and disappointment."

"Why would you want to do that?"

"Why?" The sound of the word lasted a long time. "A lot of reasons. Reasons...never mind. I have a friend who works at the courthouse. A dear, dear friend. When she showed me your letter, I offered to write, explaining why you were asking the impossible. She hates disappointing people, particularly when it's something that means a great deal to them. I'm sorry you didn't like hearing what I had to say, but then, reality isn't always kind."

"No. It isn't. But what if you don't know what reality is? That's what I'm up against."

Once again he was slow to speak. "You said you came across some information that may or may not have anything to do with you. If you'd be more specific, I could tell you whether it's something you should discount out of hand."

How could he do that? He was, what—a probation officer? "What I found—" she drew out the words to give them as much impact as possible "—made me believe that my name was once Cindy and that the people who raised me did it out of kindness, not because of blood ties."

More silence. She wanted to pound at it and demand that this bureaucrat with his unsettling voice step into the quicksand she'd been sinking in for the better part of a month. Maybe then he'd understand. "I thought it was a joke, a—a, I don't know what. But I couldn't drop it. I got out my birth certificate and told myself that it was the truth. I was the daughter of Jack and Connie Whitmore, born in Naples, Florida. But when I took that birth certificate to be verified—the one my grandparents had dug out so I could get my first job—I learned my birth had never been recorded anywhere in Florida. What I had was a fake. A fake! What did my grandparents do—pay some crook to falsify my records so I wouldn't question my background? For what purpose? I—I tried to find proof of my parents' birth. That, too, fell into the same black hole."

"I see."

No, you don't. You can't possibly! "Why was I lied to all my life? Why are there so few baby pictures of me and only a couple of my parents, none with them holding me? I always thought it was because everything went down when their houseboat sank, but now I don't know what to believe. If only I had some aunts and uncles, cousins. Anyone. But I don't." Her voice trailed off at the end and sounded too much like that of a frightened child. "I need a past. One I can believe in."

For too long she heard nothing except the sound of her ragged breathing, and she wondered if Rigg Schellion had hung up on her. She almost wouldn't blame him. After all, she wasn't anything to him. Why would he concern himself with a stranger? "What was it?" he finally asked.

"What was what?"

"What started you on this search."

"A letter," she blurted. "Old. From a woman named Juanica."

"Juanica?"

She'd been a heartbeat away from ignoring his response, but halfway through planning what she would say next, her mind caught onto what he'd said, or rather, the way he'd said it. The name had rolled off his tongue, familiar, almost caressing. *He knew Juanica! Damn it, he knew her!* "And a sand painting," she hurriedly added, because if she didn't, what she now suspected would so confuse her that she might give herself away. "It's supposed to—I don't know—keep me safe, I guess."

"Do you remember anything of your early childhood?"

She wanted to tell him that it was none of his business, but if she did, she'd sever the thread that held them together, and right now he was all she had. All. "I was only two when my parents...when the people I thought were my parents died. Like all kids, I loved hearing about things that happened when I was very young. Sometimes I'd think I remembered some of it, but I probably didn't. I used to look at pictures of my parents—of Jack and Connie, if that's who they were—and wonder why I had no sense of recognition. Wouldn't you think I'd have some memory of them? Some emotional reaction, if nothing else? After all, I carry their genes. At least I thought I did. Mr. Schellion, I feel as if I dropped out of the sky. As if I'm not connected to anyone. I need to belong, to have a sense of security."

"Do you?"

What kind of response was that? "Maybe you don't care where you came from, who was responsible for who you are as a human being. But I do."

"Sometimes it's better not to know."

Better not to know? How could he possibly say that? "I have a recurring dream. It's been with me all my life. My grandparents always said it was emotional reaction to my parents' drowning, but I'm not so sure anymore."

"What do you mean?"

"In my dream I see a little girl. She's crying, sobbing as if her heart is breaking. There are people around her—policemen, a young woman with a silver necklace and beautiful long, black hair. Who is that woman? She holds the little girl and tries to comfort her, but I feel that child's loss. I hate that dream. Every time it comes, I'm left with such a lonely feeling."

"I'm sorry."

She believed him, just as she believed he knew something about the mysterious woman named Juanica. "Then you understand why I have to pursue this, don't you? If I'm this Cindy person, I need to know why my name was changed. Why I was lied to all my life. Whether—whether I might have a brother."

"A brother?"

"The letter mentioned a boy. I don't know what else to think."

Once again silent moments ticked past until she felt she might drown in them. Finally she heard him take a deep breath that became part of the darkness swirling around her. "Sometimes, Miss Whitmore, the past needs to remain buried."

"Buried?"

"If you don't want to be destroyed by it."

Destroyed? "What are you talking about?"

He didn't answer, but then, she didn't expect him to. "I'm just glad I've always lived on the side of the law, Mr. Schellion. I'd hate to have you as my probation officer."

"Would you?"

"Yes." She barely restrained herself from screaming the word. "You don't have an ounce of humanity in you, an ounce of understanding."

Don't I? Startled by what she could swear had been his thought somehow transmitted to her across the miles, she bucked away from the receiver and then dropped it into the cradle.

Rigg had no idea how long he sat staring at the telephone after Shanna Whitmore cut off the connection. Her voice was low for a woman's, low and lonely and utterly compelling. In his mind he could see her deep gray eyes and hair that was somewhere between blond and soft brown. She would be small boned, probably not much over five feet tall. Despite her delicate appearance, there'd be a courage to her, a belief that she could do anything. He wondered what her laughter sounded like, but knew he couldn't risk hearing it—not if... Needing to do something, he pushed back from his desk and planted his feet under him.

Once, a thousand years ago it seemed, he'd believed he was doing the right thing by becoming a probation officer. He'd felt working on the side of the law might be the only thing that could save him.

But maybe it was too late and had been from the moment of his birth.

Despite the blinking light telling him that another call had come in, he stepped to the window. Nothing but a panorama of car and truck tops. He wanted out—to breathe in high-prairie air, to fasten his gaze on distant, ancient, blue-and-gray mountains and be absorbed by

space. To listen to the wind instead of to the echo of a
woman's voice. To hold back the great black cloud and believe that he was worthy of loving and being loved in turn.

But he couldn't.

He'd botched the letter to her. He shouldn't have sent her
anything, made any kind of contact. But when Juanica had
showed him what Cindy—Shanna—had written, he hadn't
been able to think past trying to prevent the woman from
coming here. When he'd sat down at the computer with
Shanna's desperate and compelling plea for the truth within
reach, the Cloud had descended on him and he'd been unable to think.

That happened too much—more and more frequently
these days. . . .

Unable to continue the thought, he whirled and faced the
wall opposite the window. Faced the picture that said everything about what was happening inside him. Starkly
black and white, it was nothing more than contrasting
squares too intense to look at for more than a few seconds.
Even now the squares began to blur, until he felt as if he
was looking into a kaleidoscope—looking into a tornado
that swirled out and down, pulling him into its center. He
hated it, hated and embraced it at the same time.

*Don't come, Cindy. If you value your life, don't get
anywhere near me.*

CHAPTER TWO

Shanna thought Farmington would be larger, maybe because so much of what she was—or could be—might be revealed here. Still, she was moved by the impact of the stark, wild country that surrounded and enveloped the community she was flying over. Although this was her first trip here, she'd always felt drawn to the Southwest. Had always wanted to breathe in dry air smelling of sage, to walk on ground rich in Native American history. How she felt about the unshakable impact of space and a sky so immense that she felt lost just looking out at it she wasn't sure, but it was impossible to ignore. If the romanticized history of the town was to be believed, Farmington had once been ruled by outlaws and card sharks. What had brought them here? Who had stayed and why?

And why did she feel as if this wasn't the first time she'd looked at an endless sky, seen starkly beautiful sandstone hills?

As the plane approached the airport, she plastered her nose to the window. What she came away with was an impression of an endless valley cradled by mountains, capable of both absorbing and isolating the unwary visitor. She hadn't expected to see so many orchards or so much cropland. This was high-desert country, wasn't it? Her seat companion, a local car dealer, explained that Farmington owed its vitality to gas, oil and coal reserves. City officials were probusiness. Sure, there was all that historic stuff like museums and monuments and kivas, to say nothing of the vast Navajo reservation, but he didn't have time for that. Most local folks didn't—just tourists and the Indians.

As soon as Shanna left the airport in her rental car, she turned on the radio and scanned stations. She picked up three strong ones, all country and western. Although her own taste leaned toward soft rock, she found something right about songs that told of hard-living, hard-working and hard-playing men and women. New Mexico was that kind of a state—rugged and timeless. Man had made his impact here, but he'd left so much intact and unspoiled. He hadn't touched the air, hadn't stripped it of its clean, dry essence—a vaguely familiar essence.

The familiarity scared her more than anything else.

Acting on directions from the woman who'd handed her the keys to the car, she headed toward the downtown area, where the public buildings were located. She tried to see beyond the commercial establishments, particularly the newer ones, in an attempt to envision what the town had looked like years ago, but it was all she could do to read street signs and keep up with the traffic flow.

When she first approached the single-story stucco building where Rigg Schellion worked, she missed the entrance and had to drive around the block. The day was hot enough to make her sweat. Still, she drove with the windows down, wind tangling her hair, and breathed deeply of air stripped of the humidity she was so used to, dry air that seemed to well up from somewhere deep in her past. That was what Mr. Schellion didn't understand—her unrelenting need for answers. For an identity.

Finally she found a parking spot in the clogged lot. She honestly didn't remember turning off the engine, but she must have. Where a moment ago her senses had been touched by guitars and a nasal voice coming from the radio, she now listened to silence.

No, not silence. The dream child was crying again, but this time she wasn't the only one. The woman, the beautiful one with long, sleek dark hair, was sobbing along with her.

Jolted by sounds that seemed to come from deep inside her, Shanna pushed open the car door and slid out. She focused on the building then, still feeling unsettled and vaguely frightened, forced her mind onto safe things.

The best part about being off work was wearing sandals—plain old leather sandals. Her blouse didn't pretend to be anything except what it was—all-purpose cotton. She wasn't sure, but she thought her slacks were cotton as well. A lot of the reservation Navajo raised sheep. Maybe she'd buy a wool blanket while she was here. Maybe she'd find a Navajo who could tell her what her sand painting meant.

A horn blast sent her thoughts flying. Smiling apologetically, she hurried out of the traffic lane, then stopped. Mr. Schellion didn't know she was coming. Maybe she should have called him back and told him she'd decided not to take his advice to let sleeping dogs lie. Instead, here she was, about to walk into his office and—and what?

Maybe—she started up the walkway that led to the main door—maybe his eyes would answer questions she hadn't been able to form in her mind, and she'd begin to understand why a part of him had remained inside her long after she'd hung up on him.

Maybe—she stepped inside and headed for the glass-enclosed directory—she'd learn from his eyes why she felt as if she'd begun a journey into the past.

After getting her bearings, she headed toward Adult Probation, her mind going no further than the faint murmur her sandals made and the greater sound of her pounding heart. Mr. Schellion scared her. No, not scared, exactly, but she hadn't been able to shake off the impact of his voice or his words.

Or of him.

A woman who managed to concentrate on Shanna's questions and speak into the phone at the same time in-

formed her that Mr. Schellion had just gone down the hall
but would be back in a few minutes. Since she was here on
personal business, it was all right if she waited in his office.

Shanna closed the door behind her, then, grateful for a
little time in which to compose herself, took in the small
room. There was a three-drawer filing cabinet, a cluttered
desk with a computer taking up too much of the space, a
couple of plastic molded chairs opposite the desk and a
window with an uninspired view of the parking lot. On the
wall behind where Mr. Schellion sat was a large, stark picture.

Drawn to it, she stood leaning against the desk while she
took in the endless and monotonous black-and-white
checks. The frame was almost nonexistent and the glass
over the picture needed to be dusted. The more she concentrated, the harder it was to keep the black-and-white
squares from running together. A person could get lost in
the simple contrast, lose all distinction between light and
dark.

Was this Mr. Schellion's personal selection? Had he deliberately chosen something that deceived the senses and
asked the question of whether there really was any difference between black and white, between night and day?

Between good and evil?

Shaken, she turned her back on the brooding design. Her
movement dislodged something on his desk and she quickly
bent to retrieve it. The moment her hand touched his desk,
she stopped, unable to comprehend what had happened.
The flat, battered surface had picked up something of Rigg
Schellion's essence.

Impossible—no hunk of wood could absorb a man's life
force.

Impossible or not, she felt *something*. Something that
spoke of a desert morning and moonless night, cold and
heat, laughter and tears. Good and evil.

Get a grip! she warned herself. Despite her firm admonition to remain rooted in the here and now, it was several seconds before she could pull herself free of whatever had tried to surround her. She should sit in one of the uncomfortable-looking chairs and wait for Mr. Schellion to come in. If she did that, she'd have time to prepare for him, be able to watch his reaction to her.

Instead, she ran her hand over her hip as if to wipe it clean and then deliberately pressed it against the desk. The positive/negative sense returned, but felt less overwhelming this time, and she told herself she was beginning to get a handle on things. Testing herself—or maybe giving in to curiosity—she straightened a stack of papers in danger of falling into the trash can. Its contents didn't look particularly interesting—a couple of memos about forms that needed to be filled out, a reminder that Rigg was signed up for some kind of workshop, a note that had something to do with his job classification.

What did a probation officer do? Oh, she had a general idea, thanks to TV cop shows and things she'd heard on the news, but what was life really like for him from eight to five every day? Did he spend it with losers, standing toe-to-toe with drug pushers and thieves and murderers? Did he have murderers in his caseload? If he did, maybe that explained his attitude. Having to be around someone who had taken a human life would harden a man, teach him to erect barriers between himself and the kind of raw emotion that went with violent death.

Maybe that was who she'd sensed when she'd looked at his picture and touched his desk—a man who spent his days with killers and then went home to a loving wife and small children.

When she spotted the two folders, she told herself she wasn't going to open them; who he dealt with was none of her business. But then she saw her fingers push back a cover and knew she'd been lying to herself. There was a name encased in plastic attached to the top folder, and by tipping her head to one side, she could make out the faded printing. Zarcillas Two Feathers.

Thump.

Her hand began to tremble and she couldn't breathe. Stumbling, she pushed away from the desk and hurried to the window. It wouldn't open. How could she get any air if she couldn't open the damn thing? Finally, she pressed first one cheek and then the other against the pane and told herself that a little oxygen was seeping in around the edges—just enough to clear her head.

Zarcillas Two Feathers. Navajo, maybe. Was she such a wimp, thrown so far off center by what she'd learned since her grandparents' death that she couldn't look at some criminal's rap sheet or whatever it was called? Angry at herself, she stalked back across the room so she could pick up the file. When her fingers refused her command, she reminded herself that she had no business prying anyway and that her conscience was causing all the trouble. Still, if she walked away from this, she'd have to call herself a coward.

Once again she watched a thumbnail slide under the cover. This time she kept at it until she could see the folder's contents, or rather one page. She found herself looking at the stark diagram of a figure that reminded her of the chalk outlines police made around homicide victims. This diagram was faceless, clothesless, sexless. There were eight marks on the body, six of them on the torso near the heart, the other two high on the right thigh.

Was this an autopsy report? Had this Zarcillas Two Feathers shot his victim eight times, or was this Zarcillas himself?

Thump.

Shuddering, she closed the file and picked up the one that had been under it. No wonder Mr. Schellion was drawn to black and white; what she'd just seen was about as black as anything could get. Barely aware of what she was doing, she read the name on the second folder. Hank Granger. This time she felt no reaction, no shortness of breath. Maybe she was already becoming hardened, she told herself as, slowly, carefully, she opened it.

There was another human outline. Six marks near the heart. Two on the right thigh.

"What are you doing?"

She jumped, dropping the folder. Something slid out of it and fluttered to the floor, but she was too startled to concentrate on retrieving it.

"Damn it, what are you doing?"

She knew that voice, remembered it from the phone conversation last week; she had been carting it around inside her ever since.

Rigg Schellion wasn't quite six feet tall; six feet of hardened muscle encased in a dress shirt with the top two buttons open and faded jeans. He wore expensive, tooledleather boots like she'd expect to find on a real cowboy. His long, tousled hair made her think of midnight. His eyes, his incredible eyes, were just as black, and she realized without shock that she'd been right about them. His flesh looked as if it had been touched by the sun all his life and was so deeply tanned that it would never take on winter's hue. Either that or the dusky shade came from his heritage.

She couldn't say how old he was—a few years older than she—but he still carried in him the energy and drive and restlessness of youth. He wore no wedding ring. His only piece of jewelry, if it could be called that, was a braided horsehair belt that rode his lean hips and was accented with a silver buckle that drew her attention to his flat belly.

He hadn't moved; maybe he hadn't so much as breathed, and yet she felt as if he was drawing something of her into himself. She sensed herself fading away, becoming more mist than reality, focused on eyes that were capable of taking her down into the underworld with him.

Impossible.

"I asked, what are you doing here?"

Not simply what was she doing with his files, but what had brought her here—as if he'd been dreading this moment.

As if he knew who she was.

"Rigg Schellion." Her voice sounded as if it had been caught in a wind tunnel, all dry and hollow. "I'm Shanna Whitmore. At least that's who I think I am. The woman out front said I could wait for you in here."

He didn't acknowledge her explanation. Instead, in a movement that took no longer than a heartbeat, he glanced down at his desk and then met her eyes again. She was uncomfortable with his eyes' boldness, but *discomfort* wasn't the right word. She couldn't ignore them. Yes, that was it—there was nothing about him she could ignore.

"You shouldn't have come."

Don't say that. "Why not?" she challenged. He hadn't moved. Neither did she.

"You can't resurrect the past. No one can."

She was about to ask him to explain himself when he blinked. By the time he'd opened his eyes again, she had somehow freed herself from their impact and could now look at him dispassionately—at least, she tried to tell herself she could. Midnight eyes. Yes, they were alluring. But they were more than that.

They were familiar.

The air was being sucked out of the room and she had to fight to grab a gulp before it disappeared completely. No. She couldn't have possibly seen him before. She'd never been to New Mexico.

"You knew who I was even before I introduced myself," she managed to say. "I don't understand."

I know you don't. Although he hadn't so much as opened his mouth, she could swear she'd read his thoughts. Feeling light-headed, she struggled for something to say, but her mind had become a dark swirl and she could only wait for him to speak and try to remind herself that it was a warm, sunlit day.

"I told you," he said in his deep, rumbling voice. "Without knowing anything except a man and a woman's first names, there's no way you can find out if they have something to do with you. Let it be—get on with your life."

"What life? I have no living relatives except maybe a brother. I don't even have a legitimate last name."

The muscles around his mouth tightened. Instead of saying anything, he stalked across the room—she could think of no other way of describing it—until he was so close she could have touched him.

Touch him? Oh, no, she wouldn't do that—even though pure masculine heat now surrounded her, tested her self-control. He was, without reservation, the most rawly sensual man she'd ever encountered. She'd had lovers, two of them, and had been attracted to a number of other men, but she'd always felt in control of her emotions.

Rigg Schellion might change that.

Reaching past her, he grabbed the files she'd been looking at and shoved them in his top desk drawer. "That's none of your business. What the hell were you looking at?"

"Don't swear. I don't like it."

"That's just too damn bad. Don't dig into things you shouldn't. Just don't." He hadn't taken his eyes off her the entire time they were arguing. She wished he would. That way she might be able to break free.

But she couldn't put a name to what she needed to be free of. She took a deep breath of air that unfortunately smelled of cotton and denim and man. "All right. So you need to keep your client files private. It's not as if I stole them."

"I didn't say you did."

This was insane. They were fighting about something that didn't matter. "How did you know who I am?" she asked, wondering if he'd answer this time.

He leaned against the desk, a gesture that should have taken him a few necessary inches farther from her but didn't. When he jammed his hands in his back pockets, the gesture was smooth and natural and told her a great deal about a man comfortable with his body. "I knew you weren't going to listen to me," he muttered. "You should have. For your own sake, you have to go back where you came from."

"Why?" The word caught in her throat and she had to try again. "You make it sound like a warning."

"A warning? You don't understand, Shanna. There's no way you ever can. Just go back where you came from."

"I can't." Why was she explaining anything to him? She wasn't one of his clients, for crying out loud; he couldn't order her around. "Not until I know who Sam and Debby were, or if I'm that child called Cindy. Why this Juanica person sent a sand painting that might or might not be capable of protecting me from something, and if she might be the woman I've always dreamed about." Despite the fear that nearly made her forget he was a man and she a woman, she forced herself to say the rest.

"When we talked on the phone, I mentioned Juanica. When you said her name, I could swear it wasn't the first time you'd done that. Do you know her?"

He became so still that he seemed to take the life out of the room with him. From the corner of her eye, she noticed the dark hairs that lay in tangled swirls on his forearm and wondered what it would feel like to have him hold her. She thought of his lean hips and the silver buckle that hid his flat belly, the comfortable way his jeans encased his thighs and calves, the massive chest she would expect to find on a bull rider.

"Does anyone else know you're here?"

The question knocked her off balance but didn't distract her from a certain reality; he hadn't answered her. "I don't see as how that's any of your concern," she told him.

He slowly, sensually it seemed, drew his hands out of his pockets and folded his arms across his chest. As he did, his strong hands caught her attention. Something had happened to his left thumbnail that had dented it inward and made a long crater of the middle.

She'd seen that nail before. Only then, the nail and flesh around it had been black, the injury new and painful.

Impossible!

"I . . ." *No! Don't let him know what you're thinking!*

"Juanica wrote that Sam and Debby were wonderful people," she said instead. "I *have* to know more, need to know who my parents were. What kind of people they were. If I do, maybe I'll understand other things."

"What kind of things?"

Oh, no, you don't. If you think I'll rip myself open for you, you're badly mistaken. "If you'll tell me why you don't want me here, maybe then we'll get around to psychoanalyzing me."

"Shanna, if certain things were kept from you, there had to have been a damn good reason. You don't want to open a Pandora's box. Believe me, you don't want that."

Pandora had nothing to do with it, Rigg thought as the whoosh of air that accompanied Shanna's closing the door behind her echoed and reechoed inside him. He should have stopped her—would have if he'd dared touch her.

Ignoring the buzzing phone, he stalked over to the window and stared out at the sun glinting off car tops. As he'd done too many times before, he fought the need to ram his fist through the glass. What stopped him wasn't the thought of cutting his fingers or even knowing others would rush in to see what had happened.

What kept his hands knotted by his side was years of a growing battle in a private hell. He'd fought the force for as long as he could remember, turned his home into as much of a sanctuary as possible. He would, he believed, go to his grave fighting.

A grave that might come much sooner than he'd believed if Cindy Parrish didn't leave. Of course, her name hadn't been Cindy for twenty-five years, and he knew better than to think of her like that. He should know better than to be anywhere near her.

She'd become a beautiful woman, not quite as delicate as he'd thought she would be, but still with an inescapable femininity that crawled over him like the morning sun inching its way down a butte. Warmth had been part of the impact, warmth and energy and a restlessness he could kill only by running until his legs gave out on him. Yet, he didn't want to put distance between himself and her sensual impact, not when she'd left him feeling this warm and alive. This hungry.

This scared.

The walls began to press in on him, but he couldn't storm out the door. There was sure to be someone out there and he'd have to answer questions—either that or smash his fist into someone's face. The thought of giving vent to the volcano building inside caused him to stare at his dark, big-knuckled hands. He'd been asked about his stunted thumb a number of times, and each time he'd said something simple about how he'd lost a fight to a bully when he was too young to know better. It wasn't the truth—like so many things he presented to the outside world.

The truth was that he'd been eight years old, riding his bicycle down one of the streets in his neighborhood, when he'd been distracted by the sight of several police cars parked in front of a stucco house where a little girl—too young for him to concern himself with—lived. When he saw the body sprawled on the lawn, he'd slammed on his

brakes and been thrown over the handlebars. No one had
paid any attention to him, and, filled with eight-year-old
bravado, he'd stuck his throbbing thumb in his mouth and
squeezed his eyes tight against the pain. When he'd finally
opened them, the inert body was still there and he'd been
drawn to it, his stubby legs bringing him closer and closer
to the gruesome sight.

The dead man had been a stranger, a thick-set Navajo, no
one he'd ever seen before.

Desperate for something to put his mind to, Rigg reached
for the file on the probationer he needed to see this afternoon. Ralph Hucker had been in trouble for nine-tenths of
his fifty years, a small-time crook and big-time loser who'd
never be anything except what he was—part of the revolv-
ing door that was the justice system.

Ralph Hucker should have never been born, never been
let out after the first time he was put behind bars. The
world didn't need Ralph Huckers, would be better off
without them.

Eyes wide open, Rigg imagined himself wrapping his
powerful fingers around Ralph's scrawny neck. He
wouldn't rush things. He'd let Ralph know what he was
doing and why, tell him that his number had come up and
he'd been found too defective to go on living. He, Rigg
Schellion, had decided on his own to put an end to a mis-
erable existence.

His fingers would tighten, cut off Ralph's breath. The
man would fight, jerking like a helpless kitten. Ralph's face
would turn red and his eyes would bulge, but Rigg wouldn't
stop. No matter how much Ralph might cry and beg and
fight, he wouldn't stop.

He couldn't.

Sweat broke out on his body. If only he was home, surrounded by cornstalks, the huge Shootingway sand painting, pictures of bears, the drawing Chabah had done of
Changing Woman. Breathing desperately, he pressed the

heels of his hands against his eyelids until all he could see was red and Ralph no longer existed in his mind. He'd destroyed the impulse to kill.

For now.

The phone started ringing again, but he didn't have enough control over himself to risk answering it. Instead, he opened the top desk drawer and took out the two files he'd thrown in there when he'd been terrified that Shanna had seen them.

She didn't know either of the names. Even if she'd read the entire files, she wouldn't have known what she'd found.

He hoped.

For the second time, he stalked to the window and looked out, his hand pressed over the small fetish bag hung around his neck by a leather cord and concealed by his shirt. The sky, a rich blue accented with trailing white clouds, called to him, and it was all he could do to remember what he and Shanna had said to each other.

Not enough. Her life was in danger here; her young, sensually beautiful, gentle life was in danger, maybe from a monster.

And maybe from him.

He had to warn her. Take the lid off the Pandora's box himself—at least as much as he dared. If he didn't, the deadly power that stalked this area and was slowly taking him over would become unstoppable.

CHAPTER THREE

After negotiating for a week-long rental of a motel room with a kitchenette, Shanna settled in and pulled out her map of New Mexico. Although it was already afternoon, she decided to drive over to Aztec so she could visit the courthouse in person instead of relying on a phone call. Someone had told Rigg she was trying to find her past. If she could locate that person and that person agreed to speak to her, maybe she'd begin to understand. And maybe next time she'd be able to carry on a civilized conversation with Rigg instead of giving in to the sudden impulse to get as far away from him as possible.

What she didn't understand, she admitted as she changed from slacks to shorts, was why the probation officer had acted the way he had, evading and deflecting questions, keeping her off balance. The man frightened her. Fascinated her.

"I don't know what you're up to," she'd tell him. "But if you're trying to act like a horror-movie villain, you've made a pretty good start at it."

"Too bad, lady. That's just too damn bad."

"But why?"

That's when she had to give up her imaginary confrontation, because she didn't have any answers, just as she had no idea why she'd reacted the way she had when he was so close she could feel his heat. He had a primitive seductiveness that made her head feel light and her belly heavy. Her only explanation, if she could call it that, was that she'd been unnerved by something in or about his office.

He hadn't asked what she was going to do. In fact, now that she thought about it, she wasn't sure he had been aware that she'd left his office. Those incredible and almost-frightening eyes of his had taken on a faraway look. It was almost as if he was being pulled into himself, to a place where no one else could follow. For a moment she'd thought he was fighting what was happening to him, but she couldn't be sure, and this particular half-baked explanation didn't make sense. After all, why should a man be afraid of himself?

Maybe, she told herself with a shaky laugh, he was trying to warn her that if she got too close to him or even breathed too much of the air around him, she'd start doing battle with her own psyche.

Her laugh quickly died in the sterile motel room. Seeking to escape both it and what coming face-to-face with Rigg Schellion had done to her nervous system, she grabbed her keys and hurried out to her car. She'd put the key in the ignition when she remembered she'd left both the letter from Juanica and the sand painting behind. Although she didn't fully understand her actions, she hurried back inside to get them and then carefully put them on the seat beside her.

There. If the mysterious and unnerving Mr. Schellion somehow tracked down her motel, at least he couldn't get his hands on what had become precious to her.

Even before she was beyond the Farmington city limits the land flattened out, unfolded, showed itself to her as a vast, unfamiliar and brooding landscape. She became aware of silvers and grays, proud, unapologetic desert. The air was so clean that the mountains seemed no more than a few miles away.

Most of all she saw the sky. Blue and bold, it dominated everything and made her feel humble.

Highway 550 dipped as it entered Aztec. She concentrated on her surroundings, taking in impressions of a small, spread-out town built along a river. Maybe water from the river nourished the piñon, juniper and cotton-wood trees growing throughout the town. Seeing all that greenery allowed her to cast off the desert's vaguely unsettling spell. Still, the town itself made an impact. It looked as if it had been in existence forever, ignorant of modern architecture, golden arches, fads. People lived here. Simply.

After a few minutes of driving around, she found the Mesa Verde Avenue building that apparently housed a number of county departments. Leaving the sand painting in her trunk, she tucked the letter in her purse and walked inside. Air-conditioning cooled her cheeks and brought her back to life. Who was this Schellion character, anyway? No one she needed to concern herself with. She searched in vain for a department of vital statistics, then remembered she hadn't been able to find anything resembling that in the Aztec phone book she'd found at the public library back home. She had wound up writing the county clerk's office, asking them to direct her letter to the proper department. She supposed she could have called, but she'd been afraid she'd sound like an idiot. As it was, writing the letter had taken two evenings.

"I might be here on a fool's errand," she told the woman she found behind a desk in the clerk's office. "I'm trying to find out something about a man and a woman who might have been here about twenty-five years ago, who might have died about that time. Unfortunately, the only information I have is their first names." When the gray-haired woman continued to stare at her from behind her bifocals, she decided to go for broke. "They might have had a daughter named Cindy. I'm sorry—that's all I know, except that the girl was around two years old." Agitated, she ran her fingers through straight sandy hair that barely reached her shoulders. "I don't know how private birth records are, but I was thinking, well—is it possible for me to look through those that were recorded around the time Cindy was born, to see if I can find her? And if that doesn't work, maybe I can search through the death records. It—I think both Sam and Debby died then.''

''They aren't here.''

''What isn't here?''

''Birth and death records. All that information is kept in Santa Fe, the state capital.''

That hadn't occurred to her. Feeling suddenly close to tears, she could only stare at the woman, who obviously wanted to get back to whatever she'd been doing. ''I wrote a couple of weeks ago,'' she finally managed to say. ''Why didn't you tell me that then?''

''Why didn't I tell you what?''

''That nothing's stored here. If you'd told me that instead of turning my inquiry over to someone else—''

''I don't know what you're talking about, miss.'' The woman's voice had taken on an impatient tone. ''Are you saying you wrote me and that I—''

''Not you, not specifically. I didn't know who to get in contact with so I just addressed it to the clerk's office, hoping it'd wind up on the right desk.''

''You see how little we are. About all that's accomplished in this building is keeping the county from unraveling—or at least we try.'' The woman's attention wandered and Shanna realized she was looking over her shoulder. For an instant she was afraid to turn around, for fear she'd find Rigg standing there, but when she finally looked, she saw a man in a slightly rumpled suit who must have come in without her noticing. She *had* to start thinking logically. Somehow.

''No vital statistics?'' she asked.

''Like I said, all that is stored in Santa Fe, and I seriously doubt they'd let you paw through old death records.''

She'd suspected that even before she mailed her desperate letter, but she'd had to try *something*. Only what? How? "Who opened my letter?" she asked, even though she wasn't sure that mattered anymore. "I included my phone number. That person could have simply called me."

"Could have, but I doubt she would have. Juanica isn't crazy about telephones. All these years of working here and she still hates the things," the woman said with a grin at the man, who grinned back.

"Juanica?"

"Juanica White Wind. Navajo, if you haven't guessed."

Feeling disembodied, Shanna could only stare at the woman in disbelief. She stared back for a moment, then turned her attention to the man, teasingly saying that she had what he needed and if he knew the meaning of the word *organized* he would have remembered to pick it up when he was in here the other day. The man shrugged and gave the woman a lopsided smile.

"I've got a suggestion for you," he said to Shanna. "You could either write or call Santa Fe. I guess you could even drive over there if you're of a mind to, but if you're trying to find out if those people you're interested in were born or died around here, you might check that out at the newspaper office."

"Newspaper?"

"The *Farmington Daily Times*. They have all the old editions. It'd take awhile, but that might give you what you need."

Juanica White Wind. Juanica. Juanica.

The name drummed its way through Shanna's mind as she stumbled back outside and tried to remember where she'd parked her car. Somehow she'd had the presence of mind to ask if Juanica was around and had been told that she was taking a few days off because her father wasn't feeling well. Pushing, Shanna had asked if it was possible to contact Juanica at home. Both the middle-aged woman and the rumpled man had laughed at that. Juanica, they informed her, lived in a hogan on the reservation and unless Shanna knew her way around, they definitely would *not* recommend she go looking out there. There weren't any street signs, they explained, not even streets in the normal sense. Most of the roads were unpaved and unmarked, and once it got dark, she'd stay lost until morning—if she was lucky.

Juanica, maybe the key to her past, lived where she couldn't be reached. Shanna would have to wait until she came back to work.

And then?

Sunlight glinted off a windshield. Although she had to squint, she made out her rental car and walked over to it. She'd pulled the key out of her pocket when something on the ground caught her attention. A large, black beetle stood only a few inches away from her unprotected toes. Almost too big to fit in the palm of her hand, it seemed to be staring up at her.

Although she'd never been afraid of insects, she slid back a few cautious inches. The bug scuttled toward her. She stepped to one side. It seemed to follow her; then, almost as if it thought better of it, the fat-bodied creature scurried away.

In the first dark underworld nine people lived; six kinds of ants, three kinds of beetles.

Shanna clutched her throat with suddenly cold fingers. Dark underworld? Beetles and ants? Where had that come from? She had to get some food in her stomach, a little sugar in her bloodstream.

That's what it was.

Please.

When she got into her car, she didn't head back toward Farmington. Instead, after taking a deep, not-quite-calming breath, she put her mind to doing something about her light-headedness. Maybe once she'd done that, she could stop thinking about dark underworlds and beetles and concentrate on the incredible fact that she might have found the mysterious Juanica from so many years ago—a woman she would swear Rigg knew.

Earlier, she'd driven down a quiet street flanked by historic structures. She headed back there and found a place to park in front of a wooden barrel being used as a trash receptacle. Because her stomach was now rumbling, she didn't so much as glance at the antique and curio shops with their hand-painted window signs before stepping inside a small café with unpainted wood paneling and rough, dusty wood flooring. Overhead, a large fan circled slowly, stirring the hot air. After glancing at the menu, she ordered something called a cactus taco.

What was Rigg Schellion doing right now? Given the way he'd been dressed, she guessed he wasn't meeting with a judge or district attorney or the county sheriff. Maybe he was in a residential area trying to find someone who should have reported in but hadn't, or whatever it was probation officers did.

Maybe he was thinking about her, remembering a discussion—an argument—that went nowhere and ended with her stumbling unceremoniously out of his too-small office. Maybe he had ways of tracking her down and would be waiting at her motel room when she returned. If that was the case, she was very, very glad she'd taken the letter and sand painting with her.

Most likely she'd allowed her imagination to go off one hundred and eighty degrees from sanity and he'd already dismissed her from his mind.

She didn't believe that.

The rumpled man's words came back to her and gave her much-needed distraction from a certain probation officer with cavelike eyes and a presence the likes of which she'd never encountered. So the Farmington newspaper kept its old issues. Maybe all the answers or at least a few of them were there. The thought both gave her a sense of purpose and made her wish she'd never come to New Mexico. What if she learned something . . . something horrible?

After inhaling half of the somewhat bland but hopefully nutritious taco, she set it down and rested her arms on the small wooden table. Through the long, thin window to her right, she could see a few people walking by. From their dress, she guessed that most were tourists. Thanks to the never-ending supply of travel brochures at work, she knew the town was near the Aztec Ruins National Monument. But what would cause someone to live here? Why would some five thousand people live out here in the middle of nowhere surrounded by high, arid land? Did they ever feel trapped?

Trapped? No. With so much sky, and land that went on forever, they couldn't think that. Only a stranger caught in a vortex of confusion would think that way.

When a dusty car with a missing front bumper lurched down the street, she focused on the driver. The woman was Native American, Navajo probably. If Shanna jumped up and ran after the car, could she convince the woman to take her to where Juanica White Wind lived?

Or would the woman look at her as if she was insane?

A striking young woman herded a couple of preschoolers to a table at the opposite end of the restaurant, distracting Shanna from her thoughts. This woman, too, was Navajo, as were the children. Unlike the driver, with her unkempt, graying strands, this woman wore her sleek black hair in neat, thick braids. She had on a single piece of jewelry, an exquisite silver bracelet that fitted loosely around her slender wrist. Her bright, sleeveless sundress showed off her slim shoulders and burnished skin.

Skin nearly the color of Rigg's. Eyes that carried the same dark depth.

Because the restaurant was nearly empty, she caught enough of what the woman was saying to the children to realize she was trying to convince them to at least give the lettuce and tomatoes on their hamburgers a try, her tone a mix of irritation and resignation.

She wanted the woman to be wearing a peasant blouse and long skirt, to have left her hair flowing like the mysterious figure in her dream. The mother should be draped in turquoise-and-silver jewelry and wearing a wool blanket and living in a hogan, not encouraging her children to eat white man's food.

After finishing her meal, Shanna started toward the door marked Rest Room. She reached it at the same time the Navajo mother did.

"Would you look at this?" The woman held up a cola-soaked napkin. "I no sooner told them to be careful—the words weren't out of my mouth—when over it went. I don't know why I bother saying anything."

Shanna laughed sympathetically, then said something about those years going so fast. She wondered if the woman would think she had children and wasn't sure how she'd respond if she started talking about things that only mothers of young children seemed to have in common. When the Navajo woman didn't answer, Shanna mentioned that she was new to the area and could use directions to the *Farmington Daily Times*. "I'm hoping to do a little research," she explained lamely.

"I guess you could do that. But why would you want to rummage around in the basement or wherever they keep those things?" She glanced at her children, who were now competing to see who could eat the most french fries. "If it was me, I'd be a lot more interested in the ruins around here. They're thousands of years old, you know. I go to the Great Kiva at least once a year and I've lived here all my life. It helps me remain connected with my heritage, helps me remember what it is to be Navajo."

"Maybe I'll do that."

The woman indicated her dress. "My grandmother doesn't like seeing me like this. She thinks I've turned my back on my roots. That isn't true—my husband and I raise sheep, and I'm a weaver, just like her." She nodded at the children. "When they're old enough to appreciate it, I'll show them some of the family jewelry and tell them its history. A person doesn't have to speak only Navajo and never get off the reservation to be Navajo. It's what's inside that matters."

"That's a beautiful sentiment." Shanna's attention flickered to the quiet, dusty street just beyond the window. "You like living here?"

"Oh, I don't live in Aztec. We have a couple of hogans out on the reservation. I know that makes it sound like we're land barons, but raising sheep is a pretty nomadic existence. I'm sorry, I don't mean to bore you."

"You aren't," Shanna insisted. "I'm fascinated by everything that happens here. You must have a lot of land then."

The woman shook her head. "We Navajo don't look at things the same way whites do. To us, the concept of owning property the way we'd have to do if we moved off the reservation is foreign to us. The land is our mother. How can a person buy or sell her mother?"

"Your mother?"

"I think you have to be Navajo to understand. I also think it was easier for my grandmother—she wasn't pulled in as many directions as I am. I have my feet in two cultures, one modern and constantly changing, the other steeped in generations of tradition and myth. It isn't always easy reconciling the two, but unlike my grandmother, I can't live totally in the past."

"No. I guess you can't. Ah, you say you live on the reservation. Do you know a woman named Juanica White Wind?"

"You've met her?"

"No, not really." Shanna struggled with the question of whether she dared say more, then decided to take the chance. "I think she sent a letter and a sand painting to my grandparents some twenty-five years ago. I was just…well, I need to talk to her about that."

"Twenty-five years? Most true sand paintings—we call them dry paintings—are created on the ground or a blanket and are destroyed within a few hours of being made. It's how we safeguard the good medicine in them."

"Oh. I—I was told it'd be just about impossible for me to find her place."

"For someone who doesn't know the reservation, yes. But Chabah, her father, is pretty well known, being a shaman and all. If you got lost and were lucky enough to come across someone, they'd get you back on track—if they were so inclined. The best I can do is give you directions to where he lives and wish you the best. Only don't take off today, because you'd never get out there before dark."

"I don't want to impose on him. I understand he's not feeling too well."

"He's a tough old bird and Juanica takes good care of him. I'll tell you what. Let me draw you a map, and that way, if you decide to drive out there tomorrow, hopefully you won't get lost."

"Hopefully. There's so much space around here."

"Isn't there," the young mother said with a laugh. Her features softened. "My grandfather said that the distance was in his soul. That he could look out in all directions and be aware of himself because nothing got in the way."

"That's wonderful. And I think I'm beginning to understand what he's talking about. Although I'm still getting used to it, I feel more cradled than lost in all this country."

"Do you?" The woman frowned. "Usually only Navajo feel that way."

"Oh." A chill—or was it excitement?—raced down her spine. "There's so much I don't know about your people. I don't even know where to start."

"There's a lot to learn. Most tourists just touch the surface."

"That's a shame. All right, the land is your mother. What else?"

"In twenty-five words or less?" she asked with a smile. "In brief, we're a nation ruled by spiritual belief, by the Holy People. It's said that we came into existence when the Anasazi came to the surface world through the Hole of Emergence. The Holy People created the mountains, mesas, deserts, springs, all plants and animals."

"That...sounds wonderful." Shanna meant it. Why then was she shivering?

"Wonderful and frightening, if you're a believer."

"Frightening?" Shanna needed to concentrate on her surroundings, but the restaurant had blurred and become indistinct. Instead she saw, or thought she saw, the endless sky stretching beyond the tired old street.

"Because of the Chinde."

"Chinde?"

"The ghosts of Earth Surface dead." The women again glanced at the children, then wagged her finger in disapproval. "There are...but I'm probably boring you. I bet you didn't know you'd get all this when you spoke to me. I love talking about my heritage, not that I probably need to tell you that. Just don't forget, the Chinde are evil, and preventing them from causing trouble keeps the shamen busy. There's one... Oh, never mind."

Evil. Shanna tensed, afraid she'd spoken the word aloud. She must not have; otherwise the woman would have said something, wouldn't she? "It sounds interesting," she muttered, hating the stupid words before they were out of her mouth.

"It's an essential part of our lives—for those who believe."

"Do you? I'm sorry. I had no right asking that. But it seems so strange, evil Chinde and ghosts, Holy People. I mean—" Shanna swept her hand to encompass the little restaurant with its dusty plastic plants and faded, red plastic tablecloths "—we're standing in a modern restaurant. Well, almost modern. We ate packaged food and drank something that was brewed and bottled in some factory. I guess I find it hard to reconcile what you just said with all that."

"I know." The woman's smile was still gentle, yet Shanna sensed that the fragile bond between them had been stretched. "Like I said, I have a foot in each world. It'll be even more like that for my children. But I grew up hearing certain things, feeling a certain presence. Those things are part of me and will never change."

Part of me. Although she felt as if she'd barely touched the surface of what being Navajo was about, Shanna couldn't impose on the young woman any longer. "If I spend much time here, I hope I'll learn a lot more about the area's past, about your spiritual beliefs."

The woman nodded, her dark eyes grave. "And the Chinde. They're integrated with everything we are."

"Are you afraid of them?"

"If a Navajo lives as the ancients were taught by the Holy People, there's little to fear."

"Oh."

"But there are so many rituals, so many taboos. And sometimes people don't know enough not to test their limits." The woman paused for a breath. Before she could say anything more, one of her children let out a squall. She rolled her eyes skyward, grabbed a clean napkin from the closest table and quickly sketched a map depicting dirt roads, rivers, canyons and crags. She marked Chabah's hogan with an X.

After thanking her, and using the restroom, Shanna stepped outside and into late-afternoon sunlight. Though she shielded her eyes with her hand, she nearly missed the edge of the sidewalk. She steadied herself and started toward her car.

Less than a foot from the driver's-side front tire, she spotted another large beetle, this one a brilliant red. Without asking herself why she was doing it, she stamped her foot. The beetle rose on spindly legs but didn't scurry away.

Again she stamped. The beetle lifted its head, met her gaze.

In the first dark underworld nine people lived; six kinds of ants, three kinds of beetles.

CHAPTER FOUR

Shanna sneezed for at least the fifth time in the last hour, then, stretching, rubbed the back of her neck. She'd gotten to the newspaper office first thing in the morning and, except for a brief conversation with a young man who showed her how the archives cataloging system worked, she'd been left alone. If she thought she'd be allowed to leave with the ancient newspapers, she would have fled the musty-smelling, windowless, lonely room a long time ago. However, she had no choice but to go on breathing air that smelled of decaying paper.

True, she could have used the microfilm, but the young man had had no objection to her making use of the real thing. She liked the feel of paper in her hands, the crinkling sound the fragile pages made as she carefully turned them. She didn't even mind that her fingertips were now discolored from ink.

The only problem with her method was that she kept getting sidetracked. So far she'd worked her way through a couple of tall stacks, pausing more often than she should to shake her head over how advertising and the price of goods had changed over the years. She enjoyed reading about governmental concerns back then, what topics were discussed in the letters to the editor, the community columns that told of family visits, trips, illnesses, even the interesting but not earth-shattering news that two brothers had painted their houses the same week.

Nowhere so far had she come across names that might help her search, but she now had a clearer idea of the world that had existed in New Mexico when she'd been a small child. It seemed simpler somehow, more centered on what was happening to people in and around their neighborhoods, with less attention being given to the larger issues of crime, drugs, world events.

When her nose started tickling again, she didn't try to stifle the urge to sneeze. Her eyes blurred and she blinked to clear them. She would have liked to tell herself that staring at little columns of print was responsible, but she knew better. Last night had not been one of her better ones for sleep. She was probably exaggerating, but she could swear she'd spent the entire night with vivid dreams running through her mind. There was no denying it—Rigg was in each and every one of them. Sometimes he stood at a great distance, with black-and-white squares forming the background; other times he was so close she'd swear she could feel his body's heat, and he held a shiny red beetle in his outstretched hand. He never spoke, or if he did, she didn't remember what he'd said.

Not that she needed a script to know what the words would be. "Don't try to dig up the past. You don't belong here, don't have any business being here."

Well, he was wrong.

Another sneeze began making its presence known, forcing her to acknowledge that if she continued flipping through disintegrating pages, she'd probably have an allergic reaction to whatever she was stirring up in the air. She bundled up the newspapers on the scarred old table and carefully put everything back on the proper shelves. Even as she moved over to the microfilm machine, a small part of her mind set up a childlike complaint. It was a beautiful day outside, with a faint breeze blowing and the sun promising the kind of warmth that would make her scalp tingle and would sunburn her nose. If she had the sense she'd been born with she'd be outside, not locked up in here.

But until she knew something, anything about her birth—

The sound of the door creaking open stopped her midthought. Certain it was the young man coming to check up on her, she did nothing more than wave over her shoulder as she picked up the microfilm cartridge he'd selected for her. "I hope no one needs this," she said. "I don't know how long—"

"It's me, Shanna."

Me. Rigg. Although he was little more than a stranger, she knew his voice, might never forget what it did to her senses. Gripping the cartridge tightly, she swiveled around and stared at him. Today he was the consummate professional, complete with dark suit and boldly decorated tie. Only his expensive cowboy boots set him apart from what she'd expect to see on Madison Avenue. "What are you doing here?" she asked, determined to reveal nothing of the kaleidoscope of emotions swirling through her.

"Looking for you."

"Me? You can't order me to leave. I have every right to... How did you know where I was going to be?"

He stepped closer, his boots thudding dully on the cement-slab flooring. There was a rhythm to the way he walked, a sway of muscles and bone that fascinated her. Although she would prefer to see him in something more in keeping with the kind of man she thought he was—earthy and natural—the suit hid just enough of his seasoned muscles that she was spared some of their impact. They were alone down here, just the two of them. With a single flip of a switch they'd be plunged into darkness.

"I called Aztec," he said. "They told me you'd been there, that someone suggested you check newspaper records."

"They?" she challenged with more courage than she'd known she had. "Or maybe Juanica told you not to let me out of your sight. Tell me something. Are you trying to keep me from meeting her? If there's some reason, I have a right to know. Damn it, I have a right."

"Not enough of one."

"Stop that!" He didn't so much as acknowledge her outburst, only continued to stare at her with those incredible eyes of his. "Look," she finally thought to say. "I'm not going to fight with you. What I am going to do is tell you that the more roadblocks you try to throw in my way, the more determined I'll become." When he didn't speak, she indicated the microfilm. "The answers I need may be in here. If I have to call a cop to keep you from denying me access to them, that's what I'll do. Sooner or later I'm going to—"

"You haven't been listening to me, have you?" He sounded weary. "You don't care what you unleash as long as you have your way."

"Unleash? It's my birthright we're talking about, Rigg. My roots."

"If only it was that simple."

What was she supposed to say now? Before she could come up with anything, he clamped his big hand over the microfilm and pulled it from her fingers. For a moment she had the unsettling and undeniable sensation that he dominated the room. She thought he might try to put the cartridge away, and she'd have to tell him he had no right, that even if he stopped her now, she'd eventually come back and learn what it contained. Instead, he reached around her and inserted the film into the machine. She moved away from the screen, letting him take over. Sitting, he worked quickly through the editions, slowing just long enough to read a date before speeding on again. It was almost as if he didn't want to see the passing of the days. Finally he jabbed a dark finger at the motionless screen.

April 14.

Looking over his shoulder, she fought off both her awareness of his presence and the sense that her life would never be the same after this moment. Then she read the front-page headline. Young Father Killed in Own Yard.

Young father? A man with a daughter named Cindy?

Suddenly she wanted to grab onto someone, anyone, for strength. But there was only Rigg, and she didn't dare touch him. Instead, she scanned the lead paragraph, then read it again when she realized she hadn't made sense of a single word.

An apparent argument between two men ended in tragedy yesterday afternoon. Before the altercation was over, Sam Parrish was dead and his suspected attacker, Zarcillas Two Feathers, had been arrested.

According to witnesses, Two Feathers had been following Deborah Parrish for several months and trying to force himself on her. When Two Feathers tried to break into the Parrish house, Mr. Parrish, who had been called home from work by his wife, confronted the trespasser.

A neighbor stated that she saw Two Feathers draw a knife and threaten Mr. Parrish, who was preventing Two Feathers from entering. Mrs. Parrish, who'd remained in the house with their young daughter, ran outside and attempted to defend her husband. Two Feathers knocked Mrs. Parrish to the ground, but it appears that she was uninjured. Then, in the presence of several witnesses, Two Feathers stabbed Mr. Parrish a half-dozen times.

Neighbors attempted to subdue Two Feathers, but he held them off at knifepoint and then, instead of running away, tried to break into the house. It took four police officers to place Two Feathers under arrest. According to hospital personnel, Mr. Parrish died at the scene.

A childlike whimpering sound rose in Shanna's throat. Although the article had been written without sensationalism, she easily imagined what remained unreported. Deborah—Debby—Parrish had watched her husband being killed. Because there'd been nothing she could do for the man she loved, she had run back inside, to protect not herself but the small child she'd left there.

Her?

"Why?" Shanna barely recognized her voice. "Why did he do it?"

"I don't know."

The room seemed to grow darker with Rigg's words, but that was impossible; she was simply in a state of shock because of what she'd just learned. "That's what the people who raised me were trying to protect me from—that my father met a violent death?"

Rigg didn't answer. In his silence she sensed not an inability to explain but something deeper, more shadowed. When she continued to stare at him, he turned toward her, eyes dusky. How long they held her like that she couldn't say; she knew only that in that time the room, the article about her father's death, the slowly gathering answers about her past ceased to exist.

His entire being had a beat to it, reminding her of the push and pull of the ocean. For as long as she could remember, walking along a beach had had a mesmerizing effect on her. It was no different now except that—except that in Rigg, she sensed a growing storm.

Storm? No. Images—memories. People yelling. Police cars with red lights endlessly flashing. A blood-soaked body sprawled on the grass like some discarded toy. A woman screaming. A child clinging to the woman's legs. A sweating man fighting, endlessly fighting the officers trying to subdue him. The child—crying. Frightened and lost, not understanding. Child . . .

No! No more! Feeling as if she'd just survived a violent ride down a raging river, Shanna fought her way free of the horrible memories and forced herself to concentrate on Rigg—whose eyes had triggered the nightmare of thought and image.

But Rigg must have decided he'd given her access to him long enough. Either that or he'd grown weary of having her gawk openmouthed at him. Whichever it was, he turned away from her, not to leave the room but to forward the microfilm to another date.

April 23.

Feeling like a prisoner being compelled by invisible hands into a web of darkness, she forced her attention onto the lead story. Young Widow Stabbed by Husband's Murderer; Killer Gunned Down by Rookie Policeman.

The whimper she hadn't been able to silence before was even louder this time. Not waiting for Rigg to move aside, she leaned closer to the screen, so that her shoulder brushed his. A sensation like that of lightning arching though a stormy purple sky flooded through her, momentarily making her forget everything else.

Then, because absorbing the past was more important than even this shock of sensation, she forced herself to concentrate.

An escaped murder suspect struck again yesterday, this time killing the widow of the man he'd stabbed a little over a week ago, before being killed himself by police. Deborah Parrish, the victim, was the mother of a two-year-old daughter. The killer, Zarcillas Two Feathers, had been arrested one week ago for the murder of Mrs. Parrish's husband, Sam Parrish.

When called to the scene, police found Two Feathers still in the Parrish house. Instead of heeding orders to give up his weapon, Two Feathers ran outside and confronted police on the front lawn. During the ensuing battle, Two Feathers was killed by rookie policeman Hank Granger. Fortunately the couple's young daughter was uninjured, although Two Feathers had briefly held her hostage. The girl is currently staying with a family friend.

Two Feathers, who had been arrested following the attack on Sam Parrish, escaped from the county jail two days ago. According to jail personnel, he was being brought back from a court hearing when . . ."

Hank Granger? Where had she seen that name before?

Thump.

Wondering if it was possible for a perfectly healthy person to faint, Shanna clamped her fingers around the table edge, using its weight as an anchor in a suddenly swirling world.

Hank Granger? Han—

A sweaty man gripping a little girl—her—with enough strength that her arm was nearly ripped from its socket. A woman sobbing, begging, reaching for her—exposing herself to the killing knife. A blow. Another . . . Screaming.

"Shanna? Are you all right?"

Someone with a deep and commanding voice was asking her a question, but although she opened her mouth, she couldn't force out the words necessary for an answer. Even with her eyes open, she saw the growing red stain on her mother's blouse, remembered her two-year-old helplessness and horror. Why was everything coming back now?

She felt strong hands grip her shoulders, and because there wasn't enough to fear in the touch, she went with Rigg as he led her through the door and up the stairs to the main floor. She caught brief glimpses of people looking at her, heard Rigg say something in response to their questions, but none of that concerned her—nothing mattered except trying to shake away the fog that had taken over. The horrible memories that had been ripped from her subconscious by two old newspaper articles—and by the depths in Rigg Schellion's eyes.

When they stepped outside, she was grateful for the clean, clear air that found its way into her lungs. But even with that it was all she could do to keep from stumbling as Rigg guided her down the street.

She hated being like this, hated knowing her world was out of control and she was unable to do anything about it. She'd taken such a heavy emotional hit that she couldn't do anything except reel.

By the time they entered a small coffee shop she could, with certainty, say that she was with a county probation officer and that she'd recently come to New Mexico to learn the truth about herself. She'd found what she'd been searching for and now all she had to do was survive that newfound knowledge. Survive that and this man who was in danger of taking over everything.

At Rigg's prompting, she half sat and half sprawled in a chair. He settled himself opposite her, elbows on the table, his face so close that she could now make out every detail in his black eyes.

Black. Everything that had happened to her recently seemed to be painted in that hue.

Rigg asked if she wanted coffee. She thought she said yes, but maybe she only nodded. At any rate, that seemed to satisfy the waitress, who toddled off, leaving her alone with him.

Alone.

In a small, crowded coffee shop on a workday morning with vehicles going by a few feet away and pots and pans rattling in the unseen kitchen?

Are you all right? He didn't ask the question aloud; she would be willing to swear to that. And yet she sensed his concern enough that she forcefully pulled herself out of the last of whatever quicksand she'd fallen into. She'd deal with her long-buried memories later, when she was strong enough.

"That's what happened to my parents," she said, acceptance in every word. "Finally, I know. They were murdered and I..."

He didn't speak. Now that she looked, really looked at him, it seemed as if he was holding himself in place with great effort. Although he didn't move, she sensed that every muscle in his body was tightly stretched, near to breaking. His breathing was quick and too loud. The why of that eluded her, as did so much about the man. She tried to concentrate on his professional attire, tried to tell herself that he was nothing more than a bureaucrat buying her a cup of coffee.

It didn't work, because every ounce and inch of her was unbelievably aware of him.

"I have to go back, read everything," she said when the silence and her unwanted reaction began haunting her. "So much didn't make sense. Why would I remember those details now? Maybe once I've studied—"

"What are you talking about?" It seemed to take all the strength in him to ask the question.

"Memories flooded back while I was reading." *Or maybe when I looked into your eyes.* "I never knew I was holding all that inside me. All these years, burying..."

"What did you bury?"

"How my parents died." She spoke automatically, forcing the words out, while emotion fought to free itself from the cage she'd locked it in. "I was there. Saw..."

Rigg hadn't once taken his eyes off her. That must be what was making it so hard for her to concentrate. Those eyes...how could anyone, criminal or lawyer—judge even—remain unaffected once he'd been fixed by that stare? She waited for Rigg to ask her to continue, but he didn't. His silence made her uneasy—almost as uneasy as his unblinking scrutiny did. Once again needing to fill the void with sound, she thanked him for realizing she'd needed a change of scene and for getting her out of that airless little room. He nodded silently.

The necessity of patching together the pieces of the puzzle reasserted itself. Seizing on that goal, Shanna forced herself to concentrate on the condiments, arranged on one corner of the table, instead of on Rigg. Rigg, whose presence had triggered so much. "What made him do what he did?" she asked. "To kill two... Hank Granger. Granger."

Two folders on Rigg Schellion's desk, one labeled Zarcillas Two Feathers, the other with the name Hank Granger.

Yesterday, when she'd looked down to see beetles staring up at her, she'd felt a half instant of cold fear. Today the reaction lasted much longer and took her deeper into an unlit, lifeless underworld, but finally she fought her way out of it. "What were you doing with their files?" she demanded. "Zarcillas's and Granger's?"

Thump.

Rigg's lips clamped together. She saw his hand snake toward her. Before she could react, he'd clamped her wrist with such strength that the circulation was instantly cut off. They were in a public place; she had to remember that—a public place.

"Don't."

"Don't what?" she managed to ask.

"Speak *his* name."

His eyes were night pools, hot at the surface but deathly cold at the bottom, and she felt a heartbeat of raw terror—or was it raw desire? She tried to hold on to the light coming from both in and outside the restaurant, but how could the sun possibly win a battle with Rigg Schellion's eyes? He spoke with such determination—determination laced with fear.

Fear?

"Don't speak *whose* name?" she demanded.

"*His*. Your parents' killer's."

Her thoughts hung not on his insane warning but on the simple and horrible fact that some man had ended her parents' lives. She wanted to tell Rigg what that was doing to her, then reminded herself that he couldn't possibly care. All he'd done since she'd first known of his existence was thwart her every move. "I don't understand," she said. She wasn't sure she comprehended anything—or ever would again.

"*He's* Navajo." Rigg still sounded as if every word had to be wrenched from him. "He was, anyway."

"I know. But—"

"Stop it, Shanna. Stop before you say another word." She'd thought he'd already got as close as he could without destroying the small table that separated them. Now he seemed only inches away, his breath touching her eyelids, her lashes, shattering her fragile ability to concentrate. "You just did something dangerous."

What did I do? Instead of asking what should be the most obvious of questions, she waited for him to continue. Waited and wondered how she could be both hot and cold at the same time, terrified of and yet absorbed by this man.

"There are ancient beliefs. Navajo traditions."

So? What does this have to do with me?

"And powerful taboos," he said in a somber tone that told her he'd got to the core of what this bizarre conversation was about.

"What kind of taboos?" she prompted when, instead of continuing, he stared at her hands with such intensity that she felt the heat of his gaze.

"That it is dangerous to speak the names of the dead."

Dangerous? What kind of nonsense was this? "That's insane!" she snapped, not trying to temper her response. "You mean I'm not supposed to ever mention my grandparents' or parents' names because they might come back to haunt me?"

"Only if they were Navajo."

Where was the waitress with their coffee? Shanna desperately needed something to distract her from this insanity. "I don't understand," she said, because absolutely nothing else came to mind.

"I know, but you have to listen to me and do as I say. If the taboo is broken, the dead person is blocked from entering the underworld. Even if the departed spent his life doing nothing but good, he is reincarnated in an evil form. And if the person was corrupt and immoral, it's even worse."

Evil. Corrupt. The words shouldn't have the power to fill her head with an unearthly buzzing, especially not in a public place like this, but she could no longer concentrate on conversation and clinking plates. "I don't understand," she repeated, her voice reminding her of a small, frightened child—maybe the parentless two-year-old she'd once been.

"I hope you never do. Just observe tradition. That's essential—more essential than you'll ever know."

His eyes . . . she couldn't see into them. It was as if he'd protected himself with some kind of night shadow. Either that or—or... No! He couldn't possibly be engaged in a war with his soul! What made her think something so insane? Still, he didn't speak, only continued to gaze at something she couldn't possibly comprehend, as if he was locked in his own private hell.

Hell?

"Why are you doing this?" she demanded. "If this is some kind of joke, I don't like it."

"A warning." His lips didn't move; his gaze remained fixed on that dark something she couldn't possibly fathom. She'd never seen anyone look more tormented, more in need of a human touch. "Do *not* speak the name of the dead—*his* name. It could mean your death. Yours and—"

"Stop it!" she snapped, because her nerves felt as if they might shatter. "What I've gone through lately is bad enough. I am not in the mood to listen to this nonsense."

"It's not nonsense, Shanna."

She believed him; for just an instant, not a single doubt remained locked inside her. Then, concentrating on salt and pepper shakers, a catsup bottle, she reached for what little sanity might remain in the day. "All right. We'll play it your way, for now. You want me to pretend my parents' murderer didn't exist, so I'll do it. There's something else. Yesterday—" *Was it only yesterday?* "—when I was in your office, you had two files on your desk. *His* and Hank Granger's, the policeman who killed him." She stopped, pulled in every possible ounce of oxygen, then faced the twin pools of night that were his eyes. "What were you doing with them?"

"Doing?"

"Yes—damn it, stop evading!"

First Man breathed on the sacred jewels, which he had placed north, south, east, west and center, and five cloud columns arose and met overhead, and midday and night began.

Shanna surged to her feet, knocking over her chair in the process. Not bothering to right it, she whirled and ran out of the café.

CHAPTER FIVE

Cars and trucks rumbled past. Fascinated by their motion, Shanna stood on the dusty sidewalk, her fingers tightly clamped around her elbows, her mind as useless as shattered glass.

She'd been sitting across from Rigg Schellion, trying to piece together her past, when something about his gaze, or maybe just the man himself, had triggered more of the eerie and nonsensical words that had plagued her yesterday. All she could think of was getting out of the impossibly small building—away from the man who'd haunted her every emotion since she'd first heard his voice on the phone.

But now that she was away from him, what should she do? Her car keys...yes, she still had them. She could, if she was able to put her mind to something so complicated, go back to the parking lot where she'd left her car. But once she got into it, what then?

"Shanna?"

Go away! Deliberately keeping her back to Rigg, she took a couple of halfhearted steps before realizing she had no idea where she was going. "I don't want anything to do with you," she said into the air. "I don't understand any of this, and you—just go away."

"I can't."

That struck her as such a strange thing to say that for a moment she forgot she never wanted to see him again. By the time she'd remembered, it was too late, because she was already looking into his eyes—his powerful eyes.

She wanted to tell him so many things, to admit that being around him terrified her but at the same time made her feel more alive than she had in her entire life. Of course she wouldn't—didn't dare—because to do so would make her too vulnerable and exposed. But the thought of opening, completely opening herself to him turned into a physical hunger that gnawed at her until she was afraid she'd go crazy with the wanting.

Fighting for sanity, she tried to concentrate on his suit, on the ordinary and civilized side of him, but a breeze caught his thick, shaggy hair and whipped it about until he looked like someone who had lived a thousand years ago in a time when nothing except survival mattered. In him was ageless mystery, a tapping of ancient secrets.

"What do you mean, can't?" she asked.

"Because..." His jaw clenched. "...there's something I—I have to protect you against." His voice sounded rough and raw.

Protect. She wanted that, wanted his strength around her, over and through her. With him standing guard, nothing evil would ever touch her.

Impossible! If there was evil, which she wasn't about to admit, maybe it came from him. "I don't need protecting," she protested. "Believe me, I'm perfectly capable of taking care of myself."

"You don't understand." He hadn't so much as moved a muscle since joining her on the sidewalk. Now he eased to one side as an elderly couple walked past.

"That might be the most intelligent thing you've ever said," she retorted. "No, I don't understand, because you won't tell me anything. Because this—nothing makes sense. Nothing!" She didn't want to sound as if she was on the brink of a nervous breakdown, but that was exactly how she felt, and she didn't know how to be anything except honest. "Some of the things you've been saying—things that have been happening to me—"

"Happening to you?" he echoed. When she saw that he was going to touch her, she nearly slapped his hand away, but in the end allowed him to place it around her forearm and draw her against him. His fingers burned her flesh. "What do you mean?"

Where should she start, what could she say? And with him so close that she could smell his faint after-shave, how could she possibly focus her mind on anything except his presence?

"Words," she muttered. "Words I don't understand rambling through my head. Seeing beetles and thinking they've been waiting for me."

Instead of telling her she was insane, as he had every right to, as she wanted him to, he spun her around until she could no longer see anything except him. "Beetles?"

"Big ones. Black and red and shiny."

"Doing what?"

"Watching me. I told you that—watching me." *Go on, call me certifiable! Believe me, I'd agree.*

"Anything else?"

"Isn't that enough?"

When he didn't respond to her outburst, only continued to stare down at her in that all-consuming way of his, she felt herself fracturing, until she wasn't sure there was anything left of her except a woman being touched by a man who'd made a city street disappear and had taken her with him to a place of sandstone mesas and ancient beliefs.

"Don't fight me, Shanna," he whispered. "Not now. Your life might depend on it." His features contorted; she could almost swear a battle raged inside him. "Yours and mine."

Whether it was the words themselves or the intensity with which they were presented that made the most impact, she couldn't say. What she did know was that she would never find peace until she'd gotten to the core of what was driving him—until she'd found the source of the lonely darkness that had wrapped itself around him. "I don't understand—" she started to say, then stopped, because so far that hadn't gotten her anywhere.

Instead, she hit him with all the honesty she had in her. "A minute ago, when we were back in the restaurant, I heard—I don't know—maybe a voice inside me."

"What did it say?"

Not "Are you crazy" or "I want nothing to do with your babbling," but "What did it say?"

Closing her eyes, trusting him to keep her from collapsing, she locked herself inside her mind, sought out the still-lingering whispers, spoke as if the words had always been part of her. "'First Man breathed on the sacred jewels, which he had placed north, south, east, west and center, and five cloud columns arose and met overhead, and midday and night began.'"

There was more, an avalanche of words determined to find their way to freedom. "'Coyote visited each column of light and changed his color to match theirs. His power increased as he absorbed these different colors. Baskets of the holy jewels were at each compass point, with a basket of evil diseases in the center where the Red-White Stone and the many-colored columns were. First Man and his companions, and Spider Ant, were all evil. The others were not.'"

Her legs felt like rubber. "What's happening to me?" she whimpered. Then, because she was suddenly terrified both of herself and him, she wrenched free and began running down the street. People stared at her, forcing her to ask herself what they were seeing. Still, until Rigg grabbed her arm again and ended her flight, she couldn't think to do anything but run.

"Don't, Shanna, for God's sake, don't."

"What don't you want me to do?" She threw the words at him after a silence that went on for a long, long time.

"To have this nonsense in my head? Don't you think I want it to go away?"

"I know you do." His voice was low, yet he didn't sound any more in control of his emotions than she did. "Shanna?" He paused, looking over her shoulder at something she couldn't comprehend—maybe the sky beyond city rooftops. "I need for you to trust me in something. To take a chance—if you're going to understand..."

Trust him? How could she trust anyone? But instead of telling him that, she felt her awareness funnel down until nothing existed except for him, standing so close that she couldn't breathe without taking a little of his essence into her. *Tortured. Splintered.* Both words described Rigg, and yet she could no more flee from him than she could battle a hurricane.

"What do you mean?" she heard herself ask.

"Come with me. Now." The very air around him seemed draped in shadows. His eyes glowed like volcanic lava. "That way... Answers."

Less than an hour later, Shanna was looking out at a massive, brooding and barren peak that rose like some magical and yet demonic growth from the nearly flat desert floor. Shiprock. She'd seen pictures of it, of course, but pictures couldn't convey this. It was overwhelming in its agelessness, its sheer sides defying anyone to scale them.

Or maybe it wasn't the monolith that was responsible for her mood. Rigg hadn't said a single word during the drive here. He seemed locked within himself, as evidenced by the way he gripped the steering wheel, his intense stare not on the road but on something beyond her comprehension. He'd barely blinked; he'd breathed so deeply that she wondered if he was trying to expel something from deep inside him.

She'd sat next to him, trying not to listen to the persistent voice of reason that demanded to know what she was doing out in the middle of nowhere with a man who seemed surrounded by a dark aura. A man who made her heart beat in a way she could neither understand nor control.

His profile, like carved stone, haunted her, dared her to touch him and discover what existed beneath the surface. It seemed to her that he would be much more in his element on horseback, with all his energy and attention focused on keeping his half-wild stallion under control. As for her, well, she would have her own horse and be somehow transformed into a fine horsewoman capable of matching Rigg's skill. They'd race over the ground, easily jumping rocks and low-growing bushes, never in danger of being thrown. At the end of their ride, they'd first care for their mounts and then walk off into the desert together, where intimate conversation would lead to sensual exploration....

What exploration? Rigg Schellion had turned her world on end; she should want nothing to do with him.

Finally he pulled off the road and killed the engine. Because they'd been driving with their windows down, the wind's quiet whispers immediately reached her. The air felt dry, clean, untouched and yet filled with something she couldn't name but wasn't comfortable with.

Silently, Rigg got out of the car, walked around to her side and opened her door. His eyes briefly met hers; the intensity she'd seen in them was still there, still smoldering. He didn't try to take her hand once she was standing beside him, but he didn't have to, because she had no choice except to follow his lead as he started toward what eons ago had been born of volcanic activity. Now it waited for them, patient and unmoving, nothing more than an overgrown chunk of rock. A dark, brooding rock with the power to reach out and touch her. Make her shiver.

"Tse Bida'hi."

"What?" she asked, the sound of his voice after the long silence nipping at her spine. Beyond the mountain, the sky was an incredible blue.

"The Navajo call it *Tse Bida'hi,* or Winged Rock." He glanced over his shoulder at her, but because her eyes were still trying to adjust to the bright sunlight, she couldn't easily read his mood.

"Winged Rock," she repeated deliberately, in an attempt to pull his mind away from wherever he'd taken it. "Why that?"

"Why? It doesn't—" He broke off, clenching his teeth; his body twitched so slightly that she thought maybe she'd imagined it. "Tradition says that once, eons ago, the Navajos took refuge on top of the rock. In answer to their prayers, it sprouted wings and took them far from their enemies, the Utes."

"Wings?" She stared at the landmark. Was what he'd just said any stranger than baskets made of holy jewels or evil diseases? "What are we doing?" she asked, her question in rhythm with the slight sounds her tennis shoes made on the hard ground. She spoke to keep from thinking, from feeling too much. From telling Rigg that she was afraid to be here, and that with every step, the fear grew.

"Here?" He gazed up at the rock, as if seeing it for the first time. His features contorted, then reassembled themselves into a form she recognized.

"Yes," she prompted. "You brought me out here, remember?"

Instead of saying anything, he turned right, and she followed—followed like a sheep being led to slaughter? Despite the day's warmth, Shiprock gave off a cool ambiance and she wondered how cold it was at its core. That must be it; thinking about Shiprock's lifeless center must have been what had filled her with this unshakable sense of dread. If she cocked her head in a certain direction, she caught a wind whisper she told herself was caused by the breeze pushing past the stone mountain. In the sound, she could almost imagine she heard the prayers of those long-dead Navajo whose desperation had made such an impact on their gods that those gods had brought *Tse Bida'hi* to life. She wasn't afraid of ancient generations of Indians, for crying out loud! Why couldn't she turn off this nearly overwhelming need to run?

Why couldn't she reach Rigg, pull him free from—from where?

Finally he stopped, his body coming to rest in a way that was unbelievably graceful. Watching warily, she noticed that he stared up at the lifeless rock walls for a long time before turning his attention to her. He'd taken off his tie and jacket before getting in the car, and somewhere during the drive must have unbuttoned his top two shirt buttons. The wind seemed fascinated by the fabric, pressing it against his chest and then lifting it away from him in turn. Occasionally enough flesh was exposed that she imagined pressing her palm flat against bone and muscle and sun-heated flesh. He wore a tiny bag held in place by what looked like a thin leather cord around his neck. The bag, stuffed with something, rested against his chest.

He held out his hand, the gesture a question and not a command. After a moment, she wound her fingers through his and stepped close, grateful when the touch calmed her a little. From where they were now, she could no longer see the road, and even when she strained, she couldn't catch the sound of passing vehicles. A couple of horses grazed off in the distance and the path they were on looked well trod, but not even a distant jet trail existed to remind her of the twentieth century.

There was only her and Rigg, her search and this man who gave out more questions than answers, who was a complex mix of darkness and challenge. Who acted as if he was at war with himself.

It didn't matter how long she stood beside him, how many silent seconds passed. Her mind was full of so many things—the past, which still lived in this place; primitive male energy; why certain people had gone to such lengths to shield her from her beginnings; why she knew without question, that Rigg Schellion was the only one who could guide her into the light of understanding. Why she desperately wanted to turn and run.

He sighed, a long, uneasy sound. His grip became stronger, until she wondered how much longer she could stand having her circulation threatened. When she felt a tug, she realized he'd begun walking again. His pace was slower now; it was almost as if he had to force himself to finish the journey he'd begun. Feeling the same way, she nevertheless followed in his footsteps. Because he was just ahead of her, she concentrated on where she was walking and allowed *Tse Bida'hi* to slip to a small corner of her mind.

There was something about where he was pointing— something dark. Dark and dead. Dangerous.

He stopped, but because she'd been all but overwhelmed by the sudden sensation, she bumped into him. "Wh—" she started to say, then fell silent. He'd brought her here; it was up to him to explain, if he was capable.

He said nothing, didn't even acknowledge her presence. Looking around, she saw that they were literally at *Tse Bida'hi*'s base. Nothing grew here. She supposed that birds and small wild animals occasionally wandered into the area, but they wouldn't stay long, because there was nothing to sustain them. Unless someone wanted to climb *Tse Bida'hi* there was no reason for anyone to stand on this spot.

She should have concentrated on disengaging her hand from his; that way she wouldn't be standing so close that their arms were touching, that his presence kept her where she didn't want to be.

''Tell me what you feel.'' As before, he sounded as if he hadn't spoken in years.

She breathed deeply, but the virgin air did little to kill the unshakable sense that she shouldn't be here. Still, he'd asked a question and she felt compelled to answer. ''It's—it feels lifeless. It might mean something to the Indians, have some spiritual meaning for them but...''

Thump.

''But what?''

Did he have any idea what was happening inside her, how close she was to falling into—into what? ''But they'll never build a shopping center here,'' she joked feebly. ''There's no reason—''

''No reason for a policeman to come here?''

''A policeman?''

''Hank Granger.''

Like a sharp knife, the name briefly sliced her free from her growing sense of fear and left her feeling hollowed out. Instead of demanding he say more, she simply looked up at him, waiting.

Another button on his shirt had freed itself, exposing even more flesh and the intriguing, mysterious little pouch he wore. She thought vaguely that she should ask Rigg about its meaning. But right now all she could concentrate on were the strange red pinpoints in his eyes. Had they been there earlier?

''This is where Granger's body was found, Shanna. He'd been killed here, shot eight times. In exactly the same places *he* had been shot.''

Thump.

She had to get out of here! Run. But where?

''That's what I saw on your desk, wasn't it?'' Her voice sounded incredibly calm, as if they were discussing the weather. ''Those outlines in each case file, the marks on them ... What are you saying?''

Rigg freed her hand, a slow, reluctant gesture that tore her apart. Leaving her, he first walked over to the base of the monolith and briefly touched it. Then he came back, but instead of saying anything, he crouched and pressed his hand flat against the ground. She wondered if there was still something there—dried blood, maybe? The spot fairly radiated sorrow and loss, and a powerful sense of evil.

"Juanica told me." He spoke slowly and so softly that she had to concentrate to hear. He didn't take his burning eyes off rock and soil; not a muscle in his powerful body moved. She had the feeling that he would have gone on speaking even if she hadn't been there. "Right after *he* died, Granger cursed him. Stood over the body, raging that *he* deserved to have been killed after what he'd done to Sam and Debby. Juanica begged Granger not to break taboo, but he wasn't Navajo. He didn't understand."

Thump.

Stand up. Stop crouching over where Hank Granger died. Now! Because she couldn't find a single word that wouldn't reveal the turmoil inside her, she stepped closer and placed her hand on Rigg's shoulder. The moment she did, a tortured bellow reverberated through her. Shocked, she started back, but almost immediately stopped, because that cry of agony came not from some demon spirit but from the depths of Rigg's being. And despite everything she felt and feared, she couldn't leave him alone, couldn't blindly run for safety—if there was such a thing. "Rigg? Rigg, talk to me. Please."

"Talk?"

"What's happening to you?"

"Happening?" He shook his head slowly, as if utterly exhausted. His hand was still pressed flat against the earth, his attention locked on that single spot. "Granger died because he didn't realize how deep evil could go—how the thirst for revenge brought *him* back from the underworld."

"No! That's nonsense!" Ignoring everything except her desperate need to free Rigg from whatever hell he was trapped in, she grabbed his arms and tried to force him to his feet. After a brief struggle he came, but she knew it was his strength and not hers that brought him up off the ground. "I don't know what you've heard, what Juanica's told you, but it's nonsense. Insane!" She was babbling, hysteria lapping at her words until she didn't recognize her own voice, but she couldn't help it.

Rigg's body felt cold. As cold as what lurked at *Tse Bida'hi's* core. "Is it?" he demanded, his eyes searing her. "What do you feel, Shanna? What do you feel?"

Something swirled around her, a storm cloud filled with dark energy. She imagined the devil at its center, had no doubt that the fiend was capable of doing anything its damned soul commanded. "Hatred. Power. So much power. And evil. Endless evil." Shocked by what had come out of her, she desperately looked around for somewhere, anywhere to hide, but there was nowhere. "I'm afraid of it, Rigg. Is that what you want to hear? All right! Whatever it is, I'm terrified of it!"

They were nearly back to the car before Rigg stopped her. Until the moment he touched his finger to her shoulder, they'd been all but running on the narrow trail.

She looked so fragile, a yucca petal being tossed about by a malevolent wind. Damn it, he should never have brought her here, but his body and mind hadn't been his own; either that or the need to have her understand as much as he dared reveal had drained him. Now, surely, she realized there were powers beyond their ability to comprehend or control; all that remained was for him to demand she get the hell away from him before it was too late. Before he jeopardized her life again.

Only he couldn't do that, couldn't force out the words when she was so close and warm and innocent and he needed that as a dying man needed sunlight.

"You're all right?" he asked, once her attention was focused on him.

"I don't know," she said, scaring the part of his soul the Chinde had, briefly, set free. "What happened? The sensations I felt..."

"Some things defy logic," he replied, damning himself for not being able to answer more fully. "We simply have to accept."

"There's no way I can do that. Rigg, something happened to you back there, not just to me. Even before we got here, you were—I don't know. Not yourself. And when I touched you, you felt so cold. Please, tell me. What's going on?"

I'm losing the battle, he screamed inwardly. Because he couldn't tell her that, he continued to stare down at her, achingly aware of how the sun had touched her hair with fingers of light until it looked like a golden waterfall. Before this moment he'd thought her eyes nearly as dark as his, but maybe he simply hadn't allowed himself to drink from the gentleness he now found in them. He wanted—needed—to tell her everything, but if he did, she would turn from him, and he'd be left feeling more alone than he could bear. If that happened, he would no longer have any reason to fight. "I'm sorry. I shouldn't have brought you out here. But..." *But I had no choice, no control over what must be done.*

"I wish you hadn't, either," she whispered. "It felt like something was—like you're keeping things from me. I have to pull everything out of you and I'm not sure I should even be trying. All right." She pressed her fingertips to her forehead, leaving white marks when her hand again dropped to her side. "You're saying Officer Granger was killed exactly the same way Z—*he* was, that the policeman had no reason for coming all the way out here.''

''That's right.''

''It happened a long time ago, didn't it? Probably the police didn't keep the kind of records they do now. If he had business—''

Fight, damn it. Fight him. ''A month after Granger shot your parents' killers. Same number of bullets in the same positions. There were a couple of mountain climbers on *Tse Bida'hi* the day Granger was killed. They saw no vehicles, no one around except for the cop. He didn't acknowledge them, didn't answer when they called down to him. They said it was as if he wasn't aware of where he was.'' *Like me before you touched me and made it possible for me to fight my way free.* ''They heard the shots—that was all. Just rifle shots and something they described as a cold blast of air.''

Her mouth went slack. Her eyes begged him to tell her something that made sense, the kind of sense an everyday woman would comprehend, but he couldn't. ''Cold air?'' When she rested her hand on her shoulder where he'd touched her earlier, he wondered if she still felt the residue of that too-brief and too-dangerous contact. He shouldn't think about how much he needed her in his arms—her breath on his flesh, lips seeking lips, bodies joining in a mindless need that would pull him out of the hell he was slipping into. No, he shouldn't think about that at all, he warned himself as he took the single step that erased half the distance separating them.

She seemed to shudder a little in reaction to his nearness, but whether the tremor was caused by fear or anticipation, he didn't know. Didn't want to know.

Juanica had told him about Cindy, a laughing, happy toddler secure in the warmth of her parents' love. He'd seen several faded old pictures of her and wondered what her laughter would sound like.

He now believed he would never evoke that emotion in her, and that, more than his own private torment, threatened to tear him to shreds. There was nothing he could do, nothing except wrap his arms around her, pull her against him, wait for her to tip her head upward, cover her lips with his own.

He began kissing her desperately, maybe hurting her with his strength. Frightening her even more because she must be absorbing his own fear. Still, he couldn't stop himself. Could only drink from her innocence and remember what it felt like a lifetime ago when he, too, had believed in tomorrow.

She should be fighting him, he thought as her soft, yet strong body moved slightly to accommodate him. She slid her arms up over his chest until they were clamped tightly around his neck. That she trusted him enough to allow him to kiss her—enough to reciprocate in the dangerous joining—flew against everything he'd thought and feared from the day Juanica had told him that Cindy—Shanna—was trying to unravel her past. But his vow to keep her out of this part of New Mexico had been the desperate plan of a desperate man. A man who hadn't yet looked into a woman's eyes and found both his own salvation and hell.

"Shanna," he whispered, her name a song in his heart. "Shanna."

She didn't ask him to say more, didn't demand the truth from him. Instead, she continued to warm him with her body's heat, and he drank from her mouth until he found the child she'd once been and the woman she'd become.

Then, when he'd all but given himself up to her and her promise of sunlight, he sensed that they weren't alone.

It didn't matter which one of them looked down first; maybe they both did at the same time. What he saw, what he knew she saw, was a long, thin, red-brown snake stretched out no more than three feet from his boots.

When the people emerged into the third world—the Yellow World—they found one single old man and his wife and another living there. These were Salt Man and Salt Woman and Fire God. Also there were all kinds of Snake People, including various colored snakes who were evil.

CHAPTER SIX

"Go back to Florida."

Shanna stared out the window of Rigg's car at her rental vehicle but made no move to head toward it. This was the first thing he had said since pulling her away from the snake they'd seen at Shiprock, and she'd be damned if she'd allow it to be the last. Alice in Wonderland had nothing on her; the thought would have made her chuckle if she could find a single, solitary thing to laugh about in this whole incredible situation.

"No," she said, proud of how calm and determined she sounded. Her reply swung him toward her, but she didn't do him the honor of looking at him—or maybe, she wasn't sure she trusted herself to gaze into his eyes before she'd rid herself of the impact of their kiss.

"You have to." He ran his hands up and down the steering wheel as if needing something to do. "After what's happened, don't you see, you have to!"

"What happened? A little snake decided to check out your boots. Maybe he wanted to see if they were made from some relative of his." *Stop making a joke of it!* she implored herself. "He ought to get together with my beetles. They'd make quite a color combination."

"It isn't funny, Shanna."

"You think I don't know that?" she snapped, her tone a powerful indication of how on edge she was. Rigg hadn't moved away from the snake, hadn't done anything to try to frighten the creature. Instead, he'd stood with his arm tight around her, whispering in time with her as she recited the strange words.

As full realization of what they'd done sank in, she reached for the door handle. She was out of the car before she gave a thought to what she was going to say to him; when she began, she was grateful only he could hear. Otherwise, she'd probably be sent to a padded room.

"'When the people emerged into the Third World—the Yellow World—they found one old man and his wife and another living there. These were Salt Man and Salt Woman and Fire God. Also there were all kinds of Snake People . . .' Go on, Rigg. Finish it. You know the words as well as I do."

"Yeah." He grunted. "I do. I wish to hell I didn't. 'All kinds of Snake People, including various colored snakes who were evil.'"

Why was she staring at him? Hadn't she warned herself of the danger in that? But did she have any choice? No, because Rigg had tapped a physical and emotional hunger she'd never known existed in her. And he was the only one capable of satisfying it. "What is it?" she demanded. "These chantings that have been going through my head—where do they come from?"

Instead of answering, he got out and walked around the front of his car to join her. She still wasn't comfortable being around him, but at least the scarlet pinpricks had left his eyes, and when he spoke, she recognized his voice. Someday, maybe, she'd understand what had happened to them out on the desert.

And maybe she didn't want to.

With his booted foot, he drew in the graveled parking lot a crude stick figure that reminded her of the protective-looking shape in her sand painting. "Those words are part of the Navajo Emergence belief," he said softly. "There's a long story—anthropologists call it a myth—about the journey the Holy People took from the underworld to the surface by way of the Hole of Emergence.''

Holy People. That's what the young mother in Aztec had talked about. Before she could say anything, he continued, ''We're living in the fifth world. The first one was utterly black. The second had a misty light. The third was beautiful, but Coyote, the child of Dawn Light, angered the water monster *Tieholtsodi,* who flooded it. Forced into the dim fourth world, the first people eventually had to leave it because it too flooded. Once the Hero Twins had slain all the monsters they found here, the Holy People created the Navajo, the Earth Surface People.''

If she'd heard that in any other context, she might have laughed, but after everything she'd been through lately, cynicism was the last thing on her mind. ''Navajo origins,'' she mused. ''Do you believe in that?''

He didn't answer and she nearly apologized, because his belief system was none of her business. But he was a modern man making his way in a modern world. He obviously had learned this emergence story somewhere; it couldn't possibly mean anything more to him than her childhood fairy tales did to her.

A wonderful explanation, logical and practical.

One that came nowhere close to answering why an ancient Indian story was emerging from her subconscious and why the man who'd taken her out to Shiprock had acted the way he had.

''Leave,'' he said, the force of his order shaking her fragile self-confidence. ''Now. Before it's too late.''

''Too late? What are you talking about?'' Reminding herself that she'd spoken to the ground, she looked up at him. Emotion boiled over inside her and made it difficult to speak. ''I can't walk away from this. Not yet.''

She waited for him to ask the obvious question, but he didn't. Instead, he held her with his eyes until she had no choice but to level with him. ''I came here to find my past,

Rigg. My real past, not the one that was fed to me all my life. Sam and Debby—I have to find them.''

"They're dead."

"I know that," she said around sudden pain. "But people knew them—people like Juanica."

His mouth tightened.

"I don't care whether she wants to see me or not. One way or the other, I have to find her. I'm not asking her to reveal any deep secrets, anything more about how and why they died. I'm not sure I'm ready for that, anyway. But Rigg . . ." She hung on the sound of his name, let it swirl through her and, strangely, took strength from it. "What were my biological parents like? How did they support themselves? Did they love each other? Were they happy they'd had me? Did—did they love me?" Exhausted, she let the words run out.

"Yes. They loved you."

How could you know? You were only a child living—living where?

"It isn't enough," she told him. She didn't have the strength to ask him about himself, not now and not here, with the memory of their frantic embrace still humming through her nervous system. "Are there pictures of them somewhere, them holding me? I have nothing. That's what keeps eating at me. Are my baby clothes packed away someplace? My baby book? Are things written about me in their handwriting?" She stopped, a sob in her voice.

"I don't know."

Hadn't it occurred to him that she'd need to piece together the fragments of her past? She wanted to tell herself that of course that wasn't true; he was a compassionate human being capable of putting himself in someone else's place. But maybe—

Maybe he was so tied up in his role in all of this that he couldn't think beyond it.

His role? What was she thinking?

"I *have* to see Juanica. Talk to her. To find me, the real me." Shanna no longer felt like crying. What she was now experiencing went so far beyond tears that she couldn't exhaust herself with that simple outburst. "If that means driving all over the reservation until I locate her house, then—"

"Hogan. She lives in a hogan."

"Fine. Whatever. A woman gave me a map. I'll drive out there this afternoon and—"

"No."

She wasn't surprised to hear him say that and should have already marshaled her arguments against orders he couldn't possibly enforce. But this morning's experiences had left her feeling fragile and unbalanced, still frightened despite valiant attempts to kill that emotion. Reminding herself that she had no reason to go on standing here, she turned toward her car. He caught her elbow and held her, not with physical strength but with a force she couldn't possibly put a name to.

"You can't find it on your own, Shanna. The roads aren't marked."

"So? I've been studying the map. There are enough landmarks that I—"

"Parts of Navajo land are Chinde land."

Chinde. Evil. Damn him for stripping her of her resolve. "What happens if I stumble on this—this Chinde turf I keep hearing about? I'm not Navajo—I can't be touched by something I don't believe in."

"Hank Granger was."

"Stop it! I've had about all I can take of this—whatever it is you're spouting! I'm not leaving until I've learned all I possibly can about my parents. If it takes a year and I wind up unemployed as a result, I guess I'll have to live with the consequences." She sounded so brave that she half believed herself. "Rigg, nothing has ever *really* happened in my life. It's as if I've been going through the motions. From the moment I realized my past wasn't what I thought it was, I've felt more alive. More challenged. More determined. I'm not going to stop until I understand everything.''

She didn't see his lungs expand, yet she knew he was drawing in as much oxygen as he could possibly hold. He hadn't released her elbow, his grip seeming to spread out to encompass her arm, her entire side. Like a slowly setting sun, the color imprinted by the day left his eyes, until nothing was left except black; and yet the darkness seemed to exist beyond his eyes, seemed to be encompassing his entire being. When she had to struggle to take a breath herself, she could no longer deny her reaction to what was happening to him. The sense of something evil, something spawned in a formless underworld, had touched her where Hank Granger died. That same sensation was back again, originating this time in Rigg.

Not caring what he might think, she yanked free and began rubbing her elbow, shocked at how cold her flesh felt where he'd been pressing. "It's my life, Rigg," she said with every ounce of bravado she could muster. "I'm going to do what I have to."

Although it was utterly, completely impossible, she could almost swear his outline was becoming less distinct, and she watched, somewhere between horror and fascination, for what else might happen. His jaw clenched and his fingers knotted into such tight fists that the flesh around his knuckles turned white.

"I'll take you," he said, the words gravel-like.

"Take?"

"To Juanica. Tomorrow. Today I've got other commitments, my job. My damnable job. But tomorrow morning." *Before it's too late for me.*

She swayed slightly, then looked around, but there was no one near them. No one who could possibly have said what she'd just heard. Besides, she already knew the truth; she'd heard Rigg's thoughts.

"Shanna?"

"What?" she managed to ask, when what she wanted to do was find the way out of this warped existence she'd found herself in.

"I need you to make me a promise."

That sounded so strange, coming from someone who seemed to exist half in this world and half in a place she couldn't possibly fathom. "What?"

"Go right to your motel room. Stay there until I can get to you."

"What are you talking about? I—"

"Don't leave the city. You're safer here. At least I pray you are."

"Stop this! Just stop it right now! If you won't tell me why you're saying these things, how can you possibly ask me to—"

"Please."

Please. The word was like a warm spring breeze after a winter of snow and ice. He still existed in that shadowy space that nibbled at his physical form, but his plea came from somewhere soft and safe. It touched the woman in her and reminded her of that earlier moment when she'd wanted him so badly she thought she might shatter with the wanting.

She felt like that again.

No one could spend the middle of the day sitting inside a motel room. After flipping through channels on the bolted-down TV set, Shanna stood by the front window staring out at the parking lot. Except for a couple of women carting cleaning equipment into rooms at the far end of the large complex, it looked deserted. She debated going out for something to eat, but she wasn't really hungry. Most likely what she felt in the pit of her stomach was backlash from the unreal morning she'd spent with Rigg. And now, because he'd asked her to, she was trapped inside four walls in need of painting.

It took her ten minutes to go through the newspaper she'd picked up on the way here. Once she'd finished, she opened the book on Navajo history she'd bought at the same place. A hardcover, it had set her back more than what she usually spent on books, but she'd convinced herself it was a necessary purchase. Nearly everything she knew about Navajos came from Rigg and that young woman, and she was determined to understand a great deal more, particularly about their spiritual beliefs.

After settling herself cross-legged on the bed, she opened to the dedication page, which acknowledged people at universities and historic societies. The author, she read, was an archaeologist with a long-standing interest in ancient cultures.

Before she'd scanned more then ten pages, she was sorry she hadn't done a better job of screening her purchase. The author might be a brilliant researcher, but as a writer he was a monumental bore. He seemed obsessed with detailing how his sources had determined that Native Americans had been in the Southwest for more than six thousand years. She didn't care about the locations of various digs or the methods used to date artifacts; she wanted to know what it felt like to sit meditating in a sweat house, to accept without reservation that following the path dictated by the Holy People resulted in a life of peace, contentment and health.

Peace and contentment. Rocking backward so she could stretch her spine, Shanna stared out at the deserted parking lot and contemplated that possibility. Yes, she'd grown up experiencing that and would always be grateful to the dear people who'd raised her as their own. It was too late to ask them why they'd hidden the truth from her. Wouldn't her energy be better served by going after answers in an objective fashion?

Good point. The only problem with that particular logic was that being around Rigg Schellion made it utterly and completely impossible for her to remain objective.

Rigg—somber and tortured. Dark and shadowy. Unforgettably sensual. Oh, yes, sensual.

With a mental shake, she tried to go back to her reading, but her concentration had been broken. Or maybe it wasn't simply thoughts of Rigg that had splintered her focus. Maybe...

Not sure why, she got up and walked back to the window. She could no longer see the maids. Because of the way her room was situated, she couldn't see either the street or the office. It wasn't anything like being on a worn path in the middle of the desert with Shiprock blocking much of her vision and only Rigg's presence to remind her that she wasn't utterly alone in an eerie, too cold world. And yet, there were similarities.

Thump.

Damn it, what was that?

Thump.

The TV? No, she'd turned it off. The room was quiet, insulated from distractions, just what she needed if she was going to wade through that darned, boring book.

Thump.

Her heart? Was that what she'd been hearing lately?

But it wasn't. Low sound, like that of a muffled drumbeat, was coming from somewhere. It had to be a distant vacuum cleaner, or agitations from the laundry room a few doors down.

Right, except that there'd been no laundromat in Rigg's office or out at Shiprock.

Dispensing with denial, she pressed her strangely cold cheek against the heated window, closed her eyes and listened. The sound continued, a disconcerting rising and lowering of volume that defied her attempt to pull it into any kind of familiar whole. She'd never heard this rhythm, if it could be called that, before coming to New Mexico; nothing in her memory bank supplied the answer—nothing except . . .

Chinde? What if the old Navajo beliefs were right and there were such things as evil spirits? She could understand their hanging around Shiprock, but a county office building and a modern motel room?

Thump.

"That's enough of that! Whatever you're pulling—" *You?* Who was she talking to? Feeling frozen and utterly ridiculous, she opened the door and peered out. Unless someone was hiding in one of the other rooms, she had this wing of the motel to herself.

Although she'd slipped off her shoes, she didn't bother going back for them before walking quickly to the laundry room and looking in. Bedding was piled high on the two washing machines, but they weren't running. Neither was the industrial-size dryer. A fly buzzed about in a disorganized attempt to find escape.

Thump.

Teeth clattering with cold, she whirled around, but there was no one there. The parking area looked massive, probably because it was empty. *Right, Rigg. I'm going to be safe here.*

Thump-thump.

She was back in her room, jarred by the slamming of the door, before she realized what she'd done. It took several tries before she managed to engage the chain lock. Feeling utterly foolish, she looked first under her bed and then into the bathroom before reassuring herself that no one had snuck in during the few minutes she'd been gone.

Thump-thump.

The sound built—slowly, erratically, with many inconsistencies, but it grew all the same. Although the window gave off heat from the sun, the room felt unnaturally cool, and Shanna couldn't stop shivering. It might be her; given the state of her nervous system, she wouldn't be surprised if her whole body was out of whack. She should do something about the way she was shaking.

As an experiment, she clamped her icy hands over her ears. She quickly learned that an inch or so of flesh and bone did nothing to insulate her from the drumming heart.

The drumming heart. Now there was a Gothic phrase if she'd ever heard one.

Shuddering, she forced herself to again focus on her surroundings. The room hadn't magically changed from sterile and impersonal into the Alice in Wonderland world she'd come so close to falling into earlier. Except for her few belongings and the indentation she'd made on the bed, it was as if she didn't exist here. As if she had no right to be within these walls. Could find no safety anywhere unless . . .

Thump-thump-thump.

She was looking through the phone book for the number of the probation department before she realized what she was doing. Angry, she dropped the book and stalked to the door. She stopped with her hand on the chain, unable to say where she thought she was going, why she felt so spooked that it was all she could do not to scream.

Once again she clamped her numb hands over her ears, pressing so tightly that now a high-pitched ringing accompanied the stupid drumming heart that wasn't a heart at all. The room was no longer simply cool; it now felt utterly lifeless. And the air—something had taken over. Something was in here with her, a presence, a—a what?

Thump-thump-thump-thump.

For the second time she reached for the chain, yanking it free and slamming through the opening with a kind of terror that made her want to laugh even as she surrendered to the insane emotion. She thought—if she was still capable of that complex activity—about running into the street, just so she would be assured that the world continued on its predictable journey. But she managed to stop without putting impulse into action, because . . .

Because the sound had followed her out here.

The sand painting.

Hurrying back inside on legs so cold she could barely command them, she rummaged frantically through the drawers until she found the carefully wrapped package under her nightgown. She first clutched it to her chest, then tore off the layers of paper. Finally she held it in trembling fingers and concentrated as she never in her life had before.

The painting hadn't changed; it remained familiar and somehow comforting. Knowing only that she had to do this, she again settled on the bed and placed the sand painting on her lap. Her fingers still shook as she began tracing the richly detailed figures and symbols, but before she'd finished outlining the godlike design, she no longer felt as if she might crack like a sheet of ice. She was once again able to make out such mundane but reassuring details as the blank TV set and the faded print on the far wall of an Indian woman surrounded by pottery.

The unearthly din that had threatened to take off the top of her head had become little more than a distant murmur. A muted and manageable thump.

"Something. Someone." The sound of her voice jolted her, and she glanced around, glad no one was in the room with her. But it hadn't been that way a few moments ago; she'd be willing to swear to that. The *thing* she'd heard had been real, real in the sense that she could neither ignore nor dismiss it.

Someone. The word kept nagging at her, forcing her to turn it around and around in her mind. But it didn't help. Still holding the sand painting in one hand, she returned to the phone and dialed the county probation office.

No, she was told, Rigg Schellion wasn't available. He'd checked in, but had gone out awhile ago and hadn't left word of where he'd be or how he could be contacted, which was unusual for him. If she wanted to leave a message—

"No," she said abruptly, and hung up. What she needed to say to Rigg had to be said in person.

"I know," she told the godlike figure Juanica's father had created. "It makes no sense. None at all. But he wasn't at his office the way he was supposed to be and I felt—heard—something."

Rigg?

CHAPTER SEVEN

Rigg stared down at the dark rainbow created by years of oil dripping on cement, but if someone had asked him what he was looking at, he wouldn't have been able to say. All he knew was that he didn't want to be standing beside his car near Shanna's motel room, that if he had any choice—any freedom—he wouldn't be here.

Choice and *freedom* were words he no longer knew the meaning of.

He could see her through the window, a still, shaded figure hunched over whatever she'd carried onto the bed with her. He could just make out the outline of her backbone. She seemed so small with her body curled in around itself, and although he knew his impression of frailty was only a result of his emotional state, he couldn't shake it.

Walk away from her. Now!

Because he knew the voice inside him wouldn't go away even though it was too late for him to heed it, he shoved it to a quiet part of his brain and concentrated on what had brought him here this evening.

He remembered precious little of the trip out to *Tse Bida'hi;* the man the world thought he was hadn't made the decision to stand on ground marred by a young policeman's death. Certainly, in his right mind, Rigg wouldn't have taken Shanna to where *he* had made his first mark as a Chinde.

His right mind? What a joke that was. The shadows had eaten away at his sunlight today until he'd wondered if he was going blind. Less than an hour ago, the D.A. had criticized him for turning in an incomplete report; Rigg had had to walk out of the room to keep himself from slamming a man he considered his friend against a wall. On the way here, a car driven by an elderly woman had nearly sideswiped him, and if there hadn't been someone riding his rear bumper, he would have run the old lady off the road.

He should be able to control the rage; hadn't he had enough experience holding himself in check? But he was splintering inside, losing himself, until he wondered if he dared ever leave the safety, the sanctuary, of his home. How much longer could he keep the monster in him from breaking free?

Maybe his sanity would be gone in a matter of days. And if the demon took over and Shanna was still here . . .

She looked up from her reading, her attention immediately going to the window as if she'd sensed his presence, and he couldn't do anything except acknowledge his need for her.

"I didn't know when, or if, to expect you," she said after she'd opened the door, her body blocking his way inside. "The way we left things . . ."

"Are you all right?"

Her laugh seemed forced and she stared at him for so long that he felt stripped naked. When she spread her hand over his forearm, he struggled against his reaction to her soft fingers. "Warm," she whispered. "You feel warm now." Releasing him, she stepped back and let him inside, but didn't take her eyes off him.

She'd been reading a book on Navajo beginnings. He'd studied the text himself, at least until he'd realized it added nothing to his body of knowledge. How she'd been able to concentrate on anything in this claustrophobic little room he didn't know, but then, her ability to focus had to be better than his. For a heartbeat he hated her, because she was an everyday woman capable of feeling sunlight. Then she took a deep breath and hatred faded like mist before a hot sun.

Need barely touched at what he felt for her. Obsession, maybe. Struggling for normalcy, he indicated the open pages. "Have you learned anything?"

She shook her head. He thought he detected something he hadn't sensed in her before—an unease, an uncertainty she hadn't had when she'd first come to Farmington. It could have been caused by what happened out at *Tse Bida'hi;* he'd certainly understand that. But he didn't think that was it, at least not all of it.

Fighting the part of him that wanted nothing more in life than to join his body with hers, he took a tentative step closer. It might work; he might be able to feel her essence without it overwhelming him. And then... "What were you looking for?" He indicated the book. "Maybe I can help."

"Help? If what you've done so far is an indication of that, don't bother."

"Maybe. And maybe what's happening is out of our hands."

Her look clearly said she wanted him to explain what he was talking about, but he had no idea how to begin, or whether he would still be in one piece by the time the telling was over.

"I don't understand you, Rigg," she said.

She glanced over her shoulder at the bed, directing his attention to the fact that her sand painting was caught in the folds of the coverlet. Just enough of it showed that even from this distance he could see it had been made by a master of the art. He'd always been impressed by what Juanica's father created, been unbelievably grateful for what he'd done for him, but to know Chabah had made this one twenty-five years ago to protect an innocent child stopped him midbreath.

"Did you hear me?" Shanna's question broke into his thoughts.

Pain stabbed at his temple and nearly doubled him over. He fought it by closing his eyes, spreading his legs to balance his weight and waiting. It was no better or worse than it had been before; the only difference was that, for the first time, he wasn't battling his demons in private. Through the mist that had become his vision, something writhed, particles and molecules not quite forming. The deeply shadowed Chinde figure—he'd come to call it that because that was as close to the truth as he dared get—wasn't hampered by gravity or any of the other rules mortals were compelled to obey. It danced just out of reach, tantalized and beckoned, spat guttural utterances Rigg knew only he could hear. It seduced and commanded. Called him to join *him* in the underworld.

He should have never left his house today.

"Rigg?" Shanna's worried voice slipped through his fragmented thoughts and gave him something to concentrate on. "What's wrong? Are you all right?"

No. Because he didn't trust his voice, he forced himself to open his eyes and focus on her. Her concern was genuine, something he would never forget. "Yes," he finally lied. "It's been a long day, that's all."

She didn't believe his explanation; every line of her body told him that. "I tried to reach you a few minutes ago," she said. "No one knew where you were."

"You tried to reach me? Why?"

"Something . . ." She pressed her hand against her forehead, as if the same pain that racked him had attacked her. "Never mind. I—you said you'd take me to Juanica. You haven't changed your mind, have you?"

Juanica. If only he'd never known the woman existed. But would it have made any difference? "No." He forced himself to concentrate on what Shanna had just asked, tried to find peace in fantasies of taking her in his arms like any mortal man. "I haven't changed my mind." Knifelike shards still darted about inside his skull, making him wonder at the destruction they were leaving in their wake. He took a deep breath, caught her feminine scent and found a little peace.

"Good..." she said.

The word trailed off at the end, proved powerful enough to wrench him free of the monster growing inside him. Ignoring the risk to his fragile self-control, he touched her arm as she'd done to him before letting him in. She flinched but didn't back away. "You're tired," he said softly.

"Tired? No."

"Then what is it?"

She looked up at him, her mouth soft and vulnerable, her eyes too large. He struggled to remember where they were, the danger they represented to each other, but none of that mattered. He wanted only to lose himself in her, to begin the journey to her heart, where sunlight and laughter waited. Where he might find salvation.

"Something happened this afternoon," he heard her say. "Something... I felt cold and I heard—"

"Cold?"

"I don't know why. The day was hot—it still is. But it was as if I'd walked into a cave. Only I wouldn't do that, not if I had any choice in the matter." She hadn't so much as blinked, her gaze on him steady and honest. "I've never had a sensation like that in my life. I don't want it again. What's that old saying? Something about someone walking on my grave."

He couldn't breathe. Fear lapped at him and he tried to shove it away.

"I almost ran," she said. "I think I would have if I'd had anywhere to go."

"You have a life in Florida."

"Stop it!" she snapped, and he knew he'd said the wrong thing, threatened the fragile bond now existing between them. "I won't give up that easily—you should know that."

"Yes," he said. "I do. Something kept you from running. What was it?"

She frowned, as if she was having to struggle to keep up with the twist the conversation had taken. "It went away."

It didn't simply go away; he knew that all too well. If *he* was after her... What did he mean, if? "What happened?"

If she found anything bizarre about the conversation, she gave no indication of it. Instead, she walked over to the bed and picked up the sand painting. Smiling slightly, she told him about unwrapping it and holding it to her breast. The shredded paper on both the floor and the bed spoke volumes. "Don't ask me to explain why I did what I did. The way I was shaking, it's a wonder I didn't break it. But the moment it was in my hands I started to feel better." She'd placed the artifact in the crook of her left arm and was tracing the outlines with her right forefinger.

He couldn't take his eyes off the sight, not just of the painting, but of what she was doing to it. Her finger caressed, tested, explored. His body ached with the need to be stroked by her. To be reminded of what it felt like to simply be a man.

"Rigg?"

The warning note in her voice was enough to pull him back from wherever he'd briefly allowed himself to go. He tried to look at her dispassionately, but that had been impossible from the moment he first saw her in his office. "What?"

"What I just described didn't surprise you. Why not?"

He thought about lying—if he could come up with a lie—but if he did, his deception might cost her her life, and he would rather surrender his soul than have that happen. "Nothing surprises me anymore, Shanna. Not about *him.*"

"The man who killed my parents. Do you have any idea how much I hate hearing that?"

"I can't help it. *He's* behind everything." She started to protest, but he stopped her with a shake of his head. "Tell me the truth. When we were standing where Officer Granger's body was found, did you feel something?"

"Like what?"

"Some presence."

"Presence? This isn't 'The Twilight Zone.' I don't—"

"Damn it, did you feel something?"

"Yes. But—"

He knew what she was going to say, that her overactive imagination had been reacting to what she'd learned about her parents' deaths and Granger's unresolved murder. "No buts, Shanna. It wasn't something you imagined—if you believe one thing I tell you, believe that. I shouldn't have taken you there. If I'd had any control..." No. He didn't dare expose himself that way. "The coldness you experienced a little while ago, the sound—those things came from the same source as what you felt at *Tse Bida'hi.*"

Her expression told him when what he'd said finally, fully, sank in. She seemed to be gripping the sand painting a little tighter, taking comfort from it. With all his heart, he wanted to believe Chabah's creation would protect her, but he knew better.

For the second time since stepping inside the motel room, he felt that tearing inside his skull. Vision dimming, he wanted to bellow his rage and hatred—to fight and attack until he no longer knew the meaning of fear.

Instead, more frightened for Shanna than for himself, he told her they were leaving. Now.

"Leaving? Where to?"

"Anywhere. Out of here."

"You're not making any sense, Rigg."

"Aren't I?"

"No!" Laying the sand painting on the bed, she quickly stepped over to him and gripped his arms with strength that would have hurt if he hadn't already been in so much pain.

"You're trying to scare me. I don't know why. But damn it, I'm not going to let you get away with it!" A shudder coursed through her body. Her eyes widened and she looked around almost frantically. "What's happening? Damn it, what's happening?"

He felt the words building inside him, knew he lacked the strength to stop them from seeking freedom, fought them anyway. "*He* knows you're Debby's daughter."

If she had the sense she was born with, she would have never gotten into Rigg's car and gone anywhere with him. He was so damnably silent, just like this morning. A remote statue of a man. True, he had brought her to a bright and too-noisy restaurant, where the smell of barbecued meat made her mouth water, but having to look at his somber features was nearly more than her nervous system could take tonight.

She'd come, she admitted to herself, because she wanted to be out of that motel room and away from the dread that threatened to drown her. And because she still sensed the living, breathing, passionate man inside the silent shell.

He knew she was Debby's daughter. Fighting tears that made utterly no sense, or wouldn't if she didn't feel so off-balance, she barely listened as a teenage girl in a stained uniform explained that she could have her hamburger cooked any way she wanted and could then select from over thirty condiments at the long counter nearby. The scenario was almost laughable; how could she possibly decide among three kinds of mustard when *he* was after her? And how could she pile lettuce and tomatoes and pickles on top of her meat with the sand painting she'd brought along tucked under one arm?

"You don't have to go anywhere?" she heard herself ask Rigg once they were seated at a window booth with a view of the rest of the strip mall. She'd placed the artifact on the table and had cut her massive burger into four sections, but

as for actually eating—well, that would have to wait until
she could concentrate on the act.

"Anywhere?"

He still looked like a man in pain, his forehead fur-
rowed, the flesh around his jaw tightly stretched, but at
least he'd spoken and his voice was deep and strong. She'd
noticed several women glancing at him, first with open interest and then with somber expressions, but sensed he was
utterly unaware of his effect on them. What was going on
inside his head?

"Home," she prompted. "It's evening. Your family—"

"No family."

Just like me. "Then you know, don't you?"

"Know?"

"Why I have to put the pieces together."

She hoped he understood what she was trying to get at,
but he said nothing. Like her, he seemed to be having trouble remembering what they'd come in here for.

"I didn't leave anyone," she added, when the silence
threatened to stretch on forever. "No man, I mean."

He didn't move, did nothing to indicate he'd heard or
was reacting to what she'd just told him.

"I don't know why that is," she went on. "My grand—
the people I thought were my grandparents were always
hinting that they'd love it if I brought a man home. I don't
mean I didn't have dates—nothing like that." Why was she
rattling on? Obviously he didn't care whether she'd left a
husband, seven children and a year's worth of dirty laundry behind. "But all they were were dates. Nothing clicked.
Clicked? Sometimes I don't know what I'm talking about."

Except for squinting slightly, he remained motionless,
eyes dancing with those strange scarlet lights she'd seen
before. The squint might be nothing more than reaction to
what she took to be his headache, but it might be more, and
more was what she wanted from him—wanted almost desperately. "I remember my senior prom, when all my friends

were waiting for the right boy, or any boy, to ask them to it. I felt removed from it all. As if I was waiting for something more important.''

Suddenly she was a heartbeat away from crying and didn't care whether he knew it or not. "That something turned out to be discovering the truth about myself.''

"You don't want to know, Shanna. Believe me, you don't.''

If he'd thrown the words at her, she would have stalked out of the room, but his voice was little more than a whisper, hungry and lonely somehow. Trying to reach beyond a barrier she couldn't fathom.

A family with two young children were settling themselves at the next table, but she didn't take her eyes off Rigg. A moment ago, the word *hunger* had flickered through her mind; it returned now, so compelling that no other sensation could possibly compete with it.

She was afraid of Rigg Schellion, afraid of his impact on her senses. From the moment he'd walked into her life, she'd felt off-balance—as if she was on a brakeless roller coaster heading into a vast darkness. She couldn't get off, couldn't even think how she might change the course of things.

The insane truth was she wanted nothing more than to continue this journey with him. To explore every nuance of it, to come to life in ways she'd never before believed possible, to never look back.

If the journey killed her—

Stop it! Tonight, in this garish restaurant, she would simply feel and react and live in the moment. She wouldn't hammer at questions without answers. She wouldn't allow fear to step between herself and the other emotions, which all said she would know nothing except regret if she didn't try to replace the darkness in his soul with something—with her.

Glad he couldn't read her thoughts, she forced herself to take her first bite. She was vaguely aware of the act of chewing, but his eyes continued to hold her. Physical need continued to be all that mattered.

He lifted his own hamburger to his mouth and imitated her actions. She stared at his hands until her eyes began to burn. "I've seen your thumb before," she said, her voice so low that she wondered if he could hear her.

"My thumb?"

"The one with the dent in the nail." Her gaze flickered back to his face and stayed there. "Somewhere in my memory...distant. The first time I saw it, the injury was new. Did you lose the nail?"

"Yes."

He wasn't denying anything. She resented the fact that they were in this public place, then acknowledged that he'd probably chosen it on purpose. "Tell me about it, please." Although she detested herself for it, she couldn't keep the begging note out of her voice. "I hate dragging everything out of you. At least tell me how I could be remembering a finger that looked as if it had been caught in a vise."

"Not a vise. A bicycle."

Before he said anything else, she had time to set down her hamburger and wipe her hands on a napkin. "I was in your neighborhood the day your mother was killed," he began. "Riding my bike. I saw the police cars, the ambulance. People standing around. I didn't pay attention to what I was doing. I hit a curb and upended, smashed my thumb between cement and bike." The corner of his mouth lifted in a grin, allowing her to glimpse the child he'd once been. "I barely felt it. I'd never seen so many police cars with their lights and sirens going."

"You were there?" she managed to ask.

"Farmington wasn't that big back then. I was eight, with a nearly new bicycle and no one caring what I did with my free time."

Something about what he'd just said rang briefly in her mind, but she lost it before she could pull it together. She tried to imagine what he'd seen because if she had a clearer image, maybe there'd be a memory for her. "Was I there? Did you see me?"

"No. Someone said you were being taken away."

She wanted to have her past back again—to have it for the first time. "That doesn't make sense." She pressed her forefinger lightly against his dented nail, as if that could take away a pain that no longer existed. "Rigg, I remember—not you, but this."

"I know."

"Don't do this to me," she moaned. "In this one thing, please, don't make me dig it out of you."

He was locked in a battle. How she knew that, she couldn't say, but she would go to her grave swearing he was wrestling with something within himself over what she'd just asked. All she could do was wait, and if she wasn't given what she needed . . .

"I attended your mother's funeral. I didn't know why then, but my grandparents insisted I go."

Again she sensed that he'd slipped something vital into the conversation, but she couldn't hold on to that any better than she had to what had happened earlier. "Her funeral?"

"Yes."

Hot wind. People crying. A woman's gentle hand and her own little one tucked into it.

"It was a warm day, wasn't it?" she asked.

"You remember?" He looked suddenly wary.

"I never . . . Maybe pieces." Closing her eyes, she gazed into the clouds of her past until something, briefly, cleared. "I loved all those flowers. Kept thinking how pretty they were. Wondering where my mommy and daddy were. I remember people crying. So many tears, and I didn't understand them."

He was staring at her; even with her eyes shut, she knew that. "What else?" he prompted.

"Not enough." She had to wait awhile, but finally the mist thinned. "I was with a young woman. The beautiful black-haired woman from another memory. I remember how soft her hand felt. How glad I was she was there."

"Juanica."

"It must have been. In my other image, she was wearing a silver-and-turquoise necklace. Today—the day of my mother's funeral—I kept holding her hand. I didn't want to be there. A man talked for a long time, and then people kept wanting to hug me, when I could hardly wait to get out of the scratchy dress I was wearing. The—the sound."

"What sound?"

"A thudding." Hating the mist now, she mentally slashed at it. "Dull thuds." She wanted to open her eyes and escape the heavy reverberation. "Dirt. Dirt hitting something. Oh, God, landing on my mother's casket."

"Don't stop now, Shanna. Keep going."

Could she? Did she dare? "I'm running. Running away from the sound. Stumbling in my slippery new shoes. Bumping—bumping into a boy."

"You see a boy?"

She told him yes, even though she was certain he already knew that. "He's bigger than me, with hair almost as dark as Juanica's. I grab his hand to keep myself from falling, but he jerks away—because his thumb is black-and-blue. It's you."

She opened her eyes and looked, not at Rigg, who was staring at her with such intensity that it made her shudder, but out the window. It wasn't yet night, but light had begun to leave the day. The shadows blurred her vision, made it impossible for her to fully free herself from what she'd just experienced.

"You didn't know me," she said in a voice muffled by emotion. "You were just a child yourself. Why did your grandparents make you attend my mother's funeral?"

"I don't know. Didn't know back then."

That damnable warning bell rang again. Tearing her attention from the unpeaceful world beyond the restaurant, she struggled to focus on Rigg.

He reminded her of midnight.

CHAPTER EIGHT

Just go away. Give me time to discover if I can still think.

Shanna had kept her hands clamped protectively around the sand painting all the time she sat in Rigg's car. Now he pulled into the parking space directly in front of her motel room, but didn't turn off the engine.

"Juanica isn't going to want to see you," he said.

"I didn't think she would. Otherwise, wouldn't she have stayed in touch with me while I was growing up? Rigg?" She'd wanted to ask her question with more confidence, but it was too late for that. "What happened? I mean, my memories are of a loving woman. Why did she walk out of my life? Was there discord between her and my parents? Maybe... was she in love with my father or something?"

"She wanted to protect you. Staying away from you was the only thing she could think of."

There was that word *protect* again. But if she didn't know what Juanica had been trying to shield her from, how could she possibly decide whether the gesture had been necessary?

"I'm not a child," she said, wondering whether she'd used that argument before. "Look, Juanica's Navajo. She believes in things I can't comprehend." *Things I don't want to acknowledge.* "Okay, going out to Shiprock upset me. I won't deny that. You told me about a young man being killed right where we were standing. Bit by bit, memory by memory, I'm piecing together my parents' violent death. I allowed that to carry over until I imagined things that don't exist."

"*He* exists. That's the only thing you have to understand—that, and that *he* wants you."

"Right!" she snapped sarcastically, although a large, frightened chunk of her wondered if maybe that was the simple and undeniable truth. "*He,* this mythical spirit or Chinde or whatever of yours, is hanging out somewhere waiting for me, and because *he* is, I'm supposed to cut and run. I can't do that, Rigg." *Because you frighten and fascinate me more than whatever it was I sensed earlier.*

She reached for the door handle, but before she could turn it, he grabbed her arm. "What do I have to do to convince you that you're in danger?"

Staring at her captured limb, she willed herself not to struggle, not to give in either to that nameless something she wanted from him or to his words. "You don't know anything about me, do you, Rigg? What kind of person I am. Let me tell you. I graduated from high school, even took some college courses before deciding to become a travel agent. I've supported myself for the past six years. I have my own place. Pay my bills, on time. I do routine maintenance on my car and belong to a save-the-manatee group. Last semester I took a course in industrial psychology and I've signed up for another about the ecosystem of the Florida coastline. What I'm saying is I'm a card-carrying member of the here and now. A logical, sensible world. I might be hearing..." All too aware of how close she was to drilling a hole through her argument, she stopped before finishing the sentence. "The only reason I'm here is to learn all I can about my parents. That's the only thing that matters."

"What any of us want and what happens isn't always the same. I wish it wasn't like that. If I could change this..."

How could he do that—with a few soft-spoken words take her from regretting she'd ever met him to wanting to spend the rest of the night with him? He was tormented in ways she couldn't begin to comprehend but felt a desperate desire to change. "I'm sorry," she whispered. Without being aware of how it happened, she covered his hand with hers and immediately felt his grip on her arm slacken. He began a gentle stroking motion, his fingers moving over her flesh until she no longer remembered why she'd been arguing with him.

She'd told him that she'd been living on her own for several years, that she had yet to find the man she wanted to share her life with. What she hadn't said was that sometimes the nights were lonely.

She shouldn't go on touching him, risking her separate self, and yet she'd shared more emotion, more of herself with Rigg in the few hours she'd known him than she had with any other man. How could she possibly walk away from him before the journey they'd begun together had fully revealed itself?

Before she learned whether she might fall in love with him?

Shaken by the thought, she tried to tell herself that nothing more than physical and mental exhaustion was responsible. Then she made the mistake, if it was a mistake, of meeting his gaze. His eyes tonight were entirely black, unmarred by crimson. She could see deep into him, to where his essence dwelled. He wasn't a quicksilver man. There was nothing superficial about him. He might keep a great deal locked away, but the lucky few who could get beyond those barriers would find a man overflowing with compassion, and passion.

She felt that passion now, a raw and uncensored reaching out by someone who'd spent too long believing he didn't dare reveal himself. Why he'd let down his guard around her, whether he had any control over what he was exposing, she didn't know. The only thing that mattered was that at this moment their hearts were being honest with each other.

He'd released his seat belt earlier. Now he slid closer, pulling her toward him at the same time. A small voice of caution warned her that she was risking everything by embracing him, but the voice wasn't strong enough. Their first kiss, with Shiprock looking on, had been a desperate impulse that left her too shaken to comprehend why it had happened. Now there was time—for softened mouths, arms finding just the right way to hold each other. Energy coming to life and building and being shared.

Eyes closed, she gave herself up to sensation, fought off her reaction to the urgency she sensed in his embrace. Tonight all she could feel was the breeze caressing her skin, the strength in Rigg's arms and chest. She felt heated and knew it had nothing to do with the temperature. The flickering in her belly and arms and legs grew. More and more of him became part of her; she sensed the same was happening to him and momentarily feared she might lose too much of herself.

The fear died, to be replaced by need.

Moaning, not caring whether he heard, she parted her lips and pressed them more tightly against his. He was ready for her, his tongue pushing past the barrier of her teeth, touching her tongue. Feeding the fire.

He drew her even closer until she was perched on the edge of his bucket seat. Leaning precariously, she felt her body rest more and more solidly against his. His hands slid lower until his fingers pressed into the small of her back.

His tongue continued to explore and challenge, darting deep and then teasing. Asking. Demanding. *Yes,* she wanted to scream. *Yes, I need this!* Instead, she continued to cling to him while her body responded to an elemental message. While she gave up more and more of herself.

De'ninaah. De'ninaah.

Suddenly quivering, she pushed free. Still trying to regain her balance, she half stepped, half fell out of the car. Rigg stared at her, his eyes asking for an explanation, but she couldn't speak. She was stumbling toward her motel room before she realized she'd left her purse and sand painting in his car. Retrieving them, she dug into her purse for the motel key. When she pulled it out, she lost her grip. The key fell to the ground and she had to stoop and pick it up.

"Don't."

That single word from Rigg was nearly her undoing; every fiber in her body ached with the need to be back in his arms. But being around him left her too off-balance and she needed to be in control of her faculties. After several tries, she managed to get the key in the lock.

She stepped inside and looked around, but darkness met her. Now even more unnerved than she'd been before, she snapped on the light switch. The lamp between the bedroom and bathroom flickered, brightened. Her attention was immediately drawn to the closet, or rather what she could see of it. She couldn't be sure; in her current state, she didn't trust any of her senses to filter the truth to her, but she thought there was a shadow there. Gripping the painting tightly, she took a cautious step.

The lamp spluttered and then went out. Panic washed through her. How she kept it from taking over, she couldn't say, except that a faint red glow from the large motel sign on the opposite side of the parking lot kept utter blackness from invading the room.

Only a burned-out bulb; that was it, a logical explanation. *De'ninaah. De'ninaah.*

"Stop it!" She shuddered when her voice echoed, and would have run if she could remember how to make her legs work.

Shanna, de'ninaah.

"Stop it! Now!" A cramp in her forefinger alerted her to the fact that she'd been jerking the light switch up and down. She held out the sand painting, all but hid behind it.

"What is it?"

Rigg! She'd whirled and was facing him before she realized what she'd done. His body was completely in shadow and the pulsing red light behind him served to make him look even more unreal. If that guttural thumping had pulsed through her at that precise moment, she might have lost her mind, but all she heard was a faint, angry whisper. Rigg's outline was too tall, too large; how could she possibly put it into perspective? Make any kind of sense of what she felt at this moment?

"What happened?"

Not sure she could or should speak, she swallowed. "A sound." If only she didn't have the memory of that earlier thumping, maybe she wouldn't feel as if she was losing control.

"What sound? I need to know."

Believing him, she struggled to reproduce what she'd just heard, stopped when her poor attempt made her shudder. "You didn't say anything?" she asked. "Tell me the truth, please! You didn't speak a word?"

She must have stumbled toward him. Either that or he'd simply taken her into his arms when he had no right—when she didn't want him to touch her. But he was holding her with the painting between them and she felt somehow strong again. Strong and safe. "It was a voice?" he asked, the question gentle. "Like the chants you heard earlier?"

"A little." *And like the thump.* "Rigg? Whoever it was spoke my name."

Rigg tensed, and although she felt unnerved by the change in him, she couldn't bring herself to pull free. Holding her tightly against him, he moved them farther into the room. His body began to chill. She was horrified by that, but he was all she had to cling to, and at this moment, she was incapable of standing alone.

"Get your things," he said, his tone low, tortured, hinting at the battle that raged inside him. "You're leaving. Now."

She hadn't asked where he was taking her because that didn't matter nearly as much as getting away from the motel room. Several times she almost told him it couldn't possibly matter where they were going because "it," whatever "it" was, would find her—might be with her at this very moment. But if she said that, she'd no longer be able to pretend she was simply a travel agent who'd come to the Southwest to do a little genealogical research.

Rigg drove west to the city limits and kept going through fields of hay and corn. Although the moon was only a sliver, the stars were out, and she saw enough of her surroundings to realize they were in a sparsely populated area. After turning off the main road, he wove his way through a neighborhood of sorts where each house was surrounded by several acres.

He entered a street with a Dead End sign. The driveway he pulled into was flanked by stalks of corn so tall and dense that she felt as if she was being surrounded by them. Finally he pulled into a carport and turned off the engine. "This is where I live."

Because she hadn't been able to see the house for the corn and now the carport blocked her view, she could only nod. "Why are we here?" she asked. "You say *he* wants me. If *he's* responsible for what's happening to me—"

"*He* is."

She wouldn't debate that with him right now, not because she was too upset but because there was nothing she could say in opposition to what—insanely—might be the truth. "What difference does it make where I am? The monster who killed my parents will just follow me."

"My defenses are here. And I don't want you to be alone."

Defenses? He didn't want her to be alone? She longed to squeeze his hand to let him know how much she appreciated his concern, but touching Rigg might fracture what little self-control she had left. Barely believing what she was doing, she reached for her overnight bag and painting and followed him.

A single outside light made it possible for her to find her way on the narrow path that led to his front door. To the left of the house was what she took to be a garden. She recognized squash, beans and, surprisingly, since she'd never seen him smoke, a large number of tobacco plants. Adding that to the list of things she was learning about Rigg, she waited for him to unlock the door. He stepped inside and flicked on the switch. At least his lights worked, instantly bringing his living room into focus.

It said male, felt masculine, spoke clearly of its owner. The entryway was pebbled. Looking down, she realized that the inlaid design echoed what she'd seen in a photograph of a sand painting. What had it been called? Shootingway ceremony?

Two large, uncurtained windows told her that Rigg Schellion sought sunlight and had no reason to hide behind closed drapes. Why should he? He had no close neighbors, and obviously there wasn't much traffic on the street. The furniture, all of it solid and timeless, reflected the muted colors of the desert. Her attention was drawn to a grouping of framed photographs on the far wall. She recognized a number of shots of Anasazi ruins, with the setting sun bathing the ancient sandstone blocks in endless shades of red and orange.

"Did you take these?" she asked.

"Yes."

She wanted more of an explanation, but he stood only a couple of feet away and she was having difficulty concentrating on anything except his presence. "I love them," she managed to utter. "You have quite an eye for color and contrast."

"I used to," he said. "Not anymore..."

"Not anymore? Why?" she pressed, but he ignored her question, simply looking down at her until, uneasy, she turned her attention to the rest of the room. The wall to her right was dominated by a sand painting so large she wondered how he'd found a nail sturdy enough to hang it. This painting, like the one at the entry, depicted two horned figures with their bodies filled by what looked like stars. "That design's called Shootingway, isn't it?" she asked.

He nodded, walked over to it and touched the figure on the left. "Mother Earth. She has the sacred plants inside her—corn, squash, beans and tobacco." Slowly, almost reverently, his fingers moved to the darker figure on the right. "Father Sky. He and Mother Earth are the two most powerful Navajo deities. His body holds the sun, the moon, the stars, including the Milky Way."

Coming closer, she took the better part of a minute to study the representations. The figures' bodies were huge, their arms and legs small by contrast. They each held what looked like baseballs in their hands but were probably symbolic of something important in Navajo culture. A thin, straight yellow line stretched from one head to the other. She pointed to it, asking what it meant.

"It's pollen, symbolic of positive energy."

"Corn pollen?"

"Yes."

His driveway was flanked by corn; corn was considered one of the sacred plants, along with squash, beans and tobacco. She'd opened her mouth, not sure what she was going to say, when he abruptly turned from the painting.

"I have a spare bedroom," he said, one hand resting over his chest as if protecting the little bag she'd seen earlier. "I want you to spend the night there."

It wasn't exactly an order; she couldn't call it a suggestion. But then what did she want—a formal invitation, maybe the covers turned down and a wrapped mint on her pillow? She'd settle for explanations.

Although she wasn't ready to end her study of his living room, she followed as he led the way down a wide and spacious hall. At the end were two half-open doors. As Rigg went into the one on his left, she glanced right and caught a glimpse of a queen-size bed, with a red-white-and-black Navajo blanket acting as a spread. A pair of jeans were tossed over a wooden chair, boots stuck out of the end of the bed and the walls were covered with pictures she couldn't make out. The faint aroma of corn and tobacco was everywhere.

The room he led her into smelled slightly musty, making her wonder how often it was used. She was glad when he opened the window a crack, both because she needed fresh air and because that gave her a little uninterrupted time in which to study her surroundings. This room, too, had a queen-size bed. She wasn't sure whether she liked the antique white spread; another like Rigg's would be more in keeping with the house's motif. There were two nightstands, one on each side of the bed. They held identical lamps with frilly blue shades and small artificial flower arrangements. The walls were decorated in a nondescript fashion—more flowers, bowls of fruit.

"This room isn't you," she observed.

"It's my grandparents'. This is where they stay when they visit."

"They don't live around here?"

"No, Albuquerque."

She hadn't detected any emotion in his short explanation, just a gaping hole. "Where do your parents live, Rigg?"

"I don't know." He was back to looking like a stranger, and an invisible barrier was thrust between them.

"You don't..." *This is none of your business. Don't push.* "I'm sorry."

"I haven't known for years where my mother lives, Shanna. It doesn't matter."

"Of course it matters," she said heatedly, then forced herself to adopt a less-intense tone. "A mother doesn't walk away from her child, not without a powerful reason. A reason like—like what happened with my parents.''

''My mother was fifteen when I was born. I was raised by my grandparents. We seldom hear from her. The last we knew she was in California.''

He wasn't going to tell her any more; Shanna understood that. If she asked about his father, he might block her off even more than he already had. It was possible he didn't know who the man was and didn't want to get into that tonight, with her. Struggling to change the subject, she indicated the room's decor. ''Do you think you'd get in trouble if you did any redecorating?''

''I won't try. My grandmother likes things this way.''

''And this is their room. I think that's sweet, that you're so willing to accommodate them.''

His features softened, telling her a great deal about what he felt for the people who'd raised him. ''My grandfather's the one who convinced me to go to college,'' he said.

''Did he?''

''Yes.'' The word had a wistful note; he looked calmer, gentler than she'd ever seen him. ''I was making what I considered to be a fortune the summer between my junior and senior years of high school, wielding a shovel for a company putting in a new golf course. Grandpa asked what I was going to do with my vast skills once the golf course was completed. Full of seventeen-year-old wisdom, I told him I'd have no trouble getting in with another construction company. He took my hand, folded it as if it was around a shovel handle. In twenty years, he said, my fingers wouldn't know how to do anything except what they were doing right now. The ache I sometimes got in my back—it would feel like that all the time and my brain would atrophy. That's what he called it—atrophy. It got through to me.''

''He sounds like a wise man.'' It was the only thing she could think to say.

"He is. Go to bed, Shanna."

He was dismissing her as if he regretted saying anything of a personal nature, as if he knew he'd dropped his guard and she'd seen into him. "And where will you be?" she asked.

"In my room across the hall."

"With two doors between us? What happens if... something happens? How are you going to know?"

"I'm a light sleeper."

Didn't he know that poor excuse for an answer wouldn't fly? She wanted to throw it back at him, would have if she'd been able to look at him without feeling as if she was flowing toward him and losing herself in the process. Instead, she stuck her hands in her back pockets in what she hoped was a gesture of confidence. "And that's all it's going to take—you sleeping with one ear open for... whatever?"

"You'll be safe here."

"How do you know? This Chinde—I can't believe I'm saying this—has, maybe, been dogging me since yesterday. Either that or I'm hearing voices and need to have my head vacuumed out." *This isn't the time for jokes, Whitmore. Knock it off.* "What is it? There's some code of behavior for Chinde? Maybe I should hang garlic around my neck."

"He won't kill you, Shanna. That isn't what he wants."

Even though it made absolutely no sense, she believed him. "What does he want?"

Rigg rocked back on his heels, steadied himself. For a long time she thought he might answer her, but silence continued until she finally understood how many barriers still existed between them. "You know more than you're telling me, don't you? Something about your house—what is it, sacred corn and your very own sand painting? That's as insane as the idea of garlic protecting someone against vampires."

He didn't respond, just continued his relentless appraisal of her, eyes darkening despite the bright overhead light. She knew it was a trick of her overtaxed emotions, but it seemed that he was becoming larger, growing and expanding until he dominated the room. She wanted to order him to quit doing that, that it wasn't at all funny and if he thought he was going to intimidate her, he had another think coming.

Only she couldn't, because in ways she didn't want to admit and couldn't understand, he frightened her.

"If something, anything, happens, call for me."

He started to leave the room. Not sure whether she wanted that or not, she took note of the utterly graceful way he swiveled away from her. She waited until he was halfway through the door. "If you think there's going to be trouble," she challenged, "why aren't you staying in here with me?"

He looked over his shoulder at her. He said nothing, but then he didn't need to, because his eyes spoke for him.

He didn't trust himself to spend the night with her.

Why not? Shanna asked herself for what seemed like the hundredth time in the last fifteen minutes. She wasn't the kind of woman to go after a man. If anyone should be reluctant about this arrangement, it was she. She'd have to be thirteen kinds of a fool not to be questioning her sanity, and yet he was the one who looked as if he'd been asked to spend the night locked in a cage with a tiger.

Angry and frustrated, wishing someone would point the way out of this unreal experience, she punched her pillow and tried to remember how people went about falling asleep. Rigg's house was so quiet that if she had a pin, she was certain she could hear it drop. She was used to an apartment complex with its accompanying sounds. If there was a radio in the room, she could turn it on and let music and voices take control of her mind until she stopped running around in the rat's cage her brain had become.

But there was no radio, only memories of the man sleeping, maybe, a few feet away. Only this continual waiting for myths and chants to make their appearance. That was the worst part, she admitted as she tried to find a comfortable position for her legs. The part that was even harder than trying to understand what drove Rigg.

The chantings were so unpredictable, so uncontrollable. By light of day she could at least give a shot at laughing off what was happening to her, but at night there weren't enough distractions. Only inescapable reality.

The beetles and snake she'd seen were somehow part of the Navajo emergence myth. Why the myth had taken up residence inside her she couldn't say; maybe it had something to do with her attempt to piece together her past.

Right! That made all the sense in the world.

She sat up, ears tuned to the night. The silence continued uninterrupted by the eerie thumping she'd first heard when she saw the name Zarcillas Two Feathers, making it possible for her to begin to believe that Rigg had been right and that nothing would happen to her as long as she was within his walls. He must have turned off his outside light; either that or shrubbery or something was between it and the bedroom window. Whichever it was, she was forced to walk with her hands outstretched to keep from bumping into anything. She supposed she could turn on one of the lamps, but from what she'd seen earlier, there wasn't anything to read in the room and she needed something to distract her.

She'd spent such a short amount of time in the living room that she wasn't sure it contained so much as a newspaper, but he must have a bookshelf somewhere. At this point, even an advertising flier would do—anything to distract her from what was making it impossible for her to fall asleep.

Groping her way in the dark, she eased down the hall toward the living room. The farther she went, the less sure she became. A bed was safe, nothing unknown waiting for her in his grandparents' frilly, old-fashioned room. But out here... No. Rigg had said she'd be safe in his house.

Her bare feet made only the slightest whisper on the cool flooring. A distant sound sorted itself out as coming from the refrigerator. She told herself that was a good sign, since in the handful of stalker movies she'd managed to peek at, everything was utterly silent just before the serial killer jumped out of his hiding place.

A green glow turned out to be a digital clock in the living room. With just that amount of illumination, she was able to orient herself in the room and again remind herself that the ordinary still held the upper hand. She wasn't going to be kidnapped or spirited off in a spaceship; she could do this. She could. Although the furniture here looked perfect for curling up in, she didn't see anything to read. Rigg was a college graduate. Surely he had at least one book in his possession.

There was a door off the living room that didn't lead to either the hall or the kitchen, and that was the direction she now headed. She supposed she could have told Rigg what she was up to in case he wasn't yet asleep and his hearing was as acute as he'd indicated, but she hadn't brought a robe with her, and her nightshirt wasn't exactly appropriate for a casual chat about insomnia.

She couldn't see either of them chatting casually about anything, she admitted as she eased her way into a room that smelled of tobacco and leather and Rigg. As in the living room, the only defense against utter darkness was another glowing clock, this one red. Because she was uncomfortable with the color that reminded her of what she'd seen several times in Rigg's eyes, she made finding a light the first priority. Fortunately, her outstretched hand soon came in contact with what she took to be a large desk. On top of it she found a lamp and turned it on. The sudden

switch from darkness to light half blinded her; she felt un-
reasonably vulnerable until her pupils adjusted.

This was Rigg's den, the walls alive with more sand
paintings and bear pictures, and a fragile, faded blanket
consisting of nothing more than horizontal lines. The
leather scent, she quickly determined, came from the recliner to the right of the hardwood desk. Although the desk
drawers were closed, he'd left a number of papers on the
top—not that she would snoop. After what she'd found on
his desk at work, she wanted nothing to do with any more
shocks like that.

There was reading material everywhere, a floor-to-ceiling
bookshelf's worth, plus a stack of magazines and at least a
week's worth of newspapers. She felt surrounded by proof
of his intelligence, his ability to live within his mind. There
was a tape player in the room but no TV. All that was
missing was a pipe rack to go with the tobacco smell.

That and the man who'd left something of himself in the
room.

In an attempt to distance herself from his impact on her
surroundings, she turned on the stereo, careful to keep the
volume low. A haunting sound, of drums and flutes, cradled her, gifting her with a sense of peace. She easily imagined Rigg walking in here after a day of work and letting the
echo of Native American music replace tension. There was
little variation in the rhythm, a simplicity that should have
bored her but didn't. It was as if these sounds had existed
for generations, spoke to her through the years. Whispered of ancient knowledge and belief.

Her mind still caught in mood and music, she walked
over to the bookshelf and began reading titles. History
books took up an entire shelf, most of them local in nature, but what predominated were texts on Native Ameri-
cana. Pulling out one that looked particularly well read, she
checked the table of contents, not surprised to find it devoted to the spiritual beliefs of Southwest Indians. With

fingers that had become less steady than she wanted them
to be, she thumbed to a section that had several pages
turned down. She scanned a number of underlined para-
graphs, reading carefully when she came to one that had a
star in the margin beside it.

At the core of the Navajo belief system is accepting
that all facets of personality are interrelated and de-
pendent both on what can be seen and what cannot.
Everything exists on two plains, good and evil, positive and negative. When in harmony, these elements
are in perfect balance, but that equilibrium is precarious and can easily be upset. Violation of taboos, contact with ghosts of the dead, being involved in
witchcraft, having evil thoughts, being disrespectful or
careless in one's relationship with the natural world
necessitate ceremonial chantways before physical and
spiritual health can be regained.

An icy chill pressed into the space between her shoulder
blades. Not breathing, she gripped the book and whirled
around. A large, unmoving shadow filled the doorway.

CHAPTER NINE

"Shanna."

Her name was a whisper, a chant, a low sound issued from a male throat. A half second before, she'd nearly screamed from fright. Now, knowing the shadow was Rigg, she waited for her heartbeat to return to a normal cadence. Still, she was a long way from feeling at ease.

"I couldn't sleep," she said simply. "I was looking for something to read."

Instead of replying, he walked over to her and took the book from her hands. He barely glanced at the open pages, making her wonder if he'd had time to see what was written on them. "That isn't going to help you relax," he said as he replaced it in the bookshelf. "And unless you understand a great deal more than you do about how traditional Navajo perceive the supernatural, its place in every element of their lives, it won't mean anything to you."

"That's what I'm trying to do—understand." She wanted to sound more in control, less unbalanced, but how could she when it was all she could do to remember what had brought her here tonight?

Rigg wore only briefs, the white fabric standing out in bold contrast to his tanned body. The amulet rested against his chest, a natural part of him. Because the room was lit only by a single lamp, much of him remained in shadow, leaving him in a quiet place somewhere between reality and mystery. He had moved slowly, as if he had precious little energy left and needed to conserve what remained. Either that or he was so sure of his position of power that he believed he could control her simply with his presence.

Maybe he could. He looked utterly graceful, so masculine that it was all she could do to keep her hands off him. The haunting music seemed an essential part of him, almost caressing his naked flesh. Like a panther in its prime, he stood above her, muscles and bone ready for whatever his mind demanded of them. She couldn't say why she thought of him in such primitive terms, as if he was more a creature of instinct and survival than anything else, but her reaction was so firmly entrenched that it would take a great deal to change it.

When he shifted his weight, now standing proudly—challengingly—in front of her, she felt torn between the desire to simply give in to his powerful message of sensuality and the urge to bolt and run.

Run? Where? How?

Why?

"I tried not to make a sound," she finally thought to say. "I'm sorry I woke you."

"I wasn't asleep."

Because he hadn't been able to let go of the day or because he couldn't stop thinking about her? "Go back to bed. I'll just sit in here awhile until I get sleepy. With this peaceful sound—" she indicated the stereo "—it shouldn't take long." The air carried his faint scent—natural, no longer cosmetically enhanced. She felt his presence more than saw him, although what she saw was enough to make her forget everything the people she considered her grandparents had told her was safe and proper behavior for a self-respecting young lady.

With a barely perceptible nod, he indicated the bookshelf. "Do something for me, will you? Right now, at least, I don't want you reading any of what I have about Navajo spirituality."

"Why not?"

"Because all that was written by people who simply studied. They haven't experienced—they don't know."

Don't know what, she wanted to ask, but something stopped the question while it was little more than a half thought. "All right," she heard herself agree. "I won't, tonight."

"Just tonight?"

He was standing so close that she could easily reach out and touch him. Fighting the aura that seemed to surround him, she concentrated on his face, on the shades and shadows barely touched by lamplight. "The time's going to come, Rigg. When I'll find out what's happening."

"You'll never learn the answer in a book."

"Then how?"

He took so long to answer, to so much as acknowledge that she'd spoken, that she all but gave up. He shifted his weight, making her ask herself if he was as comfortable with his body as he'd first seemed. Maybe he wasn't as immune to her as he'd led her to believe.

"I hope you never know any more than you do right now." His whispered reply was rough, tortured even.

What was he talking about? Surely he knew she'd want more of an explanation. Unfortunately, he didn't say anything more, and she quickly surmised he'd given her all he'd intended to. "Go back to bed, please," she said. "There's no reason you have to lose sleep."

"It doesn't matter."

He'd spoken with such a sense of finality that she felt not just sorry, but sad for him. She supposed she could have given him her layman's knowledge of insomnia, but she sensed that the usual reasons had little to do with his inability to rest. "Does this happen to you often?" she asked.

"It didn't used to but… You look beautiful in this light."

Of all the things he could have said, this was the most disconcerting. She struggled to remember other indications from him that he thought of her as a woman. Yes, the signs had been there—hot kisses, touching, a look that held and probed and took, questions about the world she'd left behind. But in many ways he kept her at arms' length. She wondered if he was ready to change that now.

"If that's a compliment, I'm flattered," she simply said.

"Not a compliment, the truth."

How many sides were there to this man? "I never thought I'd hear that from you. The way you've been pushing me away..."

"I have no choice, Shanna. At least I keep trying to remind myself of that."

The night waited beyond this room; it would have taken over if she hadn't turned on the lamp and replaced silence with quiet music. A Florida night, particularly in the summer, meant only slight relief from the heavy heat and putting work behind her. Here, with Rigg so close that every nerve in her body was aware of his presence, darkness also meant an end to the well-defined world of day. Meant entering a land of mist and promise and maybe more danger than she could survive.

"I wish I understood you," she told him. "I wish you trusted me enough to tell me the truth."

She sensed him drawing away and into himself, but wasn't sorry for what she'd said. The man had hidden behind silence long enough. "Rigg, I can't leave until I have the answers I came here for. You're going to have to accept that. If you'd help instead of putting up roadblocks, I'd have what I need and be out of here."

"I don't want you to leave."

Her body all but cried out in need, in gratitude for the simple words. She was haunted by the heartfelt tone that had accompanied his admission—and deeply touched by it. "You don't?"

"No." He drew out the word as if reluctant to give it freedom, yet incapable of doing otherwise. "You're a beautiful woman, Shanna."

He'd said that before; she should be immune to its impact. But she wasn't. Before she could think what, if anything, she should say, he spread his hands over her upper arms, his strong fingers telegraphing a power that should have frightened her. With the first touch, she had no choice but to acknowledge her reaction. Like a small bird caught in a powerful wind current, she rode out its strength. Rigg's strength.

He didn't try to force himself on her. Still, when he dipped his head toward her, she felt herself moving into him, answering his unspoken question, allowing him to cover her mouth with his, and sensed that she'd acted without conscious will.

His naked chest radiated heat and strength. She sensed more than heard the slight vibration of his heart, a vibration utterly in time with drum and flute. Pressed against him now, she parted her lips. His tongue pushed into her, taking, not asking. Despite the sense that things were going much faster than was safe, she couldn't command so much as a single muscle to pull away. Instead, she ran her hands up his body until she'd buried her fingertips in his thick hair.

A sensation of heated liquid built nearly to the boiling point in her belly and then spread quickly and surely throughout her body. She recognized it for the physical message it was, fought for a moment to deny the sensation, and then, because the hot and hungry liquid was far stronger than the need for self-preservation, she surrendered.

Rigg's hands were no longer on her shoulders. While she'd been locked in her private battle, he'd slid them around to her back, pressing her firmly against him. Against his aroused body.

Once again the instinct for survival asserted itself. Bombarded by it, she struggled to free herself from his kiss, his embrace, the invisible threads of his control over her, but he kept after her with fingers and mouth and heat, and after no more than a few seconds, she could no longer think how she might free herself.

Couldn't, because to lose him before she'd tasted her fill of him might leave her shattered.

Still caught between battle and surrender, she moved against him, taking and denying what she was doing at the same time. Her emotional war escalated, splintered her senses until she had no idea what was happening to her, only knew that she had to cling to him while the battle raged.

He continued his search for the nerve endings at the base of her spine. She responded as if his fingers had become shards of lightning, first with a quivering, then with a surrender that left her breathless. He controlled her body, took possession of it, made her ravenous for him. Taught her that, for tonight at least, her will wasn't strong enough—that he ruled her mind as surely as he did her body.

His hands slid lower, over her buttocks, pulling her fully against him until she wasn't sure any clothing remained between them—between what they both needed. Clinging to his neck now, she tried to arch away from his all-consuming kiss, but he came after her and bent her back until his strength was all that kept her from collapsing. She didn't want to feel surrounded by him, and yet the sensation drove her half-crazy. She was his, helpless and willing, the fight going out of her as surely as desire grew.

He gripped her nightgown and pulled the garment upward, leaving her naked from the waist down. She wanted, needed him to strip her so her flesh could fully absorb his heat, but he was playing with her, pushing her to the edge. To a place where drums and flutes and the rich scent of corn and tobacco waited.

She couldn't let him do that without taking him with her. As he slipped his hands under her nightgown and cupped her breasts, she managed to draw his lower lip into her mouth, holding it as surely as he held her. The struggle, if that's what it was, went on until she thought she would scream out her need for him.

He was breathing heavily, but because she was all but panting herself, she felt no sense of victory. His fingers slid over her breasts, capturing her nipples between thumb and forefinger. It wasn't torture, but there was something about his command of her that made her think of possession—of domination.

A little frightened, nearly on fire, she whipped her head to one side and pulled in enough air to keep the swirling red curtain from wrapping itself completely around her. Somehow her hands were no longer around his neck but at the base of his throat, where a strong vein pulsed. She pressed until it seemed that his blood flowed into and through her. He resettled his hands, now holding the weight of her breasts while his aroused manhood probed and promised. He still had her off-balance, still controlled their embrace.

Head pounding, body sobbing in need, she no longer cared about self-preservation.

Her ribs tingled, caught on fire as he ran his hands up her sides, taking her gown with him. Obedient, she lifted her arms and leaned forward so he could strip the garment from her. Night coolness whispered over her exposed flesh. She felt alone, lost. Impoverished. But he'd let her go only so he could free himself of his shorts, and now had hold of her again, his hands clamped over her hips. Wearing nothing except the small leather bag around his neck, he pulled her toward him, and his urgent manhood asked—maybe demanded—that she receive him.

She thought they would be joined right there, but suddenly he lifted her in his arms and carried her quickly down the hall and into his bedroom. He lowered her onto the rumpled covers and followed, his greater weight tilting her toward him. Once again something that might be fear gnawed at her, but the emotion wasn't strong enough to hold sway over what else she felt.

"I've wanted this from the moment I heard your voice on the phone," he whispered hoarsely. "Damned myself for what I knew I would try to make happen."

"Damned? Why?"

"Because it shouldn't be—you and me. It isn't safe."

She didn't care about safety, only that he wanted to make love to her and that she would starve if she didn't have him. "Don't talk, please," she begged him. "It will only ruin—"

"It's already ruined. Should never be."

If only she could think clearly enough to follow his hard and complex words, but that was beyond her. "It's going to happen," she challenged. "Unless you walk out of here now, we're going to make love."

"Is it what you want?"

Does a dying plant crave water? Letting her body answer for her, she lifted her buttocks off the bed, offered herself to him. He groaned like a man in agony.

He reminded her of a mountain, his size blocking out the world. But a mountain was cold and lifeless and impervious to emotion, while what radiated out from him spoke of nothing except life. Life and energy and desire.

Hearing nothing beyond her body's demand, she reached for him even as he slid over her. She ran her hands up his thighs, while he shuddered and covered her face with kisses so gentle and giving that they made her want to weep. She'd been wrong; how could she possibly be afraid of someone with this much tenderness in him?

He lowered his head and covered a breast with his mouth. When he drew her into him, she grabbed his shoulders with so much strength that she wondered if she might leave bruises. But she couldn't stop, couldn't temper the passion tearing through her.

Take me! Now!

As if he'd heard the words, he first gave her momentary freedom so she could lift herself to him, and then came at her with an abandon that equaled what she felt. She heard him grunt, didn't try to still the groan that first clogged her throat and then found freedom. He might have chuckled at that, but maybe what she heard was nothing more than an expression of a simpler and more basic emotion.

She tried to quiet her body. It was somehow important that she forget herself and listen to what he might tell her about himself during the act of lovemaking. But with his first thrust, she forgot everything except riding with him. Beginning the journey. Touching heat and flame. Losing; becoming lost.

Knowing nothing except his form consuming hers.

Hozhoni, hozhoni, hozhoni.
The earth, its life am I, *hozhoni, hozhoni.*
The earth, its feet are my feet, *hozhoni, hozhoni.*
The earth, its legs are my legs, *hozhoni, hozhoni.*
The earth, its body is my body, *hozhoni, hozhoni.*

Fascinated by the rhythm inside her head, Shanna tried to make sense of the words, but she was unable to shake off the need for sleep, the utter exhaustion brought about by frenzied lovemaking.

Hozhoni. The word was beautiful, that much she knew. And that the warm, still body beside her belonged—

No longer still. Moving now. Breathing a ragged cadence that frightened her and made the need to cast off sleep even more compelling.

Cold fingers touched her, trailing first over her shoulder blades in insistent exploration, then pressing more firmly until the remnants of the fog she'd been floating in drifted away and she found herself in reality.

The reality of Rigg kneeling over her, his hands...around her throat!

She concentrated on breathing, fought to. The effort brought no relief. Instinct took over and she struck at his forearms, raked her nails over his flesh. When that failed to dislodge him and a red haze began to film her vision, she kicked out, but her feet struck only air.

"Rigg! Rigg!"

His fingers tightened; her head felt as if it would explode. She'd never considered herself a particularly strong woman but, fed by fear, she bucked and writhed until she thought her bones might break. Her lungs felt hot and filled to bursting. Mindless of anything except the desperate need to breathe, she drove her nails into the skin at the back of his hands.

"Rigg! You're hurting—killing—" She couldn't finish. That outburst had spent the last of the air in her lungs. The red haze that was her vision became scarlet and then turned black. Still she fought and punished and listened to the ragged sound of two people locked in battle.

Rigg! You're killing me!

The thought was still exploding inside her when she felt his grip on her slacken. She tried to wrench free, but her strength was nearly gone. Acting on instinct, she repeated her silent message. He shuddered and groaned, the sound so tortured that she nearly forgave him.

She was free! Despite the agony it caused, she sucked deeply of blessed oxygen. One hand went around her throat in a protective gesture. Ignoring her nakedness, she scrambled to a sitting position and looked at her attacker.

Rigg stood beside the bed, arms locked at his side, head bent and tilted, muttered curses—or were they cries of agony?—escaping him. Despite the dark, she knew he was staring at her. Ripping at her with his eyes. She should run, let the night swallow her and make her safe. Wasn't that what people did when they were being attacked—think first and only of survival?

But Rigg was her only link to her past. Earlier tonight, she hadn't been afraid of him; she'd trusted him enough to share in the greatest intimacy. She couldn't forget those things. The momentary thought slid off into nothing, leaving her to battle anger far greater than any she'd ever known. Fury lapped at her, rage that might have been a cover for fear.

"What—how could you!"

"Not me."

The voice belonged to someone who'd given up on life. Someone lost. Suddenly, learning why he should sound so defeated meant more to her than anything ever had in life. When she stood, her legs threatened to give way, but she ordered them to support her, at least long enough for her to reach out and turn on the lamp by Rigg's bed.

He hadn't moved, and in the sudden, uncomfortable light, she noted that his powerful, naked body trembled. It wasn't cold; he couldn't be chilled. Then what?

Maybe something deep inside him.

An inner voice warned her not to trust him, but she already knew that. "I don't understand," she said, pressing her hand against her throat when the act of speaking brought tears to her eyes. "What do you mean it wasn't you? Who else..." She was arguing with a man who might not be capable of hearing her. One look at his red-hazed eyes told her that he was staring not at the woman in his room, but at something that existed deep inside him. Something capable of turning his eyes into chunks of burning coal. His hand went to his chest, pressing. Lips thinned, he looked down at the bed, where his amulet with its broken cord lay.

"Tell me." She didn't care if her voice sounded as if she was begging; she was, wasn't she? "Tell me! What happened?"

The coals seemed to glow, to pulse with amber lights that sent a horrified shiver through her. His body stiffened even more, and yet he was shuddering as if a battle raged inside him. A battle that might explain everything.

Driven by the need to understand, she took a step toward him. She nearly took another, but self-preservation kicked in and held her rooted where she was. "Rigg, please. I have a right to know."

He reached down and picked up the little bag, held it in his fist. He looked not frightening or imposing, but vulnerable in a way that stabbed at her heart. Another deep, agonized groan filled the air. Before she could react to the sound, he spun around and stalked from the room, his long, hard legs speeding his journey.

She slammed the door behind him and wrenched the lock into place. She tried to lift her hand to her face, but it trembled too much to allow her to direct its movement. Sobbing, she let the night surround her.

I shouldn't be here. Why I didn't leave...

Angry at the insistent question, Shanna stepped into the hall with its muted morning light. She'd spent most of the night being bombarded by the arguments that spun about inside her like debris caught in a whirlwind. In her spare moments, she'd massaged her aching throat and fought back the memories of those terrifying seconds when she'd thought Rigg might kill her.

Kill? They'd made love earlier in the evening; she'd believed in his tenderness, their need for each other. That was why she hadn't slipped out the window or picked up the phone and asked for help.

A quick glance into the second bedroom told her that Rigg wasn't there. She entered the living room, grateful to discover she had the room to herself, but uneasy because she had no way of knowing whether he was crouching in wait somewhere. Even as she told herself he might be in the kitchen, her eyes strayed to the den. She could hear music, ancient instruments and a soft chanting.

Why didn't you leave last night?

It's not that easy. We're in the middle of nowhere; we came in his car.

Anything would be better than waiting for him to finish—

I don't know why I didn't run! All right, I don't know!

Because she'd been over the senseless argument a thousand times, she knew she wouldn't now stumble across the answer; it might always evade her. Instead, courage held high and strong in front of her, she quickly dressed and began the seemingly endless journey across the living room toward the den.

Rigg was here. If pressed for an explanation of how she knew that, she would only be able to say that her body hadn't forgotten what his felt like. Whether his essence reached out to hers at this moment didn't matter. She simply knew without a doubt that when she stepped into the room, she would find him there.

He was sitting in the large recliner, his head turned so he could look out the window at the innocence of a summer morning. He wore blue jeans, no shirt, no shoes. The talisman was back in place against his flesh. The music came from the stereo, different from the tape she'd listened to last night and yet similar in many ways. Surely he'd heard or sensed her coming, but he made no indication he knew or cared that he was no longer alone.

She supposed she should be grateful she couldn't see into his eyes, where so much danger and challenge and life dwelled, but she wasn't. The simple and unalterable fact was that if he'd wanted to, he could have burst in on her anytime during the night and finished what his punishing fingers had begun. Something had stopped him; that same something would, she believed, save her now.

Remembering that terrifying battle, she pressed her hand to her throat. The touch awakened injured nerve endings, but she couldn't concentrate on that because Rigg had shifted and was looking up at her. Even with the light behind him, she easily read the agony she found there.

"What did I do?"

"Do?"

"Last night, to you. What did I do?"

"You don't remember?"

When he shook his head, he reminded her of a weary boxer at the end of a long fight. His gaze settled on her hand.

"Are you saying you're a sleepwalker?" she asked.

"No."

No. Damn it, I need more than that. "Then what, Rigg? What happened?"

"You're going to have to tell me."

He sounded so resigned. She should be concentrating on that and the essential question of why she wasn't dialing 911 at this very second. But for reasons she hoped she'd never have to explain, she believed it much more important that she draw the truth out of him than put herself in the tender care of the local law-enforcement people—law enforcement Rigg came in contact with every day of his life. It would ruin his career if she filed charges against him. He knew that. So why had he tried to kill her?

"This is insane," she heard herself say. She wanted to stop holding onto her throat, but it hurt to talk and she didn't want him to have to look at her bruises. "You're saying you don't remember what happened last night—after we made love and fell asleep—and yet you know *something* happened, don't you?"

"Yes."

"How?" Was that the right thing to ask? What difference did it make as long as he handed her the truth?

He stopped staring at her, his attention sliding to his fingers, which gripped the chair arms. Now that she was no longer looking into his eyes—eyes radiating darkness, with none of the crimson glow she sometimes saw in them—she found herself remembering last night and a lovemaking that had taken her away from everything except what he'd offered her.

"I don't trust myself around you, Shanna. You bring out... *He* took over—I prayed *he* couldn't reach us here, that I'd made it safe. I was wrong. Damn it, wrong! Just go, please..."

Despite the finality in his command, his voice trailed off at the end. If he'd speared her with his intensity or moved so much as a single muscle in her direction, she probably would have run, but he seemed incapable of shaking off the weight that had settled around him.

She hated seeing him looking trapped like this, a strong and intelligent man caught in a nightmare she couldn't possibly comprehend. "I can't," she said softly.

"You *have* to. I don't know what I might do. The next time..."

If she walked out of the house now, as she should have hours ago, it would be over between them. But an emotion far stronger than fear had wrapped itself around her and she could no more tear herself free than he could escape the hell he'd been thrust into.

Maybe it was his hell and wanting to free him from it that kept her here with him and this gentle music. Not moving any closer, but not shrinking away, either, she told him what he'd done. He nodded, now staring intently at her. Although he said nothing, she understood that beneath his shock there was a part of him that simply accepted the inescapable truth.

It was, she decided, as if he'd always known he was capable of being a danger to her.

"It's over, Shanna," he said, breaking the silence that settled between them. "What you came here to discover you have to put behind you."

"No."

"You're wrong!" His fingers dug into the leather chair arms until she thought he might puncture them. "Don't you understand? Your life is in danger as long as you're around me."

"I didn't feel in danger earlier."

"Earlier?"

"When we made love."

For the first time since she entered the room, she sensed that he was relaxing, letting go of some of the fierce control he'd clamped over himself. "I remember," he said softly.

"I hope you do," she whispered back, "because that's what kept me here. That and the promise you made."

He didn't say anything. Instead, his eyes asked the question, and despite the warning that still hummed through her, she held on to her courage—her maybe insane courage. "You were going to take me to Juanica. I won't let you renege on that. I can't."

CHAPTER TEN

Sand painting held carefully in her lap, Shanna sat beside a silent Rigg as they traveled a dirt road through miles of delicately painted, nearly lifeless land. He'd spoken only once as they were getting ready to leave, explaining that the necklace he'd lost during the night was a fetish bag filled with herbs and corn pollen, bits of turquoise and shell, tiny carved images of sheep and horses. As long as he wore what the shaman had given him, she should be safe.

Safe from what? she wanted to demand, but she knew the answer. The danger was next to her, had made love to her in the night, now stared out at the horizon as if blue sky and brown earth were the only places in the world he might find peace.

If asked, she couldn't have said what she expected to see on the Navajo reservation, land without so much as a single telephone pole. Maybe quaint roadside stands where traditionally dressed men and women sold exquisite silver-and-turquoise jewelry or handmade blankets; maybe Native American cowboys wearing dusty and battered hats with rattlesnake-skin bands. Of course they'd be riding bareback, their horses all pintos or paints or whatever they were called.

Instead she saw almost nothing in the way of life except for birds and a single, distant rabbit.

For reasons that remained a mystery to her, Rigg hadn't gone back on his earlier promise to take her out to see Juanica. And instead of running for the nearest hills or police station, as anyone with a half ounce of sense would do, she'd gotten into his car and strapped on her seat belt. Now, unless she wanted to bail out of the slowly moving car and take her chances among the sandstone bluffs or grama-grass meadows, she was alone in the wildlands with the somber-faced man whose body still called to her. Whose private agony should not be fought in solitude.

Dawn had given way to a cloudless day that touched the landscape with exquisite fingers. Because theirs was the only vehicle on the narrow track of road, it was easy to imagine that she and Rigg had fallen into some kind of time warp and had entered the primitive and isolated world that had existed here eons before the white man made his impact.

"It's beautiful," she said, breaking a silence that had continued for the better part of an hour. "Starkly beautiful. That's the only way I can think of to describe this country."

He continued to stare ahead of him.

"Why did the Navajo wind up here? There's hardly any rainfall, no rich soil. I can't imagine there's much in the way of wildlife. How did they sustain themselves?"

No answer.

"Haven't you ever asked yourself that?" she pressed. "You've spent your entire life here, haven't you? Aren't you curious?"

"I know the Navajo version of their beginning. They and the Anasazi before them. That's what I'm interested in, not what anthropologists have come up with."

Did that mean he'd discounted the carefully researched and documented records? Before she could decide whether to ask, she noticed that his attention had shifted from the thin tracks of road to a small herd of sheep grazing on a low, nearby hill. Grateful for any sign of life, she studied them. There weren't any tiny lambs, but then it was far enough along in the season that they'd probably been born several months ago. The land looked as if it couldn't possibly grow enough vegetation to sustain them and she wondered how much their owner had to supplement their feed.

Out of the corner of her eye, she noticed that Rigg was pointing. Following the line of his finger, she spotted a grayish mound some distance from the grazing flock. Several dark birds skittered around the mound, alerting her to the fact that one of the sheep had died. "That's too bad," she commiserated. "The herd isn't that large. Losing just one animal has to be a financial blow."

"It's worse to lose fifty in a single night."

"Fifty?"

"That's what *he's* capable of, Shanna."

The words were delivered with an emotionlessness she knew was studied. "How can you be sure *he's* responsible?"

"Because Chabah has been raising sheep for over forty years and nothing like that ever happened to him before. He's too good a herder—he isn't careless. It was as if their hearts simply stopped."

She shuddered in reaction, glancing quickly at the sky to reassure herself that the day hadn't darkened. "What are you saying?"

"That the existence of Chinde, at least *that* Chinde, is more than Navajo superstition. Shortly before it happened, Chabah performed a curing ceremony. *He* couldn't retaliate because Chabah's a powerful shaman. He knows how to guard himself against evil from the ghost of a dead man. But *he* could make his hatred known by killing Chabah's sheep."

If it had been a week ago, she would have laughed away Rigg's explanation, but she no longer could. "A curing ceremony? What's that?"

He glanced over at her twice before speaking, and she had no doubt that he didn't want to answer her question. "Traditional Navajo believe all sickness is caused by the loss of harmony in one's world. In order to regain the necessary balance, an elaborate ceremony must be performed."

"What about a medical doctor? A hospital? Are you saying they don't believe in such things?"

His jaw clenched; it seemed to take conscious effort on his part to relax enough to continue. "When a man's soul has been invaded, there isn't a medical doctor or hospital in the world that can help. That's why I went to Chabah."

"You?"

He'd retreated into silence again.

"You?" she repeated, last night's terror briefly reasserting itself. "What are you saying? That your soul—you thought it had been invaded?"

"I knew it had."

The words echoed inside her until she felt surrounded by them, weighed down and incapable of fighting free. Certainly Rigg didn't believe in shamans and Chinde, or ghosts. He was a modern, intelligent professional, respected by his peers, responsible for the conduct of those trying to reestablish themselves in the world beyond prison bars.

A man who'd tried to choke her.

Because *he* had a hold on his soul? "When was this?"

"Nearly two years ago. That's when the headaches began, when I knew I hadn't escaped after all."

"You? Why is *he* after you?"

Silence, heavy as lead, as impenetrable as rock. Feeling trapped by the immense weight, Shanna stared out at the land again. There was nothing here, not so much as a discarded beer can to remind her of today's world. She'd picked up just enough local history to know that the Anasazi, first to inhabit this land, had built impressive and permanent stone homes here before mysteriously disappearing centuries ago. If she blinked, would they reappear?

They didn't reach Chabah's hogan for at least another hour. Although she'd felt like screaming from the pressure of the questions building inside her, Shanna hadn't tried to break the silence. What would she say? "Why is *he* so interested in you? Does *he* think that if *he* controls you, *he'll* be able to influence the behavior of all the ex-convicts in the state?"

Chabah lived in what at first glance looked like a dirt mound that overlooked a small box canyon. Except for the canyon, there was nothing about this area to separate it from the miles and miles of dry, windswept nothingness she'd been staring at for hours. She'd seen photographs of hogans and had expected a small, snug, six-sided log structure with a modern wood stove, maybe even a door held in place with metal hinges.

When she kept staring at the earthen mound, Rigg explained that Chabah believed in keeping with the traditional style of his ancestors. This, his primary home, had been built of hand-hewn timbers and poles covered by bark and dirt; it was well-insulated and waterproof. The opening faced east, as did all authentic Navajo hogans. There was a four-wheel-drive pickup parked nearby, so dust caked that she could only guess at its color.

"He's not going to invite us in," Rigg said.

"You mean we're not welcome? But—"

"He doesn't want evil entering his home. I respect his decision."

Evil from Rigg? If she'd known how to frame the question, she'd be demanding he explain himself right now. But she was so weary of conversations that went in directions she couldn't possibly comprehend. Movement from inside the dark opening caught her attention. Not waiting for Rigg, she got out of the car and stood in the sunlight. Her heart beat painfully. Her mouth was dry, her palms slickened. Her past waited here.

A woman, not the elderly shaman she'd expected, emerged. Dressed in a green, long-sleeved blouse and floor-length, multicolored skirt, she had left her waist-length, gray-streaked but still-glossy hair to flow down her back. She wore a massive turquoise-and-silver necklace. Suddenly, Shanna knew.

Juanica.

She should have asked Rigg about the proper protocol in such situations; she should have imagined what this moment would be like and emotionally prepared herself for it. Because she hadn't done either of those things, all she could do was stand on suddenly numb legs and wait for her parents' friend to come closer.

She studied the woman. Somewhat chunky body, bronzed skin, bright and wary eyes; long, competent-looking fingers, a gentle mouth. Juanica glanced briefly at Rigg, then turned her attention to Shanna. Shanna stared back, the gaze lasting the better part of a minute. She felt as if she'd been stripped naked, taken back into childhood where memories of Juanica dwelled.

"You shouldn't be here."

"I had to come," she said, not surprised and yet hurt by Juanica's comment. She needed Rigg beside her, needed his strength and understanding. "I have to have answers."

"It doesn't matter. Only stopping *him* does."

"Stopping what? I don't understand. This—"

"You are not strong enough. *He* will feed upon you and *his* strength will become that of a fiery volcano."

She had thought she could hold her own in this conversation, but Juanica was saying things that frightened her, that made no sense—or maybe too much sense. Trying another approach, a hopefully safer one, she explained that she'd insisted Rigg bring her here because of a few snatches of memory that refused to be silenced. "I can't tell you what it's been like for me," she finished with a catch in her voice. "To find out I have parents I never knew existed.

Even if they're dead, I have to do what I can to make them real for me. It's the only way I'm going to have any sense of peace."

Juanica had folded her arms across her chest, looking for all the world like a hostile and impassive palace guard. Now she briefly closed her eyes. When she opened them, the barriers she'd erected around her emotions were no longer there.

This was her mother's best friend, the woman who'd held a terrified orphan and kept that little girl from falling apart. "I remember you," Shanna managed to say. "Your necklace—you were wearing one very much like it back then."

Juanica nodded, glanced over at Rigg. "Yes. I was."

"I held on to your hand the day of my mother's funeral. There was a hot wind blowing. People were crying. When they started dropping dirt on her casket, the sound…I had to get away. I ran into Rigg. Then—then…" *The beautiful, black-haired woman lifted the child off the ground, gently but firmly pulled her away from the boy. The woman said nothing, only turned her back on the wide-eyed boy, arms protectively around the little girl—around her.* "Why wouldn't you let me stay with him?" she asked, her voice tremulous. "I felt safe with him."

"You remember that?" Juanica sounded no more in control of her emotions than she did.

"More and more's coming back. I don't understand what's triggering it." She lifted her hand, then stared at it. She'd been about to stroke Juanica's wrinkled but strong-looking arm. But maybe—probably—she didn't want that.

Juanica's eyes glistened with unspent tears. "I prayed I would never see you again," she whispered. "Still, I've always wondered…"

"How I turned out?"

Another nod.

"All right, I guess. I'm supporting myself and that's something to take pride in. It was hard losing both my—my grandparents so close together, and hard making the decision to sell the house. That's how I found your letter, that and the sand painting.''

"I wish you hadn't.''

"I know. If I hadn't, I wouldn't be here. Your father, how is he?''

"Getting better. His horse threw him.''

"Will he talk to me? I came to see you, but—''

"He has not decided. When he has, he will let me know.''

Rigg now stood only a few feet away, making no move to touch her, and she wished she couldn't remember what last night in his arms had felt like before something took possession of him and turned him deadly. Something that might return at any moment.

"Juanica, I've come this far. Please, I can't be content with snippets of memory, all of them associated with my parents' deaths. What were they like? You must have shared things with them, had things in common. Please—what were they like?''

"She won't leave until she has that,'' Rigg said, his voice sounding rusty. "Don't deny her.''

Juanica's attention flickered to him, held. As if understanding her unspoken question, he reached under his shirt and pulled out his fetish bag.

"She knows the danger?'' Juanica asked.

"Yeah, she does. In ways I wish to hell she didn't. I showed her where Hank was killed. She sensed—*he's* getting closer to her. Working through me. Flaunting his control over me.'' Rigg reached out and trailed his hand over Shanna's arm. Then he abruptly stopped, stepping quickly away from her. She shivered slightly, aware that Juanica had taken note of both the gesture and her reaction.

"Tell me what you sensed,'' Juanica pressed.

They were tiptoeing around something none of them could deny or laugh out of existence. Shanna wanted to scream that it was time to stop acting like frightened sheep and—and what? "Strange things have been happening to me," she told Juanica, and then elaborated briefly, because there wasn't enough reason not to. She said nothing about what had happened to Rigg last night; that would have to come from him. "If I'm in danger from something that has no form, maybe Rigg's right and I need to leave. But I can't until I have more pieces of the puzzle about my past, and you're the only one who can give me that."

When Juanica neither moved nor spoke, and the seconds ticked by, Shanna fought to prepare herself for rejection. But finally Juanica indicated a blanket on the ground some distance from the hogan. Walking over to it, she sat, then patted the blanket to indicate she wanted Shanna to join her. Rigg remained where he was.

"I was raised out here," Juanica began gravely once Shanna was seated. "Like my brothers and sisters and cousins, but my father wanted his oldest child to go to white man's school. I was the first Navajo girl to attend the University of New Mexico. The dorm people paired me with your mother."

Sun beat down on Shanna's back and caused her skin to prickle, but she was barely aware of the discomfort. Rigg stood within earshot, a silent, remote figure. Shanna listened eagerly as Juanica's deep, yet gentle voice told about two teenage girls united by loneliness and curiosity about each other's worlds. Debby's parents had sent her from Arizona to New Mexico not because they wanted her to have a new experience, but because their marriage was falling apart and they didn't want their only child distracting them from raging battles and hard decisions. Debby told Juanica about being raised by fiercely ambitious people whose daughter had been the only real casualty of their single-minded drive to succeed. In turn, Juanica introduced Debby to a life-style ruled by ancient traditions and beliefs, by family values and love of the land.

They were juniors, still living together, when Sam and Debby met. Sam, going to college on a military grant, had little in common with his younger classmates, but had been drawn to the quiet, intelligent woman who worked part-time in the student-affairs office. When Sam heard that Debby's roommate was a full-blooded Navajo, he insisted on meeting her.

"We became inseparable," Juanica said with a note of awe. "I knew Sam and Debby were falling in love. I think for a little while I loved Sam myself. When we graduated, I made plans to return to the reservation, because that was the only place I ever wanted to be. Sam and Debby told me they were going to try to find jobs in Farmington. They said it was because they needed to keep an eye on me, but I knew the real reason." Juanica's voice dropped off, and her eyes glistened again. "They knew we had something special in the way of a friendship—they didn't want to lose it any more than I did."

"And they didn't have ties anywhere else," Shanna finished for her. She wished she'd brought a tape recorder or at least a camera with her, but even if she'd thought of them, she wasn't sure Juanica would have let her record this. "That's a beautiful story. Thank you for telling me. Josh and Gena? How did I wind up with them?"

What might be a smile touched Juanica's mouth. "They were teachers on the reservation. After all those years of the government insisting Navajo children had to be sent away to be educated, that insanity had been abandoned. They were good, nonjudgmental people, and they understood how vital it was to take you where you'd be safe."

Silence broken only by the sound of the wind brushing along the sparse grass seemed utterly in keeping with her mood. Josh and Gena had been good people; that's what mattered. Out here, with so few reminders of today's technology, she could almost believe it was twenty-five years ago and that her parents were just over the next hill, not dead. Not murdered.

Juanica was no longer looking at her. Instead, her attention had become focused on Rigg, her eyes telegraphing concern. He was still standing. His hands hung at his sides, his head slightly tilted to one side as if he, too, was listening to the wind—or at least Shanna might have believed that if it hadn't been for his blank stare. Had he heard anything of what Juanica had said, or was his mind somewhere else, maybe back in the hell he'd been trapped in when he, or something inside him, had wrapped his hands around her throat as a cruel joke?

"You were my parents' closest friend," she said to Juanica, keeping her voice calm and firm when she felt anything but. "Why didn't you take me to live with you after they were killed?"

"Because she did not dare."

Startled by the unexpected voice, Shanna spun around. An elderly man, his face an explosion of dry wrinkles, was walking toward them. Juanica scrambled to her feet with an agility that surprised Shanna and hurried over to the man. She presented her arm for him to grip and watched him with a loving, uneasy expression.

The man, who must be Chabah, stared at Rigg. He wore a faded blue, too-large shirt that hung on his spare frame and equally baggy pants that would have slipped off his prominent hipbones if it hadn't been for his belt with its ornate silver buckle. Because he'd rolled up his shirt-sleeves and most of the buttons were missing, she easily saw that he'd spent his life exposing himself to the elements. Despite his leathered appearance, he seemed somehow ageless. The impression came, she realized, from the life and wisdom shining in his expressive eyes.

Chabah nodded at Rigg. "You are well?"

"Not too, Shaman."

"I thought so. Are you afraid?"

"Not for myself."

"Ah." Chabah nodded and allowed his daughter to lead him closer to Rigg. Shanna stood, but the old man was still staring at Rigg. "Not for yourself. But for another?"

Rigg nodded.

"I wish I could help you, my son. I have tried—I have tried."

"I know."

"Some things defy the greatest of medicine and magic. When that happens, one must leave the place of danger. This time, go farther and don't come back."

"Running won't change anything. *He'll* follow me no matter where I go. You know that."

A stab of pain contorted Chabah's features. "Maybe more gall medicine to rid you of the corpse poison."

"Not that again. I don't think I'd survive."

If this conversation continued, Shanna wasn't sure she wouldn't scream in pure frustration—frustration and a nameless fear, not for herself but for Rigg. Because of the way he was standing, his face was almost entirely in shadow, which only added to his look of torment. "What are you talking about?" she demanded. "Damn it, I have a right to know."

"A right," Chabah said slowly. "Yes."

"No!" Rigg and Juanica said almost simultaneously.

"Yes," Chabah insisted, while Shanna fought to keep herself from trembling. "In the end, there can only be the truth."

"The truth?" she managed to ask.

Chabah indicated he wanted to sit down. With his daughter's help, he settled himself on the ground. How old Chabah was, Shanna couldn't say. Probably younger than he looked, but aged by a rugged, physical existence. Still, his eyes were no older than Rigg's, and he seemed more at peace with himself than Rigg did—a realization that made her want to clutch Rigg to her and never let go.

Either that or run from whatever lurked inside him.

Chabah cleared his throat and stared up at her until she joined him on the blanket. He smelled of sage and corn and wool. "What do you know about *him?*" he asked. "The one who murdered your parents?"

"Nothing. His name. That *he* was killed by a young policeman and that the policeman was murdered."

"*He* killed my sheep."

"Rigg told me."

"And did he tell you I lost a nephew at *his* hands because my nephew had once taken a girl from him and a Chinde does not forget? It is said that two drunken men went to a place where he once lived and cursed and ridiculed him. They died there. Your parents' house was torn down because no one would live in it. Even whites said it felt evil."

The day was no longer warm. She strained to catch a little of the comforting sound the wind made, but if it was still there, she couldn't hear it for the screams of denial inside her head.

"*He* was always different," Chabah said softly. "From childhood he was angry. Always angry. Like a storm. He turned his back on his parents' teaching. Drank white man's liquor and spent his time with other young men who drank too much and worked too little. Once when he was a teenager he came drunk to a Nightway ceremony, laughing and calling those there fools. He fell onto the dry painting we were making, ruining hours of work. I ordered him to leave, told him he was not welcome on the land of his ancestors."

"What did he do?" Shanna asked, as Juanica stepped behind her father and began rubbing his shoulders. Rigg stood apart from them.

"He left. His father was a weak man who did not know how to reach out to his own son, but I spoke with the voice of all Navajo when I told him he was an outcast and no longer welcome. As long as he lived, he did not come back to the land of his ancestors."

"Instead, he started following Debby," Juanica said.

"Why? She didn't encourage him, did she?" Shanna asked, even though the question made her feel disloyal to her mother.

"Your mother loved only your father...." Juanica's voice trailed off. A half minute passed before she spoke again. "*He* knew I often left the reservation to visit my white friends. *He* came to their house while I was there and asked me for money. He said he'd tell my father that we were lovers if I didn't give it to him. That was the first time he saw Debby. If only I'd known—"

"You didn't," Rigg said harshly. "Don't blame yourself."

"I would have given him money so he'd go away, but Sam wouldn't let me. He said that one time would only lead to others and I would never be free of him. Sam ordered him to leave."

Juanica reached under her loose blouse and pulled something out of her waistband. When the sun reflected off a shiny surface, Shanna saw it was a small, silver-bladed knife with turquoise inlaid in the handle. With the knife resting in her palm, Juanica continued.

"Debby and I were home the next time *he* came to the house, but Sam wasn't. *He* was drunk. He kept staring at Debby, trying to touch her, calling her beautiful. He told her he wanted ... The things he said made Debby and me sick. We made him leave, but he kept coming back. He'd park his old truck out front and spend the night there. If Sam ordered him to leave, he'd return later. He followed Debby everywhere. Sam couldn't be with her all the time. She talked to the police, but they didn't know where he was living. He didn't do anything, just followed her. Stalked her. Played with her."

"Obsession," Rigg hissed, his low comment chilling Shanna even more. "*He'd* become obsessed with her just as he is with me now. Nothing any of them did discouraged him."

"We used to ask each other how long it would be before his drinking killed him," Juanica said. "That was back when I believed that his dying would end the nightmare."

"There is no end," Chabah said. "My magic—it has not been enough. The day may come when *he* will win."

Although she registered Chabah's words, Shannah couldn't take her eyes off Rigg, who now looked as if he'd retreated inside himself. "That thing Rigg wears around his neck, that's part of your magic, isn't it? That and the corn and other plants."

"Sacred plants," Chabah said. "Tapes from our ceremonies. And sand paintings like the one I made for you. The Navajo believe that Changing Woman's form is too sacred to be shown in anything except a Blessingway painting, but I believed that only she would be powerful enough to stop him. That is why I made her part of my gift to you. Only she has the strength to defeat *him*."

"*He* came after me yesterday," Shanna admitted. "When he did, I held the painting against me and he went away."

"He'll be back." Rigg spoke in a hard whisper before Chabah could respond. "He always comes back."

Juanica held up her knife for Shanna to see. "My father made this for me and blessed it to keep me safe. *He* plays with me, coming close when I let my guard down and making even the brightest day dark. I believe he wants to punish me for taking you away from the land where his ghost walks. I never feel free of him, wonder if someday he will grow weary of the game and try to kill me as he did my friends. When that time comes..." She ran her finger over the blade. "I pray this will be enough."

"The lies, the secrets about my past—that was done so I'd never know about *him?*" Shanna asked.

"So *he* would not kill you as he did your parents. Or worse."

"Worse? What do you mean?"

Chabah touched her knee. "*He* wanted Debby so much that he was willing to risk his life to have her. Because the policeman broke taboo, *his* spirit didn't go to the underworld like the spirits of other Navajos who have died. Instead, he stayed here, evil and powerful. Learning the depth of his power. Becoming more and more evil. He may make you his, Shanna. Make you pray for the freedom of death."

She couldn't comprehend what the shaman was telling her, couldn't make herself believe that *he* could hold her prisoner. Or maybe the truth was she'd seen what was happening to Rigg and her mind rejected the horrible thought that the same could happen to her.

Desperate for an outlet for her suddenly overwhelming energy, she pushed herself to her feet and started toward Rigg. If he'd moved while Chabah and Juanica were talking, she hadn't been aware of it. He remained immobile now, wary and weary, with that fierce and yet trapped look in his eyes.

"*He* wants me because I'm Debby's daughter." It wasn't a question; insanely, she no longer doubted that.

"Debby wasn't Navajo," Juanica said. "When *he* killed her, he lost her. But he will not make that mistake again. He will allow you to live, as *his* possession."

A spasm nearly knocked her off her feet. She felt a breath away from being physically ill. "*He* wants me, Debby's daughter," she repeated. She stepped toward Rigg, watched as he readied himself for her. "But why you?" She pointed at his talisman. "Why is *he* doing what he is to you?"

Slowly, the gesture both beautiful and ugly, Rigg's features hardened. His eyes took her into night, showed her the depths of his soul, taught her everything about honesty.

"Because I'm his son."

CHAPTER ELEVEN

The wind changed directions, creating a sharp whining sound as it sliced past a rock. Shanna embraced the sound, briefly lost herself in it.

If she was home now, she'd be at work, maybe helping sweet little old and wealthy Nettie Harsgrove plan yet another cruise for herself and her wheelchair-bound sister. She and Nettie would laugh over how a woman always had to be on the alert for slick-talking men with dollar signs in their eyes.

She wouldn't be standing in this desolate place where the wind blew dirt into her hair and the air felt as if all moisture had been stripped from it.

She wouldn't be staring at Rigg, his confession reverberating inside her.

"*His* son?" Her throat constricted and for several seconds she couldn't speak. "You're his son?"

"Yes."

Yes. As if it were that simple. "Why didn't you tell me before—" Breaking off the rest of the sentence, she walked toward him on rubber legs until they were so close that hopefully Juanica and her father couldn't hear. "Didn't you think I had a right to know?" She sounded desperate and nearly out of control, but couldn't help it. "You took me to your house. Made me believe I'd be safe there. Made—made love to me. I had a right to know, damn it!"

"I'm sorry."

She'd opened her mouth to continue her attack before his apology reached her. Like the wind, it teased her senses, caressed her flesh and nerve endings, took her back into the night and the time they'd spent together.

Feeling her anger slip away, she made a self-protective grab at it, but it turned into mist inside her. She couldn't put a name to what she felt now; the sensation was too overwhelming. "Why didn't you?" Her voice was as gentle as his had been.

"I couldn't. Not then."

He couldn't because the truth of his parentage haunted him; she had no doubt of that. She fought to concentrate on Rigg, to listen and watch and try to understand. Her attention was drawn first to his large and competent hands and then back to his eyes, which today were clear and sane and dark. What was responsible for the change, she didn't know. Maybe *he* was somewhere else today; maybe *he* existed behind the nearest bluff, watching and listening, planning. The thought made her half-sick with fear and rage.

"Do you know?" she demanded. "When *he* comes for you, can you sense it happening?"

"It isn't like that. He never leaves me alone, not really."

A wave of compassion, sympathy, fear and even regret washed over her, but before she lost herself in those emotions, something about the way Rigg presented himself changed her mind. He'd looked so battle weary a few minutes ago and she'd interpreted it as vulnerability, but it wasn't that at all. Rigg wasn't a man defeated, someone who'd collapsed under the strain of the war being waged inside him. He might feel trapped, occasionally exhausted, but he would never surrender as long as he lived, and it was that fierceness, that intensity, that drove him.

"And you fight him with everything you have, don't you?"

Something approaching a rueful smile touched his mouth. "I wasn't ready for him last night—I'd dropped my guard, deluded myself into thinking we were safe there, and I nearly killed you.''

''No, you didn't. You were strong—''

''Not me. *He* doesn't want you dead, don't ever forget that.''

Then what? she thought, but the other possibilities were too horrid to even consider. ''How do I fight him?''

''By leaving.''

''No.''

''This is his land, Shanna. Chinde land.''

Arguments, or at least fragments of them, skittered through her mind, but she couldn't hold on to anything. She'd barely noticed what Rigg wore today; now, his snug and obedient jeans and rib-skimming T-shirt commanded her attention. She'd seen him naked last night, but then she'd been all but consumed by the hot energy inside her. They had been lovers. She'd touched and tested, embraced and recorded, clung to him because he was warmth and life and an untapped power.

That incredible experience couldn't have ended, not when it had just begun to come to life. She wasn't finished with him.

She wanted him to feel the same about her. She wanted nothing else to matter.

She wondered if Rigg needed to reach for her as much as she needed to be the one reaching. If he was battling that powerful desire, craving her, remembering last night and knowing that one night wasn't enough to sustain them for the rest of their lives, maybe his defenses were down.

Maybe *he*—

''Shanna.''

Belatedly recognizing Juanica's voice, she forced herself to turn her back on Rigg and the ecstasy and danger he represented. Chabah was still sitting quietly on the blanket, but Juanica had started walking toward them. When Shanna realized that neither father or daughter had taken their eyes off Rigg, she felt first a wave of anger and then resignation and understanding. Neither of them for a moment doubted that Rigg was capable of violence.

That because of the monster stalking him he couldn't be trusted.

Juanica waited until she was only a few feet away and then stretched out her hand. In it she held the silver-and-turquoise knife. "Take this. My father says it will protect you as it did me."

"What about you?"

Juanica's gaze sobered even more. "You are here. *He* knows that. *He* will no longer concern himself with me."

She didn't want to accept Juanica's offering, because if she did, it would serve as proof that she took the threat to her sanity, her freedom, maybe even her life, seriously. But she did; that was the awful truth. "How?" she asked. "How do I use it?"

"Keep it with you always. The shaman's blessing has made it a powerful weapon. *He* does not dare come close."

Even as the knife settled into her palm, she felt herself being pulled into an inescapable and numbing reality. Rigg had surrounded his home with the living things that the Navajo considered sacred. He'd filled a small bag with pollen and turquoise and wore it over his heart, and still his father stalked him. How could a small, ornate knife some old man had muttered over make any difference in a battle against the undead?

Thump.

Mouth dry, she half walked and half lurched toward Rigg. When she grabbed his arm, his heat flowed into her. His eyes were still black. Even if they hadn't been, she couldn't have run from him, couldn't turn her back on what was flaming to life between them. "I want to leave here," she said. "Now."

"What is it?"

Could she keep anything from him? "I hate it here. I feel as if I've stepped into the past, a past I don't understand. I want to see streetlights and shopping centers, not this—this endless nothing."

"*He's* here, isn't he?"

"I don't know!" She sounded like an hysterical child. "Maybe I'm simply reacting to what you just told me. Please, take me back to the city."

That won't change anything. He didn't have to speak for her to know what he was thinking. Still, she prayed he understood that she couldn't possibly gain control over her emotions as long as they stood on Navajo land.

The neighborhood awoke no sense of recognition in Shanna. She kept staring at the large cottonwoods that flanked the streets as she tried to imagine how they must have looked twenty-five years ago, but her imagination wasn't fertile enough for that.

And then maybe it was the man sitting beside her who made it impossible for her to concentrate.

The son of an evil Chinde.

He hadn't wanted to bring her here. With brief, terse words, he'd all but ordered her to buy a ticket on the first plane out of New Mexico. Even with Juanica's knife clutched to her breast and the sand painting in the car between them, she felt as if she was being watched. That's what she'd told Rigg when he demanded she keep nothing back. A large chunk of her mind, that portion devoted to self-preservation, had screamed at her to flee, but it wasn't that simple.

It never would be as long as Rigg lived.

"I need more," she said, although she didn't expect Rigg to reply. "More in the way of memories to make my past complete. You're sure they tore down my parents' house? A perfectly good house? It doesn't make sense."

She'd turned on the radio during the long and lulling drive off the reservation; she felt as if she'd go crazy listening to Rigg's silence and her own ragged breathing. She also hoped that song and voices would keep the thumping sound from taking over. It must have worked; she'd heard endless country-and-western songs, three repeats of the same weather forecast, two local news updates. There hadn't been so much as a single echo of the spine-clawing sound.

But then, maybe *he* was simply toying with her.

"What happened to the property after my parents were killed?" she continued, for no other reason than to keep herself occupied. "It must have gone back to the bank or whoever held the mortgage on it. Maybe they rented. Damn it, Rigg, I don't even know if my parents had enough money for a down payment."

No one should be able to drive without moving so much as a single muscle, but although the traffic had been stop and go since they'd reentered Farmington, she could swear she hadn't seen so much as a finger twitch. Because he was looking ahead, she couldn't tell whether his eyes had again become flecked with red.

What would she do if they had?

The residential area was quiet and nearly lifeless, although she'd seen several loaded buses and knew school was out for the day. She wanted to hear childish voices, voices that might trigger more memories of the two-year-old girl who'd stumbled into the arms of a slightly older boy. The air smelled of flowers, with hints of exhaust fumes and an overpowering but mercifully brief stench of tar. Turning off the radio, she leaned out the window as far as her seat belt would allow and listened. Absorbed.

"We're near where I used to live?"

"Yes."

"It's a nice neighborhood," she mused. "Settled."

"One of the older ones."

"You lived near here?" she asked, encouraged by his unexpected speech.

"East. Across the boulevard. It was a two-lane road back then."

"I want to remember." She pressed her fingers against her forehead, all but oblivious to the discomfort she was creating. "I *need* to remember."

He'd been about to challenge her, to insist she didn't need to do anything except save herself, but she cut off anything he might say by swiveling toward him and clamping her hand over his muscular arm.

The touch of him was like lightning across a stormy sky, rocketing through her, offering promise and challenge—and danger.

She stared at him—started to, anyway, but before she could determine whether he shared her reaction, something out the driver's-side window snagged her thoughts and pulled her free from something she'd spent a lifetime waiting for.

An empty lot. Weed-choked, with a random series of dirt mounds throughout. Bicycle tracks scarring the hills. Two scraggly bushes at the far end.

"That's it," she whispered. "Where I used to live."

He touched the brake and looked at her for the first time in hours. There was no question in his eyes.

"It used to be larger, a child's vision of her world," she said. Rigg pulled over to the side of the road and threw the car into park. He didn't take his attention off her and she continued, "The house was to the front of the lot, with a fenced backyard. The walk, where my father died, was there." She pointed, amazed that her finger was steady. "And where *he* fell was over there."

"How do you feel?"

"Feel? All right. It was so long ago that maybe there aren't any emotions left."

"I hope so," he muttered. Then he pointed down the street. "That's where I came from on my bike. I thought all the police cars in the world were here."

Getting out of the car, she started across the street without first looking for traffic. Rigg caught up to her before she reached the center stripe but didn't try to hurry her along. Instead, he was there, simply there. Maybe going back in time with her.

She walked onto the lot, not stopping until she stood where she knew the front door had been. "There was a screen. I wasn't tall enough to undo the latch. My daddy— my daddy would lift me up and wait for me to unlock it before he went to work in the morning. I—my mother would tell me when it was time for him to come home and I'd press my nose against the screen so he could kiss away the marks when he came in."

She crouched and ran her fingers over scars in the earth made by knobby bicycle tires. "A dirt track. The kids have turned my home into a dirt track."

"Does that bother you?"

"No," she whispered, then straightened. The movement brought her close to Rigg, and it seemed natural and right and wonderful to have him drape his arm around her shoulder and pull her against his sun-heated body.

This afternoon he smelled of sage.

"I want to trust you," she whispered.

"I want you to be able to."

"Can I?"

"No."

She'd known he was going to say that, but knowledge didn't stop the pain. She heard a door slam nearby, a normal sound on a normal day. "What was it like?" She forced herself to ask the question. "Growing up with *him* as your father?"

"I don't know."

His admission gave her a small measure of comfort, but if pressed, she wouldn't have been able to say why. Her body wanted to go on drinking from his, and despite everything she knew of his dark side, the arguments against that weren't strong enough. He was warmth, life, danger, lonely somehow. Or maybe it was she who was so lonely that nothing except ending that mattered.

She'd left the sand painting and knife in the car. Instead of going back for them, she wrapped her arm around Rigg's waist and held on, trusting in the instinct that said that, for this moment at least, it was safe for them to be together. "My mother baked. Breads and cookies. My room was yellow, yellow and white."

"It's all coming back to you?"

"Not all. Only as much as a two-year-old is capable of remembering, I guess." How he'd come to smell of sage she couldn't say. There'd been some out on the reservation, but if he'd absorbed the scent, why hadn't she?

"I didn't want to bring you here. I didn't want to take you out to see Juanica and Chabah."

"Because you were afraid I'd find out what I did?"

"Not afraid, Shanna. I am who I am—I can't change that."

Neither of them could change anything about what was happening to them. She accepted that knowledge, not with a sense of finality or defeat, but with courage. "Why not then?"

"Because I didn't want to make things any harder on you than they already were."

He was thinking of her. In an effort to express her gratitude, she ran her fingers slowly up his side, not stopping until they were resting over a rib. His breathing quickened. "I'm not the one who had a monster for a father. I was sent where I'd be safe. You weren't."

"I didn't know, Shanna. The day my grandparents took me to your mother's funeral, I had no idea who my father was. I'm still not sure why they made me go. Maybe they thought I needed to see the impact of death, that that way they could prevent me from following in *his* footsteps.''

There'd been so much deception, so much kept from two innocent children. She'd escaped ignorant and unscathed, while he...

"Tell me, please." *Now, while you can.*

He drew out of her reach, jamming his hands in his back pockets. He had a strong neck, strong shoulders, strength in every line of his body. "I was thirteen. It was five years after you'd been taken away. My mother was in and out of my life, more like a big sister than a parent. I think she would have told me the truth if her parents had let her, but they were raising me, and she did what they ordered—at least she did when she was around.''

Shanna wanted to see the house where he'd grown up, learn what it looked and smelled and felt like. She wanted to search for the love necessary to sustain a growing child.

"She had an older brother, my uncle Jeff. He was divorced, and his ex-wife had custody of his two children. I think losing contact with those children did something to him, broke him in some way.''

If she tried to touch him again, would he let her? "Your uncle—were you close to him?"

"Yes," he said simply, and in the words she found answers to questions about male influence in a parentless boy's life. "I thought of him as a great friend. Someone to take me to ball games. He had energy my grandfather didn't and, looking back, I realize he saw me as a substitute for his own children. He kept things from me just like my grandparents did. Maybe...I can't be sure, but I like to think that if he'd lived, he would have been the one to tell me.''

"If he'd lived?"

"My father murdered him.''

The day was crystal clear, with not so much as a faint haze to mute the sharp contrast between sky and earth. Although she'd felt a sense of loss from standing where her parents had once carried out their lives, she'd also been at peace. That peace ended with Rigg's words.

"Tell me, please," she begged.

Rigg was staring at the ground. She looked down, half expecting to find beetles or snakes there, but except for several tiny ants, the ground was barren. "Juanica came to me," he said softly. "She told me everything."

"Your grandparents let her?"

"I don't think they could stop her. She wasn't a stranger. I'd see her when she came to the school I was attending, to talk about Native American culture. It wasn't until that day that I understood why she always found a reason to spend extra time with me. Shortly after my uncle was killed, she rang the doorbell. My grandmother told her to go away—I remember that. But she insisted."

"Oh, Rigg! How hard that must have been for you, learning the truth right after losing your uncle."

In his eyes she found both surprise and gratitude that she understood, and she wondered if she was the first one to acknowledge how difficult that experience must have been for him. He was still standing several feet away, locked within himself, struggling to release the emotions and memories he'd kept buried for so many years. She wanted to give him her warmth and strength, but if she did, she might distract him from what he needed to say.

What she had to hear.

"Juanica had copies of the newspaper articles about your parents, the ones you saw in the archives. She showed them to me and then asked for my reaction. I told her I'd been there the day your mother and *he* died." He glanced upward, then settled his gaze on her again. "That's when she told me."

"Oh, Rigg. I'm so sorry."

"I believed her," he said hoarsely. "My grandmother cried and called her a liar, but I knew Juanica was telling me the truth. Finally they gave up and told me everything."

There wasn't enough emotion playing in his eyes. Although she continued to study them for telltale signs of another, unwanted color, most of her remained tuned to the fact that he continued to keep a great deal bottled up inside him. Last night—had it only been last night?—their bodies and minds and maybe hearts had become one. They had taken each other away from the nightmare, if only for a brief moment. If only she could to that for him again!

"Everything?" she prompted. "What did they tell you?"

A long, tortured sigh slid through him. "My mother was fifteen when she met and became infatuated with my—with *him*. Apparently he used to hang around the high school looking for teenage girls to hit on. I guess she was impressed by the fact that he had a car and dressed in black— that's how Juanica described him. He had muscles and wasn't shy and awkward like the boys my mother went to school with. He was her first boyfriend. Nothing anyone said made any difference. She was in love." He all but spat the last. "That didn't last long, just long enough for her to get pregnant."

"She isn't the only girl that's happened to, Rigg. Don't blame her."

"I don't," he said, and she believed him. "I remember what it was like to be fifteen, to think you understand life when you don't. When you can't possibly. I don't know if she wanted him to marry her—she kept that part of their affair from her parents. They started noticing changes in her. She stopped laughing. Her grades when down. *He* drank and when he did, he became violent. He put my mother in the hospital twice."

"Oh, Rigg, how awful."

"Yeah." He sounded not quite as controlled as he had a moment ago, as if his emotions were boiling close to the surface. "*He* terrorized her, terrorized the whole family. Uncle Jeff was the only one who stood up to him. He ordered him away at gunpoint—at least that's what my grandfather told me. *He* was imprisoned right after I was born. Robbery, I think."

How much longer could Rigg go on unraveling his past without exploding? And when that time came, would she be able to reach him? All she knew was that she would try with every fiber in her being. She couldn't turn her back on him. "At least they must have felt safe when he was locked away," she said.

"For a few years," he answered with a mirthless laugh. "When *he* was released, he came to see my mother. She wasn't there, but I was. He tried to walk out of the house with me and that's when my uncle stopped him. At gunpoint, because apparently nothing else got through to him. I remember that. At the time I thought he was a madman, nothing more."

"Did he stay away then?"

"Yeah."

Yeah. There was more to it than that, and in the silence that followed, she found the explanation. "Because he'd seen my mother. That's what you're leaving out, isn't it?"

He nodded, the gesture so brief that if she hadn't been staring at him, she wouldn't have seen it. "All right," she said when he didn't continue. "*He* found a new victim, another woman to chase after. Oh, God! Rigg! *He* didn't rape—I'm not—"

"No." Rigg strode toward her and grabbed her with such strength that he immediately killed the fear that had threatened to overwhelm her. "Sam was your father. Juanica told me and I believe her."

She felt weak with relief, and yet there was more to the emotion because Rigg had her in his arms and the embrace she'd needed for too long might be only a heartbeat away. This tormented man had become a part of her and she needed him with a fierceness that rivaled a winter storm. "This is a nightmare," she whispered, all too aware that whatever her reaction to *his* impact on her life was, it paled in comparison to what Rigg was going through. "If there was only some way out."

"There is, for you."

What finality there was to his words, what hard acceptance of the trap he was in. "Rigg?" she managed to say. "Your uncle. *He* killed your uncle several years after *he* died—that's what you're saying, isn't it?"

"Yeah. Except that that bastard never died—not really." He continued before she could respond. "My uncle drank. He was a good man—he tried to work and keep up his child support, but he had no tolerance for liquor. Sometimes I think..." Rigg was still holding her next to him, still allowing her access to his warmth and vitality. "Sometimes I think that as long as my uncle was in his own private hell, *he* was satisfied. But when I was thirteen, Uncle Jeff met a woman and joined AA. He was getting his life back together. That's when *he* cut my uncle's throat."

Don't be so accepting. Please yell, hit something! she cried silently. But Rigg had been living with this for years; the rage and denial had spent themselves and maybe only acceptance was left. "And that's when Juanica told you," she said aloud. "Oh, I wish I'd been there. Maybe I could have helped. Been someone you could turn to."

"No one can help me."

No one can help me.

CHAPTER TWELVE

As Shanna moved through the mass of cornstalks, they set up a vigorous rustling that all but swallowed her heart's pounding. If Rigg hadn't been beside her, holding her hand, touching her with silence and thought, she might have convinced herself that she couldn't possibly be reacting to his presence, but the connection between them was too strong and she'd come too far for denial.

"It feels peaceful. Quiet," she whispered. Much longer and she'd never find her way out of the silence. "I'm safe here. And so are you. For now, you're all right."

"It won't last, Shanna. And the next time *he* comes after me, I might not have enough strength to fight him off like I did last night."

Last night when they'd made love and then he'd tried to choke her. "Listen to me, please." She'd stopped walking, but hadn't yet convinced herself to face him, because if she did and his eyes began to glint with those scarlet lights, she'd have to run.

Flee from this man who'd swayed her heart.

"I can sense when *he's* close. I hear...I don't know how to explain the sound except that it reminds me of what I heard while they were covering my mother's casket."

"*His* idea of a sick joke. He loves that, throwing people into their worst nightmares. He's trying to work through me, Shanna." He held up his free hand and stared at her throat as proof. "You shouldn't be here with me. It's going to explode—I shouldn't have agreed—"

"I know," she said softly, quickly. "You don't want to put me in any more danger than I already am, but it's too late for that."

"No, it isn't. You don't have to stay. Damn it, you have to get the hell out of here."

"I'm not just talking about physical safety. I can't turn my back on this, Rigg. Don't you understand? I can't."

"You know about your past. There's nothing—"

"There's Chabah and Juanica and others he might go after. There's you."

She felt exposed and defenseless the moment the words were out of her mouth, and yet she wasn't sorry she'd said them. They'd been walking slowly through the corn that surrounded his house because she'd told him she wanted to experience what last night had kept hidden from her. Now, wishing this time of calm could stretch on forever, she stopped and leaned against his side, wrapping her arm around him. She felt herself flow into him, share his emotions.

Once, years ago, she'd gone to a zoo where she'd seen a panther staring out at what he could see of the horizon. The longing, the savage desperation in his eyes had torn her apart, and she'd never gone to a zoo again.

Rigg had that same look.

But Rigg wasn't alone the way that panther had been. He had her, and it didn't matter that the beast stalking him might force him to try to split them apart. Or at least, her fear of that didn't outstrip other emotions. Compassion. Determination. Need.

Rigg reached out with his free hand and gently drew something off the nearest tassle of corn. She felt herself melt a little when she saw that his fingers were coated with fine yellow pollen. He touched her forehead, slowly trailing his fingers over her left eyebrow and then the right. The aroma was so delicate that she could barely smell it.

"Positive energy," she whispered.

"A gift from the Holy People, the beings who travel on sunbeams, rainbows, lightning."

"That's beautiful." Taking his wrist, she drew his hand close to her mouth and slid her tongue lightly over his fingertips. The pollen tasted dry, slightly sweet. "What else, Rigg? I want to know more about the good in Navajo beliefs."

He smiled a little, the expression so rare and precious that she placed it deep inside her where it would remain. "I've always loved the Blessingway ceremony," he admitted.

"Chabah mentioned that. What is it?"

"A way of uniting a group, of getting the positive energy going. According to legend, it was first used by the Holy People when they created mankind. Many of the songs come from Changing Woman. A pregnant woman who wants to insure that her child will have a healthy, happy life asks that the songs be sung just before she gives birth."

"Changing Woman. I keep hearing about her."

He nodded, his features still easy, although his muscles held an energy, an awareness that mirrored hers. "She's the figure in your sand painting. Chabah wanted the deity to always look after you."

"And you," she said after a long silence during which she simply listened to what her body was discovering about the man standing beside her. "You're the other figure in it, aren't you? And you're the boy Juanica mentioned in her letter. She said she thought you were normal."

"She was wrong."

No! She wanted to hurl the word at him, but she had nothing except emotion to back up her outburst. If all Chabah's power as a shaman hadn't been able to protect Rigg from evil, if his home was turning out not to be the sanctuary he'd tried to make it, how could she hope to do more?

Maybe Rigg was right; maybe if she wanted to live, she couldn't remain near him.

"Why have you stayed here?" she asked. "If you left this area—"

"I tried. Oh, yes, I tried, but he followed me. Chabah says he found me because we share the same blood. That was the only reason he was able to leave Chinde land," Rigg said, then fell silent.

"So you came back," she prompted. "Why?"

"Because there are good forces here as well—the four sacred mountains, *Hashjeshjin* the Fire God, *Tse Bida'hi*. If I'm going to battle for my soul, I might as well do it on familiar land."

She wondered if there'd been another reason, if he'd somehow known she'd eventually come here looking for her roots, but she didn't say anything. The truth was, the longer she stood beside Rigg, the less she cared about reasons—the less she cared about anything except him. Her need to touch him was becoming overwhelming.

"It's going to be dark soon."

Until he said that, the darkening sky hadn't made any impact on her, but he was right; before much longer it would be night—a time of silence and peace. At least it could be that way for those whose souls were free and needed nothing out of the night except the chance to be together.

"Your den," she managed. "The books in there. Will they tell me more about Changing Woman and the different ceremonies?"

"I told you, there are limits. Some things, like the paintings used in healing rituals, are too sacred to be photographed. There's no way outsiders—and most of the authors are outsiders—can really understand how important *hozho* is."

"*Hozho?*"

"Harmony."

There'd been no emotion when he spoke the word, and she knew why. He hadn't felt a sense of harmony for so long that it pained him just to acknowledge its existence. Feeling suddenly restless, she turned toward his house. He nodded in that economical way of his, gripped her hand a little more tightly and expertly led her through the maze of corn.

When she entered his home, she thought she felt some faint power through the soles of her feet as she stepped on the sand painting etched into the entryway floor. Without asking what she wanted to do, Rigg moved toward his den, and she followed behind him, her hand now free but still tingling with the sense of him. He turned on the stereo, filling the air with chants and the wind song of flutes.

She felt surrounded by music that could be six thousand years old. Then she looked at Rigg. There was an agelessness to him, a strength as great as that of any panther, unbelievable courage. "You came back to fight, didn't you?" she said. "It wasn't just because you hoped sacred plants and ceremonies would protect you."

He'd sat in his recliner, his body tense as if he knew better than to ever let down his guard. Someday, maybe, she'd tell him how incredible his eyes were, how they spoke to her of pride and endurance. How she wanted to lose herself in them, and in him. He'd revealed an incredible amount today, exposed himself in ways she had never expected that had left her both in awe of him and rocked by the nightmare that had trapped him. Surely his disclosure had left him weary; what man would want to admit that his father was a monster? Still, he remained strong.

Her body heated, melted at its core. She wanted to come to him naked and laughing. Offer herself to him. Demonstrate with fingers and mouth and body how much she trusted him.

How much she needed him.

Could he possibly guess what she was thinking? She tried to see into him for the answer, but it was dark in the house, and although she'd embraced the memory of his eyes, all she had now was that memory. Maybe she was nothing but shadow to him.

Shadow and mystery and promise, and maybe as much danger to him as he was to her.

There was a chair to her left. It would take no more than two steps for her to reach it. She could sit down, lean back, dig within her for ordinary words to hand him so he wouldn't guess that she was utterly, completely willing and ready to continue as his lover.

Lover.

Weeping inside, she folded her arms tightly around her middle. She felt the small but solid weight of the knife Juanica had given her and acknowledged a tidal wave of hatred toward it. Then she stared at the dark and compelling silhouette sitting just out of reach.

The music wasn't loud enough. Despite the pounding rhythm of drums, she could hear Rigg's heart beating. That was impossible; the rational part of her knew that need and imagination were creating a sound that couldn't possibly reach her.

Rigg's heart, not the thumping that signaled *his* presence. She believed that; with every fiber in her, she believed that.

She slid a few inches closer to him. Her flesh, already sensitive, now felt as if she was standing naked in a sandstorm. She thought of the ocean, of walking along a sun-heated beach with Rigg, of searching for tiny and perfect seashells to gift him with, of sharing a sunset with him.

"Don't touch me, Shanna."

Pain, the horrible and nearly unsurvivable pain of having to obey him, nearly brought her to her knees. She didn't ask why he'd said that; she didn't have to.

Just as she knew that his pain matched hers.

"I love it here," she heard herself whisper. "The smell of this room—sage and corn. The rhythm of ancient chants. All those sand paintings."

"Don't."

"I have to!" She should turn her back on him, walk away from the risk; any sane woman who wanted to go on living would do that. "If I don't, you'll never know who I am."

"I don't want to know, Shanna. I don't dare."

The panther she'd seen that long-ago day had screamed once, a lonely and powerful sound she'd never forgotten. At this moment, Rigg's emotion seemed no different. "I don't care. Damn it, I don't care!" Restless, she paced to the window and looked out. Her back felt hot, and she had no doubt that he was staring at her, stripping her naked with his gaze, learning things about her he shouldn't.

Night was coming slowly. It was as if the sun couldn't bring itself to put an end to its journey across the sky. Maybe one of the Holy People was traveling on a sunbeam.

"Were you happy as a boy?" she asked.

"Yes."

"I'm glad. Ignorance can be a wonderful thing, the ignorance and innocence of childhood." She hadn't wanted to turn around, knew she wasn't yet strong enough to face him, but the fading sun and sky belonged to the Holy People and she needed Rigg to be a part of her. He still hadn't settled back in his recliner. Tension continued to wrap itself around him—tension that, maybe, had everything to do with her and nothing to do with *him*. His left hand still gripped the chair arm but the other was now reaching for something on the nearby table.

She barely noticed what he was doing until he handed it to her. It was a picture album, one of those compact little books that held only one picture per page. With an unshakable sense of foreboding, she carried it to the window and used the Holy People's sunbeam for light.

Rigg as a child. Little more than a mound in a frightened-looking girl's arms—his mother's arms? A two-year-old with chocolate frosting smeared over his face. A toddler sitting in a rocking chair, little legs barely reaching the edge. Kindergarten self-confidence perched on a bicycle with training wheels. A grade-schooler dressed in a red-and-white baseball uniform standing at the batter's box. A teenager in rented tux with a rosebud in his lapel and his arm around a much-shorter girl, her glowing, him looking as if he'd rather be playing baseball. Shanna absorbed the images, made them part of her understanding of him. She wondered why there were only two pictures of him with his grandparents, and if the lanky young man with the already-receding hairline was his uncle. His murdered uncle.

Her fingers stopped, curled slightly, resisted turning the last page. She found herself looking at a grainy and faded picture of a black-haired, stony-eyed man, shaggy bangs obscuring his eyebrows. His face was round and yet there was nothing soft about him. The mouth was held in a firm line, nose full and wide nostrilled as if he'd been startled. His wrinkled shirt was open to at least midchest, where the picture ended, an invitation to sensuality that failed because his flesh was too soft, the beginnings of a double chin hiding his short neck.

"That's *him,*" she said softly.

"Yes."

Telling herself she needed a better look, she pulled the snapshot out of the plastic sleeve. The paper felt brittle, as brittle as the man's gaze. "Why is it here with pictures of you?"

"So I won't ever forget where I come from."

Rigg wasn't a product of those barren eyes. She wanted to study the girl who'd been holding Rigg as a baby, the girl she took to be his mother, to see if she could find him in the features of someone who was more child than woman. But her fingers wouldn't let go of the old snapshot. Turning it so that the last of the daylight fell on the indistinct image, she asked herself what her reaction would have been if she hadn't known the truth about *him*.

No one home. She could have said a thousand things about the man, analyzed his background, his personality and education and work record, the fact that his nondeath was beyond his control, but it all boiled down to one inescapable fact: Rigg's father had been born without a soul.

The image fractured, wrinkled, became a tightly compacted ball in her fingers.

"Don't!"

"It's too late," she told Rigg without regret. Unclasping her fingers, she waited until the picture partially uncurled before tearing it first in half and then in quarters. She let the fragments fall to the carpet, only then aware of how cold her fingers felt. "Let *him* know what I think of him. Let him feel my hatred. What he did to my parents—damn him!"

Rigg was standing, stalking toward her, trapping her thoughts. She nearly shrank from him but stopped herself in time; she would not cower. Because he was facing the window, she got a good look at his eyes, his dark, dark eyes.

"You don't know what it's like. You have no idea what *he's* capable of."

No, she didn't, she admitted, although now that she'd met his son and become his son's lover, she probably understood far more than anyone else was able to. Juanica's knife pressed against her middle, acting as a reminder of danger, but she would deal with that later. Now there was only Rigg.

Only the command in his body.

Stepping deliberately on the shredded photograph, she met Rigg in the middle of the room. Every wall of his den had been covered in sand paintings—not real ones, created out of ground-up, colored rock by patient Navajo men and soon destroyed to protect their power. Still, she felt comforted by them.

She couldn't lift her arms, could only stand while he traced the contours of her throat, her chin, the ridge of her collarbone. She felt soft and warm and new, as if she'd come to life at this moment and would be content if her existence went no further than today.

Hours and hours ago she'd put on a wrinkled cotton blouse she'd pulled out of her overnight bag. It had serviceable front buttons, buttons that Rigg was now gently and slowly unfastening. He pulled the hem out of her waistband, looked down at the ornate and fragile knife, looked back up at her.

"I told you not to trust me, but it's all right—for now."

"I know." She wrapped her fingers around the knife and handed it to him. He cradled it in his palm before laying it on the table that held the little photograph album. When he didn't immediately touch her again, she ran her hands around his waist and boldly pressed herself against him.

He was ready for her.

Strength slid out of her legs, her torso, left her feeling nothing except a volcano of heat. She wanted to strip herself for him, offer herself freely so he would understand how much she believed in him, but he was way ahead of her. Taking her so deep within herself that she lost her reason and knew only wanting.

She hated his shirt, all but tore it from him. Hating his belt, she fumbled with the fastening and loops until she'd dropped it beside the shirt. She saw her hands start toward his jeans, felt numbness grow from fingertips to palm, sagged before him.

His turn. The blouse first and easily, followed by the zipper on her own jeans. She barely remembered what happened next: holding on to him so she could lift one leg and then the other, evening air on her newly exposed flesh, his nails raking lightly over her thighs. Her whimpering. His deep chuckle.

His hands roamed, torching her skin wherever he touched. She couldn't say when he removed her bra; she didn't care. There was a couch in the room, too short and narrow to accommodate them, and yet they made it work. He crouched over her, so large and yet everything she'd ever dreamed of. He must have laid her down because she couldn't remember doing that herself. After that he didn't have to guide her. She—the instinct that she'd become— knew what to do, how to help, how to make room for him despite the confined space.

His hands and lips were knowledge. He sensed when to press deep and possessively, when to tease gently. He kept at her mouth, kissing, nipping, probing until she became lost in his assault. His hands roamed her, traveled her curves and valleys, found kindling and turned it into an inferno. She began calling for him. Begging. Opening herself to him.

He took her, took and gave at the same time. She felt full and yet starving, fed upon him and tried to satiate herself. The hunger grew, building like trapped volcanic energy until she knew she was going to explode.

Until he showed her where freedom lay.

What joy meant.

They lay on the carpet, legs draped loosely over each other. He must have placed her there and then covered her with a throw before stretching out beside her. She vaguely remembered his leaving her for a brief period, but she'd been so lost within herself, so utterly content, that the memory of him had sustained her until he returned.

He was sleeping, and by the moonlight coming through the window she could see that his features had become peaceful. He'd been like that as a small boy, smiling and happy, content with what life had given him. There'd been a difference in his teenage pictures, a kind of lost and angry look to his eyes that maybe no one else would have noticed. At least in sleep he could forget.

She couldn't.

You can trust me, for now, he'd told her, and she'd believed him because she needed to. But he'd satisfied her, and her body was no longer hungry, and it was time to think. Time to face reality.

She tried to roll away from him, but his leg was angled over her hips, his weight holding her in place. The pressure awakened a small note of alarm that would continue to grow unless she stifled it. But should she? Maybe now, alone with the night and his sleeping body and her thoughts, she'd be a fool if she didn't look at the truth.

Chabah believed Rigg capable of violence; that's why he'd shown him how to surround himself with the magic and power of Navajo beliefs. Juanica had tried to warn her by insisting that she carry a sacred knife, but she'd let Rigg take the knife from her. The sand painting was still in his car.

Rigg's car. Rigg's house. Rigg's body pinning her to the floor.

Fear had a taste, hot and acidic.

With terror looping around her like a coiling rope, she forced herself to slide out from under him. She started to roll away, then stopped with her fingers poised an inch over his thigh. Tears stung her eyes and regret became stronger than fear. She knew she couldn't put her emotions into perspective until she was away from him.

Until she no longer drank in the smell of him.

She grabbed for her clothes and the knife, but didn't dress until she was in the living room. He'd said he was a light sleeper; he might wake and come looking for her. If he did, could she tell him the truth—that she'd been a fool for letting him claim her again?

The knife felt solid and strong, a work of art meant to punish and protect, but she could never use it on Rigg. The sand painting, which had protected her from *him* earlier, was in the car, only a few easy yards away. It suddenly seemed important to get her hands on that right now; she felt unbelievably defenseless when she needed to be strong and brave and in control.

Free from Rigg's impact.

When the front door gave easily, she asked herself why Rigg hadn't locked his door. Maybe he hadn't been capable of placing thoughts beyond the moment, beyond her. It was nearly the same for her now. She should have put on her shoes; that would have made the journey over the pebbled walkway easier, but tender feet and night darkness only faintly disturbed by the moon weren't the only reasons she made so little progress.

Rigg was back there. Rigg with his demons and battles, his understanding and hungry hands. The body that gave and gave and gave. His body would never comprehend why she was leaving like this.

The night was cold. Too cold.

Realization of that elemental fact came slowly, like whispers of alarm cast aside by a disbelieving mind. Angry, she forced herself to ponder what she intended to do once she had the sand painting. If Rigg had left the keys in the car, she guessed she could drive it back to her motel, but the last time she'd been there *he* had been, too.

What a joke that was, so funny that she nearly laughed. *He* couldn't possibly be waiting inside her motel shower because...

Because *he* was here.

CHAPTER THIRTEEN

There was a shadow. A form.

If anyone ever asked her what it felt like to stare her own mortality in the face, Shanna would have to say that it had a cold taste, felt like icicles moving through her veins. Or a vise clamping down around her throat and lungs and heart.

Go away! Just leave me the hell alone!

Someone was laughing, but it wasn't a sound like any she'd ever heard before. The laughter came from a throat that had forgotten how to speak, raking like fingernails on a blackboard until she nearly screamed.

Leave, damn you!

The shadow moved, wavering slightly like leaves in the wind but without the gentle hypnotic quality that went with that image. As it came closer, she thought she detected an unpleasant odor. In a dim and distant way she realized she was gripping the knife so tightly that she risked slicing herself on the blade, but the knife was reality and the only protection she had.

The shadow was gray, different from the night, a lighter shade and yet more impenetrable than the total absence of light. The image began taking on a curious kind of substance, one without heat, accompanied by a raw and brutal laughter meant to taunt and terrify.

"You want me." Her throat tightened and for too long she couldn't speak any more than she could run. Then she forced out the necessary words. "I know you do. But I'm not Debby, not my mother. Why—"

Revenge.

How simple, how utterly and completely simple.

"She didn't have anything to do with your death. She was a victim. Your victim."

She hated me.

And hatred was a crime in his eyes, for all but him. Now it was her turn to laugh, or rather she would have if she could have made the sound. It came out a squeak, quick and weak, letting him know too much about her tenuous hold on sanity. *He*—she could no longer call it a shadow—was taking on more and more substance. Zarcillas—there, she could think it; it didn't make any difference. Did it?

Zarcillas was a man and yet he wasn't, all form but without any depth or substance. It seemed terribly important to have discovered that he was one-dimensional, that his head was all outline and no eyes, mouth or nose. He wasn't really speaking; it was more like sound bytes penetrating her brain. Did that mean he couldn't see, couldn't smell?

What the hell did it matter?

Rigg! Be careful. Help me. Be careful.

He stood on the lawn in front of Rigg's house, his shadowy feet not quite in touch with the earth. The smell was getting stronger, that of death and decay. The stench of hatred.

"What do you want?"

You.

"You can't have me—I won't let you."

He didn't respond, did nothing except become even less mist and more reality. He was bulking out; she knew of no other way to describe what was happening to him. Becoming stronger, darker, until the night lapped at his edges and she began to lose him. It wasn't fair! She wanted to fight a man, not this—this what?

Don't panic! Don't, don't, don't!

Her teeth were clenched tightly together. When she tried to release the pressure, she realized she'd done that instinctively to keep herself from screaming. Jaw aching, she peered into the night and watched. Waited. Pointed the knife at him because she had nothing else.

Rigg! I need you!

He was coming toward her, taunting her with the slowness of his approach, daring her to turn and run. But she had nowhere to flee, no place of safety.

Except, maybe, the small field of corn.

Nausea rolled through her and made her weak. When another wave followed on the heels of the first, she realized her stomach was reacting to the stench as much as to the unbelievable horror of what was happening. *He* must be opening his mouth—she had no other explanation for the movement in the middle of his blackened head shape. She tried to ready herself for whatever might come out of him, but there was nothing—nothing except a puff of frozen air.

Closer. Closer still.

Rigg!

You can't run.

I'm not going to, she wanted to tell him, but that was for brave and stupid movie heroines. This was her, a normal and mortal woman face-to-face with—

With a creature, an undead monster now gliding toward her.

When her left knee threatened to go out from under her, she realized she'd taken an involuntary step backward. Despite her precarious balance, she slid away again, stopping only when she backed into a bush. Her heart was fighting to escape her chest. She felt on fire and frozen at the same time.

Gravity meant nothing to him. He kept coming closer, not moving and yet eating up the distance that had separated them. She tried not to breathe so the smell wouldn't make her even sicker than she already felt; she tried to think. But nothing in her life experience had prepared her for this.

I will have you.

She would choose death over that; didn't he know it? But maybe he would only follow her; maybe there was no escape.

No!

Rigg!

No, not Rigg, because he might sacrifice himself for her.

Instinct took over and she squared off to face the human nightmare. His face was still wreathed in darkness, but she felt the power in his non-eyes—power and hate and obsession. A shadowed mass that must have been his arm stretched out from the black-bulk of his body. She felt cold tentacles touch her cheek; she all but shattered, but couldn't command her muscles to move. There was no life-force to him, nothing with the slightest hint of warmth, of compassion. It was as if all the malice in the world was centered in him.

His frozen fingers explored her nose and eye socket, marched arrogantly to her lips as frantic no's reverberated inside her mind. Despite her revulsion and horror and disbelief, she wanted to clamp her teeth over him and bite down with all her strength. But the thought of having the taste of him inside her made her want to gag.

Mine. You are mine.

Her body was utterly without muscle, except for the hand that clutched a small and—she prayed—sacred knife. *He* kept singing, kept chanting that she belonged to him, kept touching and caressing. Testing how far she'd let him go. What if he believed she wanted this?

Like a panther charging through a suddenly open door, she lunged out, certain she'd found his belly. She drove the blade into him, drove and drove and twisted and tore.

There was nothing.

Only air.

You can't hurt me. Nothing can hurt me.

"No! Damn you, no!"

No longer thinking, she lowered her head and hurtled at him, wanting nothing except escape. She felt herself sinking into air, and then frozen vises clamped around her throat and forced her back against the bush. She tried to scream, but he'd cut off her air. Her vision became a red veil, trapping her, closing her in the world he controlled. She slashed again and again, tearing at nothing. Her mind fought to make sense of the horror and then skittered off, rejecting hell.

"Let her go!"

Rigg! She wanted to sob in gratitude, to throw herself at him and beg for protection, but *he* still had her. He was choking the life from her.

"Let her go!"

A car door opening and closing. Running feet. A sharp intake of breath—Rigg's breath. Somehow she managed to twist around so she could see him. The moon licked at him and gave definition to his naked body, highlighted the small object he held as defense between himself and his father.

Her sand painting.

"Take me, damn it! Leave her alone!"

I'm not ready for you. Not yet.

The vise around her neck tightened. She felt herself being lifted off her feet; she kicked out, stabbed and tore and fought. She thought she'd screamed, but surely that horrible gurgle wasn't all she was capable of.

Out of the corner of her eye, she saw Rigg charge his father. She wanted to warn him that there was nothing to fight, that the Chinde would consume him, but the need for air was too rapidly becoming all she could concentrate on.

Rigg leveled a powerful fist at the shadow, but his features registered no surprise when he connected only with air. He rocked back, gripped the sand painting in both hands, hurled it. She thought she heard a muffled thud, but maybe it was only her tortured lungs warning her that they were on the verge of bursting. The sound was almost immediately followed by that of something shattering like glass.

She could breathe!

Forcing her legs to hold her, she gaped, not at the place where *he* had been, but at Rigg. Despite the inadequate light, she recognized the fight and desperate determination in him, the total concentration on this horrid and incomprehensible battle. His form seemed to expand, to fill with muscle and bone and nerve, and she knew that if that long-ago zoo panther ever tasted freedom, he would look the same.

Her shattered sand painting lay at her feet. Silence blanketed her. She felt warm, not quite so splintered by fear.

"Shanna?" Rigg took a step toward her, then stopped, as if sensing she didn't know whether she dared trust him. The night continued to take on a blessed gentleness, a soul-grateful quiet. That, more than the easy way she now drew air into her hungry lungs, told her *he* had left.

"*He* was here. I saw him," she managed to say. "A form. Substance. Evil."

"I know. Shanna? Are you all right?"

She couldn't answer that; she might never be "all right" again, but at this moment it didn't matter. Rigg was lean, powerful strength, a man unashamed and unaware of his body. Moonlight slid over him like a lover. She needed him next to her, holding her, making her world right again; if he so much as touched her, she would want to spend the rest of her life making love to him.

She already did.

"*He* won't be back tonight."

"How do you know?" she asked, even though she believed him.

"He's playing a game, a game that exhausts him. He'll need to rest." Rigg dipped his head, indicating the ruined sand painting. "I'm sorry. I don't know why—I just acted."

"He's gone, that's all that matters," she said, despite the dread in the pit of her stomach. She wondered if Rigg was aware that he was naked, wondered why she should be thinking of that and not the simple fact that a dead man had held her life in his hands. Not sure of what she was doing, she took a half step toward Rigg before her knees buckled. She felt strong arms go around her and then the heat of Rigg's body as he pulled her against him. "Damn, damn, damn," he hissed. "He can't—I won't let him— Shanna! I almost lost..."

After that she knew nothing.

Rigg's bed smelled faintly of spice and wool. She lay on it, her head at a slightly awkward angle on the pillow, but she couldn't think how to remedy that. Every time she swallowed, the act brought tears to her eyes. She couldn't decide whether to curse what *he* had done to her or let terror have the upper hand.

Rigg, wearing only jeans, sat on the edge of the bed. He'd given her a cool cloth to drape over her throat and had watched her so closely that she felt raw and vulnerable from his scrutiny. Except for asking if she wanted to see a doctor, he had said nothing.

She could hear him breathing, almost believed she felt the tension in him. She wanted to tell him that she didn't in any way blame him, that she was fine, that she trusted him.

She wanted to give him those reassurances, but they remained out of reach.

"*He* could touch me, but I couldn't touch *him*. The knife was useless," she whispered, then paused while she repositioned the damp cloth. "I couldn't see his face—maybe there wasn't one."

"It's there when he wants it. When it serves his purpose."

This was an insane conversation, one she didn't want anything to do with. In the perfect world she tried to insulate herself in, Rigg would join her under the covers. His body, his lovemaking, would take over, and she wouldn't remember anything about the nightmare she'd just lived through. "How did you know *he* was there? The way you came running—"

"I heard you leave, Shanna. I was at the window when *he* appeared."

"You heard me le—why didn't you say anything?"

His eyes remained fastened on her, honest and accepting and wounded at the same time. "It was what you wanted. I wasn't going to try to stop you."

No, she nearly corrected him. She didn't *want* to walk away from him, but her confused mind had needed time and isolation, and she'd been unable to ignore its demands. She couldn't explain why she'd felt that way. After what she'd just been through, the rest of the night seemed as splintered and irreparable as the ruined sand painting. "Were you afraid?"

"For you? You must—if anything had happened to you . . ." His jaw clenched and she remembered the words that had been torn from him just before she passed out.

"No, what I meant was, were you afraid that you wouldn't be able to stop *him?*"

His hands had been clamped over his knees. He lifted one and began running his knuckles over her face. They touched where his father had touched, erased the horrible memory of that other contact. His knuckles felt cool, blessedly cool and gentle and safe. He'd turned on a lamp but was situated so that his features were cast in darkness.

"What I felt went far beyond fear, Shanna. Listen to me—for once, listen to me. I'm going to put you on a plane in the morning. You've got to go back to Florida. That's the only way you'll be safe."

"You tried to leave, but he followed you."

"I'm his son. It's different for you." Straightening his finger, he slid it over her cheek, gave her a little more of himself.

Fighting her body's response, she concentrated on what she needed to say. "You're asking me to run. To leave you here to fight him alone. Someday he's going to win. Damn it, Rigg. Someday—"

His lips stopped her. They settled over her mouth in an arrogant, nearly possessive gesture. When his father tried to control her, she fought with every ounce of strength in her. This was different. Rigg was no Chinde; he was life and passion and commitment wrapped in a body and mind struggling to remain free. A man searching for what other men took for granted—the right to be with a woman.

A man capable of stripping her mind of everything except her need for him.

Cool lips. A faint chill radiating out from him, imprinted on him by the night—the nightmarish night.

Still, she wallowed in him, wound her fingers through his rich hair and held him against her. Drank from his strength and gave in return. Felt her breasts and belly and the intimate place that had already known him grow hot and hungry.

Thump.

No! No!

One more moment, just another instant with Rigg's arms clutching her to him, his mouth and tongue possessing her, eating away at her senses. Consuming her.

Thump.

"Rigg," she managed to say, although his lips were still pressed against hers. "Rigg."

What? he asked without the word coming from his throat.

She pressed her palms against his temple and turned his head so that lamplight spilled across his face. His eyes pulsed and glowed, red slowly swallowing the deep black she so loved. "*He's* come back for you," she said.

"No!" She sensed something heavy and night-shadowed building inside Rigg. Sensed him curse and rage at whatever was consuming him. Maybe she should be terrified, but her heart remembered what it was like to lie beside him and she couldn't be afraid.

A whisper, so deep and hollow that it seemed as if it had come from the bottom of a well, tore through him.

"Run. Go to Chabah. He'll—get out of here. Now!"

"I won't leave you. I can't!"

"Damn it, Shanna..." He surged to his feet, nearly knocking her down in the process. His fists were raised, his features contorted. "Get the hell out of here! Please."

The driver's seat had been imprinted with the contours of Rigg's body. Sitting behind the wheel as the night slid past, Shanna tried not to think about how much the car felt like Rigg. He was back at his house. She'd taken his vehicle; he had no way of following her.

But should she be fearing Rigg? Maybe *he* could desert his son's body as easily as *he* entered it and in a few minutes or seconds she'd find *him* sitting beside her.

Rigg had been wrong. Zarcillas hadn't needed to rest, after all.

"What do you want?" Her voice echoed in the close interior. "Me? If that's what you're after, just take me."

There was no thump.

"What are you doing? Torturing your son? Tearing at him? But why? Why put your son through hell?"

Silence.

"Don't I have a right to know?" She came to a deserted intersection and sat watching as the light turned from red to green to yellow and then red again. The digital clock on the dashboard said it was 3:16 a.m. Except for her, the city was asleep.

Rigg wasn't sleeping; she knew that.

"Why do you hate him?" she asked as she pressed on the gas and the car slowly picked up momentum. "He was a child when you died. He had nothing to do with your death. Damn it, why do you hate him?"

Thump.

Although she had to clamp her teeth together to keep nausea from rolling through her, she was barely aware of the state of her stomach. In a strange way she felt at peace.

"You're here, aren't you? At least trying to reach me. She hated you, you know that, don't you? My mother hated you."

Thump.

Don't give in; don't panic. "Rigg does, too. That's why he's fighting you. Leave him alone—can't you just leave him alone?"

Thu...

"What's the matter?" The challenge in her voice made her proud; she could only pray that Zarcillas couldn't sense her emotions. "Are you tired? Did having to fight your son exhaust you?"

Nothing.

"Just leave us alone. Go back to whatever hell you came from. Die, damn it, die!" She was approaching another red light. There was no cross traffic. Barely slowing, she eased through the intersection until she could see the ruby light reflected in the rearview mirror.

Was that color back in Rigg's eyes? Had his father returned to feed off him?

Would the time come when there was nothing left of the man she'd fallen in love with?

Rigg sat in his den, head tipped back, eyes shut as he tried to lose himself in sound. His mouth moved slightly as he echoed the chant playing on the stereo. "Today I will walk out, today everything evil will leave me, I will be as I was before, I will have a cool breeze over my body, I will have a light body."

He sighed and drew in a fresh breath, but it did nothing to quiet the turmoil within him. Shanna was out in the night somewhere. He prayed she was alone and safe, hated the sense of helplessness that made it nearly impossible for him to gain any sense of comfort from songs that had sustained the Navajo for generations. Chants that had always before rejuvenated him.

His father. Zarcillas. What the hell difference did it make whether he said his name or not? The man—the Chinde he'd become—existed in a place between life and death, and nothing he did or tried to do would send him to the underworld where he belonged.

Nothing?

No, Rigg couldn't accept that, not any more than he could accept that Zarcillas was capable of destroying Shanna!

He felt drenched in sweat, unable to tell whether his body had begun to grow cool again, which would be proof that Zarcillas was no longer eating away at his sanity. He could go back to Chabah and tell the old shaman what had happened. Maybe there was something else they could do, magic that hadn't been tried before, a way of evoking the power of the Holy People.

A way of keeping safe the woman he'd fallen in love with.

He half pushed himself out of the chair, then fell back again. He had no idea where she was. He'd let her go because he'd believed himself to be the greatest danger to her. There was nothing he could do tonight—nothing except listen to the songs of his ancestors and take strength from them. Maybe enough strength to fight for Shanna's life.

Her life, not his.

"I will be happy forever, nothing will hinder me—I walk with beauty before me, I walk with beauty behind me, I walk with beauty below me, I walk with beauty above me, I walk with beauty around me, my words will be beautiful.''

If only he could believe.

CHAPTER FOURTEEN

What had created this land? The starkly beautiful sweep of orange-pink sandstone buttes, a horizon that seemed to stretch forever before becoming part of the sky were beyond Shanna's ability to define or describe. She should have learned more about the forces responsible for these intricate and delicate and yet proudly enduring sculptures, or at least brought along a camera so she could capture the subtle earth colors, the dark and ominous clouds. But she had nothing with her except a silver-and-turquoise knife.

What seemed like hours ago she'd gone through a stretch of green-and-yellow-dappled cottonwoods, the by-product of a thin ribbon of creek, but she was now back in arid, soilless land. Rigg's car and the dust it kicked up had barely disturbed the sheep that had been sleeping in the trees' shade. Except for them and the birds, she hadn't seen anything living since dawn had put an end to the night.

When the sun found an opening among the clouds, she squinted and winced as her heavy lids scraped over grains of sand that had built up on her eyes. The sleepless night had left her with aching muscles and a dull headache, and only the vaguest idea of what direction she needed to head in in order to find Chabah's isolated hogan. She was hungry, but because she was somewhere deep in Navajo wilderness, she would simply have to accept a gnawing stomach.

Chinde land.

Land that Rigg had returned to because it called to something deep inside him.

Looking out at the endless nothingness, she tried to accept that this was where the Navajo dead were said to dwell, where *he* ruled. But she could find nothing to fear in endless, peaceful shades of brown and gray and rust. Sturdy bushes somehow clung to land that looked incapable of nourishing the smallest plant.

Something she'd heard earlier chased through her mind. Although still groggy from lack of sleep, she captured it and brought it back so she could play the words again.

"It increases and spreads. In the middle of the wide field, the white corn, it increases and spreads. Good and everlasting one, it increases and spreads."

It was from Rigg's stereo, from the store of chants and songs he'd surrounded himself with. When she realized she'd started to smile, she held on to the discovery until a little of the lost and frightened feeling that had been stalking her faded.

Rigg had laughed once, been a curious boy capable of the empathy necessary to comfort a confused little girl. He deserved to be like that again. Somehow.

And if it was too late . . .

If *he* came after both of them—

No! That thought might drive her insane, and she needed to keep her head clear, to learn how to fight—if this was a battle they might possibly win. Win? How?

What she was on couldn't be called a road, more like a narrow strip firmly packed by countless hooves and generously salted with tire-punishing rock. She should have stayed on the more well-defined "road" where she occasionally spotted a track in the dirt, but as dawn kissed the land, she'd felt herself being drawn toward a series of distant bluffs, no longer caring whether she found the illusive hogan. She'd become aware of nothing except that magnet of stone, and the need to follow her instincts.

Distances were deceiving; it had taken twice as long to reach the bluffs as she'd thought it would, which meant even further delay in getting to the hogan, maybe the risk of never finding it.

Still, there was something about the stark rock sides etched by wind that continued to call to her so incessantly that she couldn't possibly ignore the command. When she tried to swallow, her throat felt as if it was closing up. She'd drunk from the creek upstream from where the sheep were, but would have been parched if she hadn't found a thermos in Rigg's trunk and had the foresight to fill it. Reaching for it, she drank sparingly.

She was alone out here, just her and an occasional bird silhouetted against menacing purple-blue clouds. The wind had picked up and was now ripping over the ground. She loved the sound, wondered if she could find a way of duplicating it so it could join with the rhythm of drum and flute and old men's voices.

Rigg should be here. Surely he'd achieve peace in this land carved and created by forces stronger than she could imagine. As she neared the largest butte, the one that had exerted the greatest influence over her, she sent Rigg a silent message, telling him that Zarcillas hadn't found her this morning and that she was safe. The realization that Zarcillas might be wreaking vengeance on his son filled her with dread, but Rigg's house was a world away. She couldn't help him; he'd ordered her to leave his side.

She could only follow her heart to the base of the cliff, get out of the groaning, dusty car and stare up at mass and weight and power. It was barren, exquisitely painted in an incomprehensible array of gentle colors, endless and timeless, the sum and substance of her existence now. She must have disturbed several swallows because they darted about, occasionally hiding themselves in the deep shadows near the top. She spotted a spider a few feet above her, seemingly suspended in air. Instead of swiping at it, she moved to the side so the tiny creature could continue its downward journey undisturbed. Thinking of the beetles and snake she'd seen as she was beginning her journey into this place of constantly changing rules and dangers, she tore her eyes from the mountain mass long enough to study the ground. She spotted several pinpricks in the earth that could be entrances to the homes of tiny ants. But except for the spider, she couldn't see anything for the swallows to feed on.

The vast sandstone sides called to her again. The dun color looked as if it had been blown onto the surface and would come off on her hand if she touched it. Curious, she walked close enough to press her hand against the rock. It felt dry and warm, utterly lifeless. Timeless.

The wind threw itself against the sandstone and made a curious thudding sound before fading away. Although she detected similarities between that and the sound that accompanied Zarcillas's presence, there was enough of a difference that she continued to feel relaxed and peaceful. Content except for her need to be with Rigg.

I'm all right, she told him. *It's quiet here. Quiet and beautiful and ageless. I feel... as if I'm coming home somehow. But I'm scared for you. And of you.*

A flicker of movement high above distracted her. Squinting, she recognized a sparrow's lean movement. There was something just behind where the bird was flying, a huge, deep-set ledge of some kind. When she moved so that the sun was behind her, she realized it was much more than a natural outcropping.

She'd seen pictures of Anasazi ruins created from stone and mud so that they seemed an inherent part of the cliffs they'd been built into. This, unless she was badly mistaken, was one of those. *It should be larger,* was her first, sleep-deprived thought. *More impressive.* More appealing to a tourist's camera. A moment later she acknowledged heartfelt gratitude that there was no real road leading here, no signs erected to describe the obvious.

This was her ruin, her quiet, intensely private cliff dwelling. Its appearance was so unexpected that she half prepared herself to see it fade away, but it must have been here for hundreds, maybe thousands of years. Thousands. A rare and precious sight impervious to the passage of time. Was this why she'd been drawn here?

She could see steps carved into the stone that led up to the long-abandoned homes and wondered about who'd built them and what had made the residents first choose this site and then leave. And once again she wondered what had drawn her here.

She'd tied a loose shoelace and put her foot on the first step before it struck her that the dwellings themselves had no magnetic hold on her. She stood without moving for the better part of a minute while the breeze brought her the smells and sounds of Navajo land—land Rigg hadn't been able to leave. When she turned and began walking parallel to the butte and only a few feet from it, she couldn't say what was directing her. The only thing that mattered was that she knew she was doing something she had to.

Her mouth already felt dry again. Her stomach growled indignantly. She ignored those discomforts as easily as she did her exhausted body. She was here; something had pulled her to this spot.

Something that had to do with Rigg.

The butte curved in on itself until she found herself all but wedged into a tiny space where sunlight seldom touched. After about a hundred feet, the sliver of canyon widened out a little. It was still so dark and close that she felt slightly claustrophobic and nearly unable to determine how far she'd come. At least the length of a football field, maybe two. No creature would come in here; there wasn't so much as a single weed growing. Finally the need to push on eased, and she stopped walking. Almost as if she had no control over her actions, she looked up, uneasy because she saw only shadow and felt as if she'd entered a cave.

The wall here had enough of a slant to it that if she had suction cups on her hands and feet she might be able to climb. The thought of her imitating a spider's movements made her chuckle unexpectedly. The sound rose and echoed, drawing her attention upward again. The few clouds she could see, compliments of the cliff's tunneling effect, still held that same deep purple hue, but they'd parted enough so that a ray of sunlight could escape. It glanced off the sandstone wall high overhead, illumination holding just long enough to allow her to see that something had been etched into the surface some fifty feet above her.

A petroglyph? Could she have stumbled across one?

Simply accepting, she reached out. Her fingers found something to cling to, and there was enough of a ledge about three feet off the ground that she was able to lift herself onto it and stand in relative comfort. Making the most of the faint sunlight and what her fingers could tell her, she began a slow and hopefully not too precarious climb. With each step she reassessed her chances of getting back down in one piece. So far so good.

When she figured she'd traveled about half the distance, she came to another shelf wide enough to allow her to stand flat-footed.

The sun must have decided to quit playing with the clouds and to gift the day with its heat and brilliance. She'd loved the rich hues of a potential storm, but the sunshine was safer, less filled with energy she couldn't match. Except for the sound of her breathing and the occasional whisper the wind created as it bounced off one outcropping or another, the silence was so deep that she felt as if she might drown in it. Still, she was grateful for the opportunity to exist quietly within her thoughts.

Something was keeping her in New Mexico. A couple of days ago it had been the lure of the past, but that was no longer true. Rigg had been fighting his father's impact for a long time. He knew how the battle must be fought, he and Chabah and maybe Juanica. Certainly her presence only increased Zarcillas's determination to rule and dominate. Increased the danger to Rigg's sanity, to his soul.

If she left, maybe Zarcillas would return to the nothing place he existed in when hatred didn't catapult him into deadly action; then Rigg might have the precious time he needed in order to gather his strength for more battles.

And maybe Zarcillas sensed Rigg's exhaustion and had decided that the time had come to control and dominate.

To strip away Rigg's sunlight and replace it with darkness.

Thoughts of what Rigg's eyes might look like if his essence no longer lived within him filled her with dread. She felt her fingers slip off a handhold; half sobbing, she grabbed so tightly that she tore a nail. She looked down but could see little more than her feet. Above her, with sunlight washing over its ageless surface, was a lonely and yet powerful-looking figure etched into the rock.

Changing Woman.

Despite the heat on her head and shoulders and the additional warmth created by her climb, Shanna felt cold. Another ledge, maybe the one the artist had stood on while carving Changing Woman, wasn't that far above her. Gathering her strength, she forced herself to stop shaking and scaled the last few feet until she was able to place her hands flat against the deity's face. It felt eternal beyond the limitations of time and weather.

Tears stung her eyes; she didn't try to tell herself the sleepless night and her exertions were responsible. She wished she knew more about the Navajo deity, about everything spiritual where the Navajos were concerned. Still, for this morning, this was enough.

"Did you bring me here?" she asked Changing Woman. "Are you responsible for my being drawn here?"

Or was she simply losing her mind?

Falling into the abyss that was claiming Rigg?

* * *

It was noon by the time Shanna stepped on the brakes and sat looking out at Chabah's hogan and the quiet land around it. The house might be only a few years old; the Navajo woman she'd met in Aztec had told her that her people moved frequently while tending their sheep, and each family had several hogans they considered home. But the way this hogan had settled into its surroundings, as if it had long been a part of the environment, made her think it was different.

She found more to love in this simple place of earth and rough wood than she ever would in her modern apartment. To live here where TV and other modern conveniences never touched her… Of course, she couldn't really do that; she was too much a product of today for that kind of existence. Still, if it wasn't for Zarcillas's presence, this land could renew her.

Maybe answer her questions about Rigg's place in her life, in her heart.

He was here. Although she'd never seen the older-model pickup before, she somehow knew it belonged to Rigg and not someone else who'd come to visit Chabah and Juanica. Last night he'd told, ordered, her to go to the shaman. This was the place he would come looking for her if he was in control of his faculties.

And if Zarcillas ruled his son? She couldn't answer that any more than she could turn around and go away. Driving slowly so as to kick up as little dust as possible and to give herself time to prepare for Rigg's presence, she made her way along the randomly twisting path that led to where the old Navajo lived.

When she shut off the car, she sat for a minute, breathing deeply, thinking of the time she'd spent with Changing Woman. Then, after tucking Juanica's knife under her blouse, she opened the door and stepped into the sunlight.

A shadow filled the hogan entrance, a shadow born of strength and warmth and danger. Rigg had had to bend over to clear the low doorway. When he straightened, he did it slowly, as if he was giving her time to adjust to his presence—to run if that was what she wanted.

"He isn't inside me, at least he isn't now."

"You always know? There's never a time when..." This was insane. She was trying to ask Rigg a question and she couldn't even think how to finish it. "Does Chabah know I'm here?"

Rigg nodded. It was then that she noticed he hadn't shaved. He looked weary, drained, and she could only guess what the night's battle against demon forces had cost him. If Zarcillas returned, would Rigg's strength be spent before his father's was? "I needed to talk to you first," he said. "To ask if you'll have anything to do with me."

"I don't know how to answer, Rigg. I want to believe I can trust you."

That made Rigg laugh, although there was no warmth in the sound. "I haven't been able to trust myself for a long time. How can I expect you to do what I don't dare?"

"You can't." She raked her fingers through her hair, unmindful of the riot of windblown tangles. She hadn't so much as looked at herself in the rearview mirror today, but could guess what she looked like—haggard and trapped. Like Rigg. "All I know is, this *can't* go on. We have to stop *him*. Somehow."

"Somehow? Don't you think I've been looking for the answer to that for longer than I want to admit? It isn't too late for you. You can go where *he* can't find you."

Yes, she could find safety, as long as she never saw Rigg again. Meeting his eyes, she simply shook her head.

He said nothing, only returned her gaze.

"I saw something this morning," she told him softly. "I want to tell Chabah about it, to ask him—"

"When you weren't here when I arrived, I was afraid *he'd* found you."

There was too much distance between them. How could she gain a greater sense of what was going on inside Rigg if she stood so far from him? Yet there was danger in getting any closer. Taking the risk, she moved away from the car. His shirt looked as if he'd slept in it. His boots were dust caked. She guessed he hadn't had any more to eat than she had and that although his body craved sleep, he couldn't relax long enough to let that happen. "I'm sorry if I worried you."

That elicited another of his rough laughs. Still, the haggard look remained, giving her unwanted insight into the torment he'd gone through while waiting for her.

"Tell me about it," she made herself say. "Everything that's happened to you since *he* began whatever it is he's been doing to you. He killed Hank Granger and your uncle and others. He slaughtered sheep. Why—why is he doing what he is now instead of—of simply killing you?"

"I used to ask myself that," Rigg said wearily. "I'd wonder what a knife would feel like, a gun. Finally I told Chabah about my nightmares, the urges to commit violence. Chabah said that *he* was different, more evil than any other Chinde because he had already been evil in life. *He* wants immortality."

"Immortality?" Just the thought made her shudder. "But—"

"Don't think like a white woman, Shanna," he interrupted, a finger pressed to his forehead. "If you do, you'll never understand. A Chinde is like a corn plant—his time is limited. Although the Navajo fear the spirits of the dead, they know they'll eventually find their way into the world below. They'll forget they were ever one of the Earth Surface People."

"Why didn't that happen to *him?*"

"I don't know, at least not completely." Rigg spoke calmly, without a hint of disbelief or question in his voice. "For years after Hank Granger's death, the Navajo believers were careful to not speak of my father, and even Chabah thought that *he* had left this place. Then something happened. Maybe someone who didn't know what he was doing mentioned *his* name. Maybe it was Juanica telling me about my past. Maybe—I was changing from a boy, taking on the energy and strength of a man. Chabah believes *he* wants that, wants to become me."

"Oh, Rigg, no."

He didn't change expression, making her realize he had accepted that a long time ago, had resigned himself to the battle. "He wants me. He will never stop fighting me for possession."

"For possession of your body and mind? To know he'll live for as long as you do and never have to go back to—to wherever other Chindes go..."

She wanted to finish what she'd started to say, but even after everything she'd been through, she couldn't forget a lifetime of beliefs. In the world she knew, there weren't such things as deities called Changing Woman and Mother Earth and Father Sky, and certainly the souls of those who died didn't hover around waiting to take control of their offspring. But this was ancient Navajo land, and she didn't understand anything except that Rigg Schellion was engaged in a battle for his very existence.

"You told Chabah what's happened since we last saw him?" she asked. "He knows that *he* entered your home, got past your protection?"

Rigg, again looking like that caged panther, nodded and half turned toward the hogan. When he swung back around, his determined stare nearly stole her breath. He'd told her he was exhausted by this endless battle with his father, and yet she had no doubt that he wasn't ready to give up. There was more at stake now—her role in this drama.

Zarcillas knew that the daughter of the woman he'd lost his mortal life over was here.

Sick and scared, she started walking. She stopped just outside the hogan's entrance, no more than five feet from Rigg. "I'm frightened for you," she whispered.

He shook his head like a weary runner at the end of a marathon. "Shanna? My father killed your mother. Stabbed her because she wouldn't become his lover. Maybe nothing will stop him from doing the same to you if you resist."

She couldn't concentrate on all this, couldn't sort through what should be an insane conversation, yet might be the most sane and real thing she'd heard in her entire life. "Then we have to stop him," she said.

"How?"

I don't know! Angry and trapped herself, she grabbed Rigg's arm with every ounce of strength she possessed. Pain shot through her; she dimly realized that the discomfort came from the finger she'd injured while climbing. Releasing Rigg, she showed him her jagged nail. "I saw Changing Woman," she whispered. "A petroglyph of her. If Zarcillas is here in some form, then maybe Changing Woman is, too."

She expected Rigg to recoil at the sound of his father's name, but maybe he was beyond that emotion. "Do you believe it?" he asked.

She didn't know what she believed about anything anymore. Everything in her background and training was screaming at her to run to the police and demand they protect her from—from what? Someone who had died twenty-five years ago? "You surround yourself with corn and sand paintings. Juanica, who went to college and works for county government, carries a knife her father blessed. I don't question what either of you are doing—don't you question me, either."

"I don't want you to be a part of this. I want you safe."

Maybe she should have felt comforted by Rigg's whispered comment, by the way he'd laced his fingers through hers and pulled her against his side. But although she immediately felt a strong pulse of desire, she knew he couldn't insulate her from this nightmare anymore than she could free him.

"I am a part of it. Because of who I am, *he* isn't going to stop until he has me. He won't try to kill me, Rigg. I'm not Navajo—I won't become a Chinde. If I'm dead, he'll have nothing. He learned that with my mother. He wants me alive..." *Don't stop. Revulsion won't change the truth.* "...where he can put his hands on me whenever he wants."

"I won't let him! Damn it, I won't!"

Rigg couldn't stop his father; he already knew that. Feeling as if she was being torn apart, she yanked free and started into the hogan, stopping only when she remembered that strangers weren't welcome inside the old shaman's home. If she expected help from Chabah—maybe their only hope—she would have to be careful not to anger him.

She called out softly, waiting with the sun to her left and Rigg behind her, not touching her. Maybe not even breathing.

One minute passed. She again called Chabah's name. Juanica, her features tight, stepped outside. "He's coming. I told him not to, but he insists."

"You don't want him to see her? Why not?" Rigg demanded.

"He's a tired old man, Rigg. I don't want him to risk his life for an outsider."

Outsider? Once Juanica had loved her enough to find people to take her parents' place; the years shouldn't have made that much difference. But when Chabah emerged and Juanica positioned herself between the others and her father, Shanna understood. The Navajo woman had once loved the little girl known as Cindy, but her loyalty now was to her father—and she was afraid for him.

Ignoring his daughter, Chabah stared at Shanna. Her eyes still burned from lack of sleep, but she forced herself not to so much as blink. Love radiating out from Juanica encompassed her father and made Shanna hungry for something she'd never experienced. Barely aware of what she was doing, she glanced at Rigg. His eyes, quieter and more somber than she'd ever seen them, told her that he, too, sensed what Juanica felt for her parent. Maybe he was thinking of what he'd never had with his own father. At least, she admitted, they had that in common.

"I knew you would return," Chabah said in a rough tone. Something dangled from his gnarled fingers. She recognized it as a little bag like the one Rigg wore around his neck. She wondered if he still had it and whether he still believed in it. "When Rigg told me what happened last night," Chabah continued, "I knew you would turn to me for guidance. For protection."

"I had to," she said in a rush. If only she could hold on to Rigg and take strength from him. "*He* came after me. *He* wanted—he wants me."

"He is testing his power over you. Waiting for the time when his strength is greater than yours."

The sun was so hot she felt nearly desperate to escape its intensity. If only the promising morning clouds had remained. "I know."

Chabah shifted his weight. For a moment she was certain he meant to walk over to Rigg. Instead, he straightened and glanced at his daughter before running his tongue over dry lips. "I will tell you what I told Rigg. Go. Now. Run."

"What?"

"You must. There is nothing I can do for you."

CHAPTER FIFTEEN

Rigg had almost no reaction to the shaman's words. When he'd heard them for the first time a half hour ago, it had been all he could do not to shake Chabah until he told Rigg he hadn't meant a thing he'd said. That, yes, he would use every bit of magic learned through a lifetime of training to save Shanna's life.

Now Rigg accepted the truth behind Chabah's words.

Shanna looked incredible. He sensed her exhaustion, guessed that, like him, she'd had nothing to eat since yesterday. He didn't doubt that she felt like a trapped animal—just as trapped as he did. She was still the most unbelievably beautiful woman he'd ever seen.

The desert had become part of her.

"There's nothing Chabah can do," he told her as gently as possible. "Everything he guided me in, all the precautions, the ways he directed me to protect myself—none of that worked."

"I know." She rocked on her feet a little. "I'm sorry. Sorry and scared for you."

He'd guessed she would say that. His heart swelled at this proof of her loyalty. Loyalty? No, damn it, what she felt for him must be stronger than that; otherwise she wouldn't be here, risking further harm to herself. If he dared hope, dared think beyond today, he could explore the depths of both their emotions, but this wasn't the time for that; maybe it never would be.

"Listen to me," he insisted. "There are no miracles here." He jerked his head at the new fetish bag Chabah and Juanica had wanted him to wear. "No magic cures."

"What are you saying? That you're giving up?"

Giving up wasn't an option he had; she knew that. Still, he nearly threw the words back at her; he would have if he hadn't been aware of how much he'd lose if he did. He gripped her arms, drew her so close that he caught the hint of sage she now carried in her hair. The scent was nearly his undoing.

"There has to be something," he challenged Chabah fiercely and insanely. "Something you haven't thought of, haven't already tried."

"There is nothing."

Shanna shuddered in Rigg's grip. He held on to her with a strength he felt from the depth of his soul. If Chabah was right—and despite his outburst, he believed that with every fiber in him—there was only one course left to him.

To give up Shanna.

Face hell alone.

"No," Shanna said, before he could begin to pull his thoughts together. Her voice carried more determination than it had before. He nearly believed in the word, nearly wrapped it around both of them.

"Listen to him, Shanna," Juanica insisted. "We're not living in a world of ancient belief and ritual, a simple and good world kept that way by walking a narrow, righteous path. He—"

"I know there's nothing simple about what's happening," Shanna interrupted heatedly. "Believe me, I know that all too well. But, Chabah." She struggled to free herself from Rigg, and when he reluctantly released her, she didn't stalk away. Instead she stood staring at the old man with eyes that looked every bit as haunted as Rigg's ever had. "Chabah. There's magic in the sand painting you gave me."

"Was," Rigg reluctantly reminded her. "I destroyed it."

Her features contorted at that. "Because you tried to defend me with it. But before that, the first time I felt *his* presence, it worked."

He listened, simply absorbed the sound of her voice, the strength and courage in it. With an economy of words, she told Chabah and Juanica about clutching the sand painting to her when she'd first sensed *his* presence in her motel room, and the almost-overwhelming feeling of relief and peace that had spread over her when she realized the presence had slid away.

"I know that's why he left," she finished emphatically. "No one will ever convince me differently. Something about the painting repelled him. Was stronger than him. If that happened once—"

"Shanna." Hating what he was doing, Rigg nevertheless continued to throw his logic at her. "Chabah created a painting for me, more than one. But that didn't stop *him*. Neither did hanging trinkets and keepsakes around my neck, or anything else I tried. Juanica's knife was useless."

She was going to slap him. He saw her lift her hand, saw unreasoning anger contort her features. Then, whimpering low in her throat, she slumped forward. "The knife," she whispered. For the better part of a minute no one spoke. He heard the wind, felt the day's heat, fought off the need for sleep. Most of all he was aware of the presence of the best thing to have ever entered his life. It was too late for them; they'd never had a chance. And when she was gone, he wasn't sure there'd be reason to continue fighting.

To find a way to destroy what couldn't be destroyed.

"There must be belief," Chabah said, his usually scratchy voice harsh with conviction. "One who does not believe with one's heart cannot be touched by magic."

Chabah had told him that before, more times than he wanted to think about. He'd tried. Damn it, when he'd planted his corn and worked an ageless design into his entryway, when he'd memorized countless chants and songs, he'd told himself he believed in the faith that sustained traditional Navajos. But white blood flowed in his veins and he'd been raised in a culture a world apart from the one that had sustained Chabah and Juanica's ancestors.

Juanica. She'd gone to white man's school and earned her living in the white man's world, but when her time there was over, she returned to an old hogan and deliberately wove flaws into her exquisite wool blankets so there would be room for her soul to escape, as her mother and grandmother and great-grandmother had taught their daughters.

"I didn't believe in the old ways, in your tradition," Shanna was saying. "There was no way I could, because I didn't understand anything about it. I had no idea what I was doing when I held a piece of artwork to my breast. I was desperate, nothing else. But it stopped him—because..." She spun around and for a heartbeat seared Rigg with a look filled with questions. Then she turned her back on him.

"Because what could not be was happening to you," Juanica supplied. "An essence that all your logic said couldn't possibly exist was in the room with you and you acted out of instinct. You became a believer, at least for those moments."

Shanna hadn't taken her eyes off Juanica while she was speaking. She'd nodded, slowly, gracefully, wrapping a satin loop around Rigg's heart with that simple gesture. How in God's name was he going to order her out of his life?

What did it matter what happened to his heart? For her sake, and maybe for his as well, he had to make her leave.

"Maybe I did believe," she said. "I don't know. Can you make another one?" she asked Chabah. "If one worked, why not another?"

Chabah shrugged. Rigg was shaken by how old the man looked. "It is not a simple thing, not something easily done. The design is important. The wrong one..." He stared tellingly at Rigg. "And one in the hands of someone who does not fully believe is useless."

He knows. Rigg tried to tell himself that couldn't possibly be, but who was he to say what dwelled inside Chabah's heart? Hadn't he done everything he possibly could to embrace Navajo beliefs? But bits of colored sand sprinkled on the ground and nonsensical, repetitious words, a fragile turquoise-and-silver knife—how could those things possibly defeat what was eating away at him?

"What do you mean, the wrong one?" Shanna pressed.

"Before I create something with my hands, it exists only inside my head," Chabah explained. "It may be beautiful, but it also may have no power."

"Recreate what you did for me the first time," she insisted, her features tense. "You remember it, don't you? The childish figures, Changing Woman."

"You believe?"

"Yes!" Shanna insisted. "I felt drawn to it from the first time I saw it. That's why—something enticed me to the petroglyph of her this morning. I'm not a climber. I don't like heights or closed spaces, and I knew I should be getting here as fast as I could, but when it started calling to me, I didn't try to fight."

"What are you talking about?" Rigg demanded.

"The etching of Changing Woman." She pointed vaguely off into the distance. "Near the cliff houses."

Before he could ask for a further explanation, Chabah told him there was a small group of cliff dwellings near Cinder Gorge. "But there are no petroglyphs there," the old man said, his eyes closed to slits, his attention fixed on Shanna. "Not unless someone has come recently and desecrated the rocks. Or unless..." He glanced at his daughter.

"What do you mean, no petroglyphs?" Shanna insisted. "I know what I saw. I climbed up there and put my hand on the drawing. It's faded, faintly outlined, but I could see it from the ground. It's Changing Woman. I have no doubt of that. No doubt."

"Shanna." Rigg reached for her hand. Although she didn't draw away, neither did she respond to the contact. Before he could ask her what was wrong, a shaft of pain sliced through him, so raw it nearly forced him to his knees. He fought it as he'd fought such things too many times in the past, cursed the monster who, even now, refused to give him a moment's peace. He'd been about to tell Shanna that she'd been emotionally overwrought when she thought she saw something in the rocks, but now all that mattered was keeping her safe—from him.

"Rigg!" Her voice was heavy with alarm. "What's wrong?"

"Nothing," he lied. "I'm just...tired." He took a half step toward his pickup, belatedly realizing he still had a hold of her hand. He released her, fought off the anguish of that loss. "I'm going back home."

"What? Damn it, Rigg. What's happening to you?"

Nothing, he tried to repeat, but the monster wouldn't let him speak. He was vaguely aware of three pairs of concerned eyes staring at him and wanted to tell them that he'd been through this before and knew what he needed to do to survive.

"*He's* after you, isn't he? Don't lie to me, Rigg!" Shanna pleaded.

He couldn't form a single sound, could barely keep his feet under him.

"Chabah! Do something!" Shanna gasped as Rigg closed his eyes and clamped his hands tight against the sides of his head in a futile attempt to stop the agony.

Both Chabah and Juanica were saying something. Rigg sensed hands on him and thought they belonged to Shanna, but couldn't force himself to focus long enough to be sure. He should be used to this; he'd always been able to battle his father until the monster withdrew in momentary defeat. But this was worse than it had ever been, a ripping and shredding of his brain.

His knees turned to water and he started to sink to the ground so he wouldn't injure himself further in a fall. Warm, strong hands—Shanna's hands—guided him. He felt hard earth, tried to straighten. The knife buried in him became a sword that tore great chunks out of him. Bellowing his rage, he shook his head from side to side, cursing the man who'd given him life. He wondered if he'd survive long enough to place himself in some psychiatrist's care. A padded cell. Endless drugs. Was that his future?

No!

"Rigg. Rigg. Rigg."

Her voice, something to cling to. A promise of normalcy. Maybe a shared hell if he couldn't fight his overwhelming need for her.

The sword jabbed, twisted, robbed him of his sight. Although Shanna was holding on to him, her warmth the only thing between him and a barren, embattled future, he fought her. He pushed clumsily, tried to scramble away, fell back against her.

His father was shrieking at him, *No! I will not—you can't—I'll kill—hate. Hate! No, no, no...*

Shanna was whispering, "Rigg, I'm here. Rigg, I won't leave you. Rigg, fight. Fight."

He did, with strength that should no longer exist, with a fury that tore at his stamina as much as the attack itself did. Energy came from the woman beside him. Her voice kept him from becoming lost, gave him something to focus on. Made him strong.

He might have passed out. He didn't know and maybe it didn't matter as long as he no longer felt as if his mind was being shredded. As long as he felt Shanna's arms around him and her whispered singsong filling him with a sense of peace he'd never found in the chants he'd tried to surround himself with.

"I'm... all right," he gasped.

"I know you are." Crooning words. "You're strong. Strong. But Rigg..."

She didn't have to finish. He knew what she was going to say—that a wounded man couldn't survive many more attacks. He didn't care, not now, not with her next to him. She'd started talking again. It took several minutes for him to realize she was speaking to Juanica and Chabah.

His weakness filled him with an anger that rivaled the fury he felt whenever his father launched one of his cruel assaults. He wanted to be the one Shanna could lean on, a hard-muscled man to counter her softness, but he didn't feel anything except beaten.

No, damn it, not beaten.

Although the effort took all he had in him, he managed to haul himself to his feet. Somehow he held his head high. Shanna was standing so close that when he breathed, he felt as if he was taking a little of her inside him. She clutched something in her hands. When he realized it was the fetish bag Chabah had just made for him, he thought about refusing to let her get any closer to him with it; he couldn't stand to see her delude herself. But it had taken all his will to remain erect, and she was all desperate determination. When she stood on tiptoe and slipped the leather strap over his head, the small weight against his throat felt somehow comforting. Not enough, but comforting just the same.

"There's nothing left inside me, Shanna." Although he hated it, he wasn't surprised by the note of finality in his voice. He also knew he wouldn't lie to her again. "Once *he* has me, I don't know what's going to happen."

"Nothing's going to happen. I'll protect—"

"You can't! You have no idea what he's capable of. Tell her," he ordered Chabah. "Everything."

Features grim, Chabah described what fifty dead sheep looked like. What had been done to Hank Granger and Uncle Jeff and others. He spoke of things Rigg had hoped he could protect Shanna from—like the unmarked grave no Navajo or animal went near because of the sense of evil that still surrounded it and the shack *he'd* lived in while he was stalking Debby. "It was left like your parents' house," Juanica continued for her father. "Abandoned. And then three years ago, a couple of liquored-up white men spent the night in it. When they were found, their throats had been slit."

Rigg thought Shanna might blanch at that, but she didn't. "Simply because they'd spent the night in a shack?" she asked with no tremor in her voice. "Why?"

"Why not?" He forced out the words. When she stared up at him with wary and desperate and still-determined eyes, it was almost more than he could handle. "Before going there, they'd boasted they weren't afraid of any ghost. They cursed *him*. Their friends admitted it after they were killed. They'd cursed him and spoken his name in a place he claimed as his own. They ridiculed him and he sought revenge."

Shanna nodded. Then she touched her palm to his chest so that the talisman was caught between them. Although he should warn her of the danger, he couldn't make himself speak or move. Couldn't deny himself her warmth. "*He's* going to return," she said softly. "And when he comes—"

"Maybe this time he'll finish what he began with me."

"No!"

"I know what I'm talking about. He'll never give up."

"Then we have to stop him."

"Damn it, he can't be stopped, Shanna. Don't you know that? You tried. Remember, you tried last night. He's going to take me over and when he does, he'll have my strength. Before I allow that to happen, I'll have myself locked up."

"No."

"What else is there? You have to see—you're the most in jeopardy."

"I don't care!" Despite her brave words, her eyes were huge. "You'll be as good as dead if a mental hospital gets a hold of you. Locked up? Rigg! I can't let that happen—I can't!"

"Enough." Chabah's quavering voice echoed in the vastness. "White men and women speak too much. Shanna, you talked of Changing Woman. Take me to that place. Now. I must see—"

"What?" Rigg interrupted. "We don't have time for that. She's got to get on a plane. Get her the hell out of here—before I kill her."

Juanica had given them some cornbread before they all left Chabah's hogan. If it hadn't been for that energy boost, Shanna wasn't sure she'd have been able to keep going. But the simple food might have come hours too late. She'd been operating on empty too long and probably had only imagined she saw something on the side of a cliff. Chabah had spent over seventy years here and he'd never seen what she'd described. Illusion, that's what it was. Illusion, or maybe delusion.

They were wasting time chasing after hers and an old man's hope when she should be getting Rigg to a hospital.

A hospital where they'd declare this fierce fighting man insane and pump him full of mind-numbing drugs.

Anything was better than that.

The first to exit Rigg's car, Shanna stared up at the half-dozen cliff houses. They were heavily draped in shade now and at first she hadn't been able to see them. Even now she wasn't quite sure whether they existed or if they and the petroglyph of the Navajo deity were something her sleep-deprived brain had concocted.

She wanted to believe; for Rigg's sake, she *needed* to believe. She didn't dare ever lose sight of that.

And if it turned out that she'd found a previously undiscovered prehistoric carving, so what?

"Rigg," she called out when he remained in the vehicle. "Please tell me the truth. Do you have the energy for this? If you don't—"

"Chabah wants a miracle, Shanna." He sat clutching the steering wheel. "Despite everything, I want to give it to him."

Even if it meant sacrificing himself? Wishing she'd never said anything about what she thought she'd found here, she blinked back hot tears. It was like Rigg to put Chabah's needs before his. Maybe he believed himself lost and saw nothing positive in his existence except the knowledge that he'd given an old man a reason to go on clinging to his primitive beliefs.

Despite the unrelenting sense of urgency that demanded she get Rigg to some kind of professional help—if there was such a thing—she acknowledged Chabah's presence. In that rusty voice of his, Chabah repeated what he'd said before they left the hogan, that Changing Woman had taught the Earth Surface People how to live in harmony with nature, that she had built the first hogan out of turquoise and shell and had given the people the gift of corn. Changing Woman was powerful and wise. If a person believed in her and came to her honestly and humbly, the request would be answered.

Even before Chabah finished, Shanna was forced to admit how deranged the quiet speech sounded. Nothing had "drawn" her to this place. She'd been punchy and disoriented from lack of sleep, barely able to think. She'd risked breaking her neck climbing up to something that even Chabah hadn't been aware of.

And now Chabah wanted—what? For Rigg to haul his tired and weakened body up a cliff face? To what purpose?

"It isn't going to change anything," Rigg said. He'd gotten out of the car. His eyes, black as obsidian, whispered of soul-deep exhaustion.

Risking his life; we're risking his life.

After a few seconds during which she wondered if maybe he'd simply drift away like a puff of smoke, he started toward Juanica who was gazing up at the cliff houses. When he was as close as he could get to the ruins, he lifted one hand to shield his eyes. The other hung at his side, fingers empty.

At Chabah's insistence, Shanna headed in the direction she'd gone this morning. Although she kept waiting for a sense of purpose, a feeling that there was a reason behind what she was doing, it didn't come.

The land here looked so utterly devoid of life. Had it been like that this morning? She couldn't remember. "He needs help," she told Chabah when she was sure Rigg wouldn't overhear. "There must be some doctor who—"

"White man's medicine cannot understand a Navajo ghost, Shanna. Rigg does not believe—that is why my medicine has not helped him. But you . . ."

He was waiting for her to verify that she'd experienced something wondrous when Zarcillas fled from her motel room, but she couldn't. Terror did unfathomable things to the human mind and she'd been desperate when she'd grabbed the sand painting and used it as a shield. Maybe Zarcillas had been playing yet another of his sick games. Maybe he'd disappeared because it suited him, not because of Changing Woman's power.

Maybe? The monster was capable of anything.

"Where?" Chabah asked. "Tell me again. You were drawn here—you could not fight what was happening to you?"

"I didn't try," she admitted. "The feeling seemed over-powering at the time, but right now—now I feel nothing."

She expected Chabah to look disheartened, but he merely grunted and started walking in the direction she'd pointed. He stumbled slightly while stepping over a rock and she quickly steadied him. She sensed movement behind her. She didn't have to turn and look to know that Rigg had joined them. His long legs quickly caught up to Chabah. He casually looped the older man's arm through his and slowed his pace.

Because of the hard contrast between sunlight and shadows, Shanna was unable to clearly see his features and had to rely on instinct—if she had such a thing. Rigg was still deeply tired, still pushing himself to the limit of his endurance. If she was incapable of tapping into his emotions, she might have no way of knowing whether Zarcillas had begun a fresh assault on his son.

Rigg was scared, not for himself but for her. And despite his weakened condition, he would never give up.

She'd been close to tears too many times in the past few days; she should have built up her defenses. But how could she possibly pretend that Rigg's future, his life, didn't mean more to her than her own did?

"There." She pointed. "Up there."

The sun by now was no longer overhead. Heavy shadows draped the narrow channel between sheer cliff walls. No matter how hard she squinted, she couldn't see the outcroppings she'd balanced on earlier, let alone spot a faded outline. She offered the opinion that maybe no one had seen the etching because no one had been here during that brief window of opportunity when sunlight touched it. Juanica nodded, but neither Chabah or Rigg said anything. Instead of moving any closer to the mass of sandstone, the shaman stood with his arms stretched toward the sky, eyes closed, chanting softly.

Shanna waited for Rigg to give her a telling stare, tried to prepare herself for the disbelief she was certain she'd see in him, but he simply stood near the older man, arms loose and yet not easy at his side.

If the wind hadn't been blowing, it would be uncomfortably hot out here. Still, although she was grateful for the breeze, it kicked up enough dust that she had to squint to keep particles from getting into her eyes. Like her father, Juanica seemed oblivious to the elements. After a minute, she too lifted her arms and joined in the chant. The words made no sense to Shanna; she assumed that they were Navajo and simply listened to the syllables, to the emotion, to the prayerlike quality their voices had taken on.

She wanted to believe. With every fiber in her body she wanted to believe that Rigg would find salvation here.

"You must climb," Chabah said. "Both of you."

"No."

Ignoring Rigg, Chabah grabbed Shanna's arm with so much strength that she winced. "Listen to me. Changing Woman works through you. She trusts you, an outsider. I cannot say why. It is beyond my wisdom. You must place yourself in her hands. You must believe."

Rigg reacted first. "No. Damn it, Chabah. You can't—"

"Stop it, Rigg." Shanna needed his arms around her, his warm and life-giving arms, but didn't dare let that distract her. "You've been fighting *him* for so long that you think you have to fight everyone. Do this for us. Nothing you've tried has worked, has it? This—"

"I haven't asked to be locked up yet."

"And you're going to. You're sacrificing yourself for me." Spurred on by that knowledge, she planted herself in front of him. "I'm going up there," she said softly, determination riding every word. "And I need you with me."

He sighed, long and low. The deep whisper nearly tore her in two, nearly left her lost and lonely and hungry. "All right," he said. "But first I want you to promise me something."

Knowing what was coming, she couldn't speak.

"Don't try to ignore me," he insisted. He hadn't tried to touch her, not that that made any difference because she wouldn't have been able to leave his side if her life depended on it—which it might. "Don't ignore me."

"I'm not." *I can't.*

"A promise," he said fiercely. "Yesterday *he* said something to you. I asked Chabah. *De'ninaah* means "come here." *He's* calling you. Don't ever forget that—he wants you. If there aren't any miracles up there, promise me you'll get on the next plane out of New Mexico. You are never to come back here, never to try to get in touch with me again."

I can't; you're asking the impossible!

"Shanna, listen to me! I've never been more serious in my life. I'm doing this for you. Maybe everything I've been going through since he started trying to take me over has been because of you. If I lose, I want to go down knowing you're safe."

He was talking about dying. "Rigg, please." Hating the desperation in her voice, she struggled for normalcy. It helped, nominally. "Don't ask this of me. I couldn't stand—"

"I don't care! I don't care about anything except knowing you're safe."

She believed him with every fiber and molecule in her body. Was her absence the only gift she could give him? Was isolation and endless battles and eventual defeat his only future?

Yes, unless Changing Woman...

"All right." *No! Don't say this.* "We'll do this one last thing together, and if it doesn't work..."

"Finish it, Shanna."

"If it doesn't work, I'll never see you again."

CHAPTER SIXTEEN

Shanna was above Rigg, her foot just out of reach of his outstretched hand. When she pointed out that she knew the way, he'd allowed her to begin the climb ahead of him, but he was far from comfortable with the arrangement. If she lost her balance, he hoped he'd be able to catch her.

He hadn't told her how he felt, had said nothing about the waves of weakness that relentlessly washed over him. Still, he had no doubt she'd sensed that—just as he sensed her despair.

What did it matter? No matter what separation might do to both of them, he didn't dare release her from her vow to leave the land his father had claimed. It was the only thing that might keep her alive.

This slow and laborious climb when he should be husbanding his strength for the next attack was insane. But Chabah had insisted and Shanna had agreed, and Rigg couldn't let her go up there alone.

Maybe he should have.

Maybe he should walk off into the wilderness and let *him* claim him.

"It wasn't this hot earlier," Shanna said, sounding out of breath. "My hands are sweating. It's hard to hold on."

"You don't have to do this. It's nothing but an old man's dream."

"Stop it! You don't know."

But he did, because he'd lived with hope, and with hope shattered. He was vaguely aware of the hot wind and the darkness, but those considerations paled next to the soul-deep sense of desperation ripping at him. Before today was over, Shanna would be gone. Safe. He'd never see her again.

"Rigg?"

"What?"

"My hair's in my eyes. I think I'm almost there, but maybe it's wishful thinking."

He looked up, hoping to be able to tell her how close she was to the squiggles that were supposed to be Changing Woman, but her body blocked his view. Her presence made it all but impossible for him to concentrate on anything else. If his father came after him now, he didn't want Shanna to see, but maybe he had no choice.

Maybe?

He'd had no freedom since the assault on his sanity, his soul and his body began.

A long sigh alerted him to the fact that Shanna was no longer climbing. Looking up again, he saw her slide to one side on a narrow ledge and indicate she wanted him to join her. Careful not to bump her, he took the final cautious step that brought him up beside her. Her sun- and work-heated form was within reach if he dared. Because he knew he'd never be able to let her go if he so much as touched a fingertip to her hair, he remained on his share of the ledge and waited.

"Look."

Belatedly reminding himself of why they were here, he first closed his eyes in an attempt to clear his vision and then focused on the rock just above him.

There was something—faint lines that curved and straightened, stopped and started, etchings that might be nothing more than tiny cracks in stone.

"You saw this from the ground?" he asked in disbelief.

"It was absolutely clear. So obviously Changing Woman. But now..."

"Now you're no longer sure?"

"I know what I saw."

He didn't like that she was speaking in the past tense, but he couldn't give her back her short-lived hope that she'd found the embodiment of a powerful entity. Now, maybe, she would accept what he had long ago—that no one could save him except himself. Only could he? "I'm sorry," he said.

"Sorry? You don't believe—"

"Don't, Shanna, please. Don't hold on to false hope."

He could hear her breathing, the sound hard and ragged. Unable to see enough of her features to know whether defeat had yet entered her eyes, he turned his attention back to why they'd made this climb.

Changing Woman had always been a dark figure outlined in corn yellow, her slender arms lifted to hold the symbols of nature and reproduction. He'd thought of her as a benign and benevolent figure, gentle and slightly built when a deity that powerful should be much larger, stronger.

He'd wanted to believe; despite his grounding in modern-day reality, he'd wanted to believe, but nothing he'd done or thought or prayed had evoked any response from Changing Woman, and he'd stopped asking for the impossible. He'd faced the fact that he might have to spend the rest of his life locked up so his father couldn't feed off his strength and youth.

Yet Zarcillas had fled when Shanna held a depiction of Changing Woman to her breast.

And something had compelled Shanna to come here this morning.

He was getting punchy, losing perspective. Seeing a logic in random designs that wasn't there. Wanting to put his hand on what might be the figure's head and experience the depth of belief Chabah took for granted.

"What is it?" Chabah called up to them. "What do you see?"

"Lines and cracks," he said before Shanna could speak. "Just lines and cracks."

"Enough! I will not hear this. Silence the arguments inside you, Rigg. Open your mind and heart to possibilities. Experience as a child does, without reservation."

"Do it, Rigg!" Shanna whispered.

Do it, Rigg. For me. For us.

With her plea tight inside him, he waited out the slight cramp in his right calf, then again faced the rock. Heard the wind. Smelled the desert. Felt Shanna beside him. Let his mind empty and waited for it to fill.

He has a voice, he has a voice. Just at daylight the Mountain Bluebird calls. The bluebird has a voice, He has a voice, his voice melodious, His voice melodious, that flows in gladness. The bluebird calls, the bluebird calls.

Forgetting to breathe, Rigg continued to stare at lines and curves. The chant repeated itself inside him; he belatedly recognized it as part of the "Daylight Song," which had been among the tapes Chabah had given him. He was punchy. The sleepless night had caught up to him, that and his fear for Shanna's life. That's all.

No, not all.

He has a voice, he has a voice.

"Rigg?"

It didn't matter what Shanna thought, how insane it made him sound—he had to share this with her. When he whispered the words, she stared soberly at him and he had no way of judging her reaction.

He watched her chest rise and fall, noted that she hadn't so much as blinked. When she spoke, her lips barely moved. "'Among them I walk. I speak to them—they hold out their hands to me.'"

"Where—"

"I don't know where that came from," she interrupted. "I don't understand any of this, but Rigg—" Attention still on him, she flattened her hand against what might be

Changing Woman's breast. He waited for her to say something more, but she remained silent. The wind danced and sung around them. Swallows darted about at the corner of his vision, their wings a peaceful whisper of sound that made him long for the gift of flight. He remembered another snippet of a chant, but not what it was part of. Something about walking. Yes, walking.

" 'Today I will walk out, today everything evil will leave me, I will be as I was before, I will have a cool breeze over my body, I will have a light body.' "

"Rigg?" Shanna whispered, alerting him to the fact that he'd spoken aloud. "What—"

"It's inside me—that's all I can tell you." *A cool breeze. A light body.*

Raw hunger gnawed at him. The need to have back the freedom of the boy he'd once been grew and expanded until he felt engulfed by a child's memories and hope and promise. His shoulder now pressing lightly against Shanna's, he touched what he'd climbed up here to see. The slab of rock was sharp edged, but he was barely aware of the projection that bit into his palm. The rock was cool because it spent most of the time in shade, and yet, shouldn't it have been colder than this? Lifeless instead of imprinted by something he couldn't comprehend?

Although he remained aware of Shanna's presence, he deliberately focused attention on his hand and what was happening to it. The longer he kept it against the dry rock, the warmer it became. He felt warmth in his palm and fingertips, became aware of energy spreading to his wrist, up his arm, sending tentacles of heat to his heart.

"Rigg, what?"

Before he could think how he might possibly answer, how to tell her that the impossible had happened, something hit him between the shoulder blades. Grunting, he turned quickly and was instantly grateful that he stood on a relatively wide ledge. The blow was repeated, this time with enough force that he nearly lost his balance.

"Rigg, what—"

"Zarcillas. He's back."

Shanna couldn't say how much time passed before what Rigg said sunk in. A moment ago she'd been aware of nothing except the almost reverent way he was touching the petroglyph, that and her reaction to having him close and quiet and calm.

That had changed. Horribly.

"You're sure?"

"Yes," Rigg answered, but already his response was unnecessary. His eyes, the midnight eyes she could easily lose herself in, were no longer pure. Fire danced in them, fire and danger.

She didn't know how he could survive another attack.

She yelled down to let Chabah and Juanica know what was happening. Chabah's response was instantaneous. "Hold him. Protect him. Give him your belief. Your strength."

Although she'd already gripped Rigg's hands, she knew that wasn't enough. If love had the power to heal, Rigg wouldn't now be under attack.

Chabah had said something about belief. No doubts! She didn't dare doubt!

As Rigg's body became rigid, she clutched him to her. Words of love boiled inside her, but she cast them aside. They would come later—if there was a later for her and Rigg. Ignoring what she knew she would see in his eyes, she fastened her attention on Changing Woman, let thought become words. "'Dewdrops and pollen may I enjoy. With these may it be beautiful in front of me. With these may it be beautiful behind me. . . . All is beautiful again. All is restored in beauty.'"

Rigg twisted away. Calling on strength she didn't know she had, she refused to let him go—refused to let him fall.

"Say it with me, Rigg. Now! 'Dewdrops and pollen may I enjoy. With these may—'"

"No!"

For a moment she thought he was fighting her, but when he clasped her so fiercely he'd leave bruises, she knew his anger was directed at what was attacking him. "Don't!" she screamed. "Damn you, Zarcillas, don't hide from me! I know what you look like, what you're capable of. Stop torturing him!"

A shriek slashed through the air; her head felt as if it might explode. Rigg's grip became even fiercer, but she didn't care.

"Leave her!" Rigg bellowed as he whipped his head first one way and then the other, as if searching for whoever was attacking him. "She doesn't deserve—"

"You coward!" Shanna accused. Only after the words were out of her mouth did she realize what she'd said. It didn't matter; Zarcillas already knew she hated him. "You're afraid, afraid of your own son's strength!"

"Shanna!" Rigg's voice was tight with desperation. "Don't! His wrath—"

She stopped him with a kiss, held his body still with nothing more than the force of her will. For a moment he tried to break free, and terror nearly overwhelmed her. But he must have understood what she was doing and was compelling himself to relax. She sensed him throughout her, his life force, the incredible determination that had kept him from surrendering even when he must have believed there was no way out of this hell. He burned her with his kiss; his arms protected her and kept her safe, when he was the one in the most danger. The wind seemed to be picking up strength, whirling and beating, trying to knock them both from their precarious perch, and still Rigg held on to her and she felt no fear.

"*He'll* never let go. Never." Rigg's words pressed against her mouth—hard, inescapable words. "Once *he* has you—Damn you! You can't have her! I won't let you!"

With one arm, Rigg continued to hold her close. With the other he struck out, a fighter's punch that nearly unbalanced them both. She clung to him, forcing him back against Changing Woman's silhouette. Her left shoulder flattened on the rock, and even while she strained to see what Rigg was attacking, she felt heat sear her shoulder. Strength poured into her, strength and a courage that might have come from sandstone and a prehistoric etching, and maybe was a gift from Rigg.

"You can't have him!" she told the shifting, darkening swirls taking shape within the twisting air. "I won't let you."

You can't stop me.

"Yes, I can! You're evil! Evil! A Chinde afraid to join others of your kind in the underworld. Afraid. A greedy coward sucking the life out of your son. Killing innocent people."

I will have you.

"No, you won't," she started to say, but Rigg acted first. Although he now shuddered almost uncontrollably, he squared off to face the darkening, bunching wind. A moan rolled up from somewhere deep inside him. She knew he was at war, with himself as well as with his father. Good and evil spinning closer and closer.

"She is morning, Rigg," Chabah called out. "Touch the morning. Take strength from it."

Again Rigg moaned, the sound so tortured she didn't know how she could stand it. Although she was ready to sacrifice herself for him, some greater wisdom compelled her to wait. To let him listen to the shaman's wisdom.

"Morning?" he whispered.

"I'm here."

He swayed toward her, laced butterfly kisses over her eyes and forehead and throat. He looked at her as if she was made of turquoise, as if they'd found each other after years of painful separation. She responded, not as a woman being brought to life by a virile and desirable man, but as though she was a delicate spring flower touched by dawn. She could laugh with Rigg, laugh and sing and find beauty in the shapes and shades of this land. Together they would explore its secrets, its wonder, its quiet splendor.

Unless Zarcillas destroyed his son.

The wind howled, sounding like a tortured soul, a vengeful demon. Although she continued to try to gentle Rigg with her touch, his attention had again been wrenched back to his tormentor.

"No, no, no," Rigg chanted. His features were tightly drawn, the furrows between his eyes deep. She imagined broken glass flying about inside him, tiny spears seeking to destroy what was good about him. When, in his battle, he wrenched free of her, she threw her body against him and pinned him to the rock, his back now flat against the petroglyph. In her mind's eye she imagined him absorbing the deity's essence. Becoming even more powerful. Fighting what couldn't be fought and winning.

"Believe in Changing Woman!" She sounded demented and didn't care. "Rigg, believe in her power."

"Stop it—you can't have me—I won't let you—" Rigg sucked in a ragged breath. "Damn it, I won't let you win."

"Don't think about him!" she insisted. "He doesn't matter. Only Changing Woman does. The chants. Rigg, remember the chants!"

Chabah yelled something to them. She thought she heard Juanica cry out, but couldn't concentrate on her voice. Rigg was trapped in a tornado, his body in danger of being torn apart, the war awful in his fire-flamed eyes.

The shadows and shapes stopped their wild flight and settled into the form she'd seen—had it only been last night?—at Rigg's house. If anything, Zarcillas looked even more fleshless than he had then. His mouth was parted as if he was panting. Yellowed, snaggled teeth lay in disarray in the dark opening. His eyes were hollowed out, empty, like twin holes punched into bone.

Her heart pummeling against her chest, she placed herself as a shield between father and son. Rigg tried to push her away. Then, when she took a stumbling step precariously close to the edge of the ledge, he yanked her against him.

"Don't touch her!" he warned the weightless creature floating before them. "If you do, I'll jump. You'll never have me. I'll come back as a Chinde."

No.

"Yes!"

I want you.

Feeling as if she was both on fire and frozen, Shanna stared into that dead face. Rigg's death? No! She couldn't let that thought swamp her! "Did you hear him? He'll haunt you, drag you into hell. Do you know what hell is?" she demanded. "Do you?"

Yes.

Suddenly, irrevocably, she believed Rigg's father. Zarcillas was trapped in a nonexistence she couldn't possibly comprehend. That limbo maybe more than anything else was what had filled him with hatred.

It didn't matter. Only Rigg did.

Another of those horrible shudders consumed him. Although she desperately needed to feel the rock's heat, she knew Rigg needed it more. She levered herself against him with such force that her muscles screamed in protest, but she didn't dare let him go because—

Because if they were going to win this unholy battle, they needed Changing Woman's help.

Zarcillas was coming closer. She was terrified he'd finally succeed in joining himself with Rigg, but what could she do? They were trapped up here. There was no way they could leave without risking their lives.

And even if they remained here, they might end up dead.

"Changing Woman!" Her throat cried out in protest when she screamed, but she ignored it. "Changing Woman, help us!"

"'Today I will walk out,'" Rigg said firmly. "'Today everything evil will leave me, I will be as I was before, I will have a cool breeze over my body, I will have a light body.'"

Made braver by Rigg's words, Shanna shifted position and pressed her cheek against the petroglyph. Rigg had been staring at Zarcillas as if he didn't dare take his eyes off the constantly moving and deadly mass, but for the briefest of moments their gazes locked.

I love you.

I love you.

A scream, like that of a soul in agony, reverberated off the cliff walls and was then carried into space. Shanna would go to her grave believing that she heard the rock sigh and that the vibration emanating from it was that of a massive, beating heart.

Rigg's fierce gaze told her he'd heard and felt the same things.

"You won't win!" he challenged Zarcillas, who whipped about as if caught in the hands of a demented giant. "You can't have us! Changing Woman is here. You can't fight a god. You can't win!"

No, no, no, no.

"Yes!" Rigg hissed. His heart pounded and beat double time. Either that or the sound came from a force older than the rocks themselves. "Listen to me," he taunted. "I'm not alone, not anymore. Changing Woman—"

No, no, no, no.

"'Today I will walk out, everything evil will leave me, I will be as I was before, I will have a cool breeze over my body, I will have a light body.'"

No, no, no!

Zarcillas was now so close that Shanna felt trapped by the cold that surrounded him. Prayers, pleas vibrated through her, but he was so big. So powerful. He reached for Rigg, blackened fingers clamping around his wrist. In slow motion, Rigg was being dragged away from Changing Woman. He formed a fist and struck at his father's throat, but there was no impact; Shanna remembered the horror of being attacked and having nothing to attack in return.

"Rigg!"

"A Chinde," he threw at his father. "Kill me and I'll come back—"

Not kill—never that—possess.

When Zarcillas continued to pull Rigg toward him, Shanna screamed. Her voice echoed off the rock and catapulted her into action. She reached inside her shirt for Juanica's knife, but instead of wasting her energy in a useless thrust, she took a moment to hold the knife against what had breathed and beaten, what she believed with all her heart was Changing Woman. The handle heated; the silver blade glowed. Gathering her strength, she slashed at what held Rigg prisoner. Watched as Zarcillas jerked away.

No, no, no!

Shanna felt as if she weighed nothing, weighed everything. Still, although the knife slipped from her fingers, she managed to reach for Rigg's hand. He gripped back, pulled her around so that her spine, too, was welded to the rock. His eyes seared hers, telegraphed what he needed from her.

They spoke as one. " 'Today I will walk out, everything evil will leave me, I will be as I was before, I will have a cool breeze over my body, I will have a light body.' "

No!

Zarcillas threw himself at her, clawing fingers reaching for her throat. She scratched and fought—fought nothing. Rigg spun away, his hands going to his chest. But instead of protecting himself, he yanked off the fetish bag and flung it at Zarcillas. The bag seemed to melt, to burn its way into Zarcillas's chest. The demon tried to tear it from him, but it was imbedded in him now. Smoking, smelling like death. Before her eyes, his body began losing form. She could breathe again.

"Go!" Rigg screamed. "To the underworld. That's the only place you belong, with others of your kind."

No!

"Yes! You can't have me, or her!"

No!

Still melting, becoming colorless. Feeling victory within her grasp, Shanna hurtled her own insult at the creature who'd murdered her parents. "I would never—I'd kill myself—No! Changing Woman will protect me. Always. Do you hear me? You'll never touch. Never!"

Mine, mine, mine.

"I hate you, loathe you. I believe—Changing Woman, I believe in her."

Mine.

"So do I," Rigg said with a glance in her direction. "I believe. Do you hear me? I believe."

Mi...

Rigg looked like a mountain, muscles contracting and expanding like those of a newly freed panther. She heard what couldn't possibly be his heart beating, but maybe was; the truth of that would have to wait. Only one thing mattered—Zarcillas was fading. Sliding off into nothing.

The wind became a gentle breeze.

"Changing Woman," she whispered through tears she couldn't begin to stop. "Thank you."

The cliff face warmed, glowed, softened. For a moment sunlight spilled over them. Shanna smelled spring flowers, corn pollen, thought of the peacefulness of dawn.

"Changing Woman. Mother of the Earth Surface People." The simple words rumbled from Rigg's chest.

* * *

The climb down to where Chabah and Juanica waited seemed to take forever, and yet Rigg was in no hurry to reach the ground. Even as he concentrated on where to place his feet, his mind—his unbelievably clear mind—continued to replay what had happened up there.

None of it made sense, at least not to the logical part of him. But for a long, long time now he'd felt too much like a cornered animal, ruled by nothing except an instinct for survival, and that animal could accept. So, finally, could the man, and he sent his own silent thank-you to the deity Shanna had led him to.

Shanna was drenched in sweat. The pulse at the base of her throat beat erratically and reminded him of what his own heart had felt like while he was trying to protect both himself and her from his father. Her hair had been whipped about by the wind until she looked as if she'd always lived here. Dust marred one tanned cheek; there was a faint scratch on the other. The knuckles on her right hand were red and sore looking. He wanted to bury his face in her hair, to hold her and hold her until he could close his eyes without seeing the end to him, to both of them, flash before him.

"It is over."

Reaching for Shanna, Rigg acknowledged that Chabah had spoken. Shanna pressed herself against his side, the gesture telling him that he wasn't the only one who'd been shaken to his core. "I know," he told the shaman, with a conviction that came from a part of him that believed the unbelievable. "He's gone."

"Forever."

"You have no doubt, do you?" Shanna asked Chabah, her voice stronger than Rigg expected. She'd clamped her arms around his waist and was holding on with surprising strength. "You always believed he could be beaten."

Chabah nodded. "But only by someone who believed totally."

Rigg wanted to kiss Shanna endlessly and never lose the touch and feel and wonder of her lips. But he forced himself to do nothing more than stand there with their bodies sharing the same heat. "I did believe," he admitted in wonder. "What I felt up there—"

"It *was* Changing Woman," Shanna said.

"Changing Woman? You have no doubt?" Juanica asked. Her attention was focused on Shanna, and Rigg wondered if she was remembering Shanna's mother. He hoped Juanica would send Debby a message that her daughter had become a courageous woman.

An exquisitely beautiful, courageous woman.

"No doubt," Shanna answered calmly.

When Chabah turned sharp eyes on Rigg, the message was clear: they needed to talk, soon. It was time for him to understand completely. He nodded, eager to be guided by Chabah's wisdom.

For both him and Shanna to be led into full understanding by the shaman.

They. Both. The words eddied about inside him. Although his sense of exhaustion grew with every passing minute, he knew he was a long way from being able to relax. Other things would come first—like taking Chabah and Juanica back to their hogan, like returning to civilization so he and Shanna could clean up and get something to eat.

So he could make love to her.

Again and again.

She was pulling out of his arms, leaving him. He reached for her with a fierce determination before he realized that she'd simply squatted so she could pick something up off the ground.

In her hand, her lovely and shaking hand, she held both Juanica's knife and the fetish bag. When she started to hand the talisman to him, he bent his head so she could slip it around his neck. Once it rested against his chest, she leaned close and layered kisses on his flesh there, heating him even more.

Heating him in a way totally different from what he'd felt when Changing Woman touched him.

"You're safe," Shanna whispered. She handed the knife to Juanica. Then she loosened the cord that had held the pouch closed, making an opening large enough to accommodate her fingers. When she withdrew her hand, it was coated with a fine yellow dust.

"Corn pollen." She smiled as she pressed her fingers to his mouth. He tasted spring and promise and life. This time when he folded her in his arms, he heard nothing except the beating of her heart.

Their hearts.

EPILOGUE

They were the only two people in the Great Kiva. Shanna didn't know how or what strings Rigg had pulled so they could be alone inside the Anasazi ruins. For now it was enough that he was beside her and that when they left here, they'd return to his place.

His place.

"I wish Chabah was here," she said softly. "I think he could tell us a great deal about the people who built this."

"Maybe. Maybe not. He's committed to keeping alive the old Navajo ways. I'm not sure how much he knows about those who were here generations before that."

"Maybe." She took a step toward one of the restored sitting areas, then rejoined him and nestled against his side. He smelled wonderful, a mix of the shower he'd taken before daylight, the cornstalks they'd walked among when they'd stepped outside, even the faintest hint of desert air.

How could she think about anything except making love to him when he smelled like this? As he held her against him, she looked around, taking in the dim, artificial lighting and a modern roof—the original one hadn't survived the thousands of years since the kiva had been built. She noted the stone walls and seats, the packed earth, enough space that she felt dwarfed by it. Although the Anasazi who'd once lived here had used the Great Kiva as a common meeting place, it held an aura of mystery for her. She sensed the presence of ancient spirits and souls, wondered if they were in any way aware of her. Wondered if they approved of what they saw today.

"*He* never knew this kind of peace, did he? Your father. I can't help but feel sorry for him. To be ruled by anger and hatred—what a terrible existence."

"You can say that after what he did?"

Because she wanted to give Rigg as honest an answer as possible, she deliberately stared at the ground and surrounded herself with the memories she had of her parents. She wanted more; it would be a lie if she said different. But she couldn't change reality. All she could control was her reaction to that reality.

"Juanica found some wonderful people to raise me. They loved me, nurtured me. They kept things from me because they felt they had to protect me. They were doing what they believed was best— and I don't blame them. The important thing is I was raised in an atmosphere of love. That's something *he* never had, or never believed he did. It twisted him, made him bitter and angry. Yes, I feel sorry for him."

"I never did, not until today."

"But you do now?"

"If you can forgive him, I can do the same. Say his name, Shanna. There's no longer any danger."

She couldn't help but smile. "You believe Chabah, don't you? You know Zarcillas will never return."

He sighed, smiled a little himself. "Juanica's father can be pretty persuasive." His smile expanded, filled her heart with its beauty. "I'd forgotten what it feels like to be at peace with myself. To have that back again..."

"I know. I'm at peace, too."

"No more nightmares?"

"None. I slept last night...." Remembering what had happened before they'd finally let go of each other in the dark, she let the words trail off. They'd been back from the Navajo reservation for three days and nights. At first they'd been too tired both physically and emotionally for anything except quick meals, long showers, quiet hours spent locked in each other's arms. Simply holding on.

But they were rested now. They'd talked about what had happened. They'd come to accept, to fully believe as Chabah and Juanica did.

Rigg was free. She felt his freedom in the gentle way he held her, whispered endearments as their bodies became one, laughed.

How she loved his laughter!

"I'm going to have to go back to work," he said before she could tell him that.

She stared at a gray wall, tried not to listen to the way his voice echoed in the dark and empty chamber. "I know."

"And you?"

They hadn't spoken of tomorrows. All their time together had been spent in today, the moment, because they'd learned how precious now was. "What do you want me to say?"

"I'm not going to put words in your mouth, Shanna. I'll never do that. It has to be what you want."

I want what you want. Although she hadn't had enough of having his arms around her, she pulled free so she could look into his eyes.

His dark eyes. Dark and clear. Filled with the love that all but boiled out of her, too.

"I need to be with you," she whispered.

"Enough to start over in New Mexico?"

"It wouldn't be starting over. I'd be coming home."

"Home," he whispered, and that was all it took. She couldn't stand apart from him, after all. The idea of their separating was unthinkable.

The soft white lighting dimmed—at least it seemed that way to her, but then it might be that she didn't care about her surroundings, about anything except him. He held her even tighter, the gesture both possessive and incredibly comforting. "Listen," he whispered. "The Anasazi are calling."

"What are they saying?"

"That they want you here."

"They?"

"And me. But it's more than wanting. I love you, Shanna. I *need* you. For the rest of my life. My life," he added with a hint of wonder. "I never thought I'd be able to say that again. To believe..."

She waited, but he seemed lost within himself. Guiding him back to her in the only way that mattered, she lifted herself onto her toes in silent invitation. He responded, drawing her into him, folding himself around her, answering her.

Kissing.

When the light dimmed even more, she thought briefly of Changing Woman and of returning with Rigg to where they'd found her.

And then he ran his fingers into her hair and pressed his palms against her temple and there was only him.

And all their tomorrows.

It is lovely indeed, it is lovely indeed.
I, I am the spirit within the earth.
The feet of the earth are my feet.
The legs of the earth are my legs.
The bodily strength of the earth is my bodily strength.
The thoughts of the earth are my thoughts.
The voice of the earth is my voice.
The feather of the earth is my feather.
All that belongs to the earth belongs to me.
All that surrounds the earth surrounds me.
I, I am the sacred words of the earth.
It is lovely indeed, it is lovely indeed.

—Song of the Earth Spirit,
Origin Legend

*   *   *   *   *

COMING NEXT MONTH

#59 SHADOW OF THE WOLF—Rebecca Flanders
Heart of the Wolf
At every full moon he strikes. TV journalist Amy Fortenoy wanted
to be the one to collar the elusive "werewolf killer." After all,
capturing the nocturnal predator would boost her career—and, she
hoped, her standing in her family's eyes. But P.I. Ky Londen had
his own, very private, reason for joining the search—one that *never*
should have involved the sexy and determined reporter. For Ky was
on a quest to find his true father—and all the evidence pointed in
one deadly direction.

COMING IN TWO MONTHS

#60 'TIL WE MEET AGAIN—Kimberly Raye
Mishella Kirkland had the healing touch, and she desperately
sought to harness its power to save her sister. Yet stranger
Raphael Dalton knew the truth behind her gift—particularly the
evil source bent on reclaiming its power. To save her, Dalton
assigned himself to act as Mishella's protector—and lover—only
to discover that he was her greatest threat.

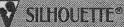
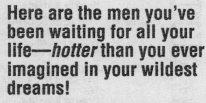

ANGELS AND ELVES
by Joan Elliott Pickart

Joan Elliott Pickart brings you her special brand of humor tales of the MacAllister men. For these carefree bachelors, predicting the particulars of the MacAllister babies is much easier than predicting when wedding bells will sound!

In November, Silhouette Desire's *Man of the Month*, Forrest MacAllister, is the reigning Baby Bet Champion and a confirmed "uncle." Until his very pregnant, matchmaking sister introduced him to Jillian Jones-Jenkins, he never would have thought that the next baby he bets on might be his own!

Experience all the laughter and love as a new MacAllister baby is born, and the most unpredictable MacAllister becomes a husband—and father in *Angels and Elves*, book one of THE BABY BET.

In February 1996, Silhouette Special Edition celebrates the most romantic month of the year with FRIENDS, LOVERS...AND BABIES! book two of THE BABY BET.

BABBET1